The Soul of Mary Stuart

Holly-Eloise Walters

Churchill Publishing UK Ltd
2021

1st Edition

ISBN: 978-1-63821-005-4

Churchill Publishing UK Ltd.
71-75 Shelton Street
Covent Garden
London
WC2H 9JQ

www.churchillpublishing.com

Ode on the death of her husband, Francis II

by Mary Stuart

In my sad, quiet song,
A melancholy air,
I shall look deep and long
At loss beyond compare,
And with bitter tears,
I'll pass my best years.

Have the harsh fates ere now
Let such a grief be felt,
Has a more cruel blow
Been by Dame Fortune dealt
Than, O my heart and eyes!
I see where his bier lies?

In my springtime's gladness
And flower of my young heart,
I feel the deepest sadness
Of the most grievous hurt.
Nothing now my heart can fire
But regret and desire.

He who was my dearest
Already is my plight
The day that shone the clearest
For me is darkest night
There's nothing now so fine
That I need make it mine.

Deep in my eyes and heart
A portrait has its place
Which shows the world my hurt

In the pallor of my face.
Pale as when violets fade
True love's becoming shade.

In my unwonted pain
I can no more be still,
Rising time and again
To drive away my ill.
All things good and bad
Have lost the taste they had.

And thus I always stay
Whether in wood or meadow,
Whether at dawn of day
Or at the evening shadow.
My heart feels ceaselessly
Grief for his loss to me.

Sometimes in such a place
His image comes to me.
The sweet smile on his face
Up in a cloud I see.
Then sudden in the mere
I see his funeral bier.

When I lie quietly
Sleeping upon my couch,
I hear him speak to me
And I can feel his touch.
In my duties each day
He is near me alway.

Nothing seems fine to me
Unless he is therein.
My heart will not agree
Unless he is within.
I lack all perfection
In my cruel dejection

I shall cease my song now,
My sad lament shall end.
Whose burden aye shall show
True love can not pretend
And, though we are apart,
Grows no less in my heart.

This book is once again dedicated to my Nan, Susan.

I would not be half the woman I am today were it not for her love and influence. Although she is no longer physically with me, I carry her with me each and every day, like a handprint on my heart. Thank you for the wonderful life you gave me.

Everything I do, I do in your honour.

Don't weep at my grave,
For I am not there,
I've a date with a butterfly
To dance in the air.
I'll be singing in the sunshine,
Wild and free,
Playing tag with the wind,
While I'm waiting for thee.

(Poem by Helen Steiner Rice)

Susan Margaret Walters
11-01-1949 – 25-12-2017

I would also like to dedicate this book to all the people who have sadly lost their lives to the Covid-19 Pandemic. My heart is with everyone who has lost loved ones to the virus.

An Eternal Love

Chapter 1

I love him. I have always loved him. I will always love him. He is the air that I breathe and the life that sustains me. He is perfect. He is mine. From the time we were small children together, up until this moment when I am readying myself to marry him, I have loved him. He is everything I want and more. He is the flower that grows so gracefully. The petals that fall from the rose and make the spring mornings smell so sweet. He is the sunshine on a summer's day. The calm after a storm. He is the birds that so gently wake me each morning. He is my everything. He is mine, and I am his. He is the reason that I feel as if I float just a little above my body. He lifts me up and makes everything crystal clear. He is perfection in every sense of the word. When we are alone, I can think of nothing except those fabulous blue eyes of his, staring straight through me and into my very soul. Together, the fragility of this life fades away. I feel immortal when I am beside him. He makes me a better person. He makes me stronger. He is the reason for my existence. The reason I wake in the morning. The reason I sleep so soundly. I do not know that I can put into words the reason why I love him so well. Is it the fact that when he smiles the rest of the world disappears? Or maybe it is because he can make me laugh like no one else. Or the way he says my name like it is the most precious word. It is because he puts my needs and the needs of all his loved ones above his own. Because he would die for the people he cares about. Because he understands the inner workings of my mind more than I do. Because he is kind, loving and loyal. When we are together, my responsibility fades away. The pressure that weighs heavy on both of our shoulders does not feel so hard to bear. We do not feel as if we are a Queen and a Dauphin. He sees Mary, and I see Francis. We do not see France and Scotland. He sees me, and I see him. No more, No less. We can see the heart that beats in the other's chest. We see that we are more than just our nations. More than the crowns that sit on our heads. We have needs and wants. We have plans for our future. Above all else, we have each other. He is more important to me than any kingdom will ever be. No matter where life takes us or what this world expects from us, it all comes back to him. And it always will.

Oh, how I love him. My love for him consumes me, and today it will become official before the whole of France and God. I am breathless as I think of our future—a future of unconditional love—a future filled with the children we will have together—a future of unrivalled happiness. Today, we finally become one. I am so blessed. Today, I have one thing in mind. And he waits for me at Notre Dame. I have dreamt of this day for a very long time. I can hardly believe that it has finally dawned. I could scarcely sleep last night. My mind was abuzz with excitement. Francis is the only man in the world for me, and I am honoured to have him in my life. I do not think that anyone had expected us to fall so hopelessly in love. Ours was always supposed to be a political marriage. A joining of our two countries. It was supposed to make my rule in Scotland stronger. Love was just a happy accident.

We have known each other for almost our whole lives. I have been here in France since I was just five years old. I am now fifteen and Francis fourteen. When we were younger together, we felt as if we had the whole world at our feet—my hand in his and nothing else to concern us. We would not go anywhere without the other close behind. I would take Francis' hand, and he would follow me wherever I would go. He was like a little doll. Always at my side and pretty as porcelain. I loved how he followed me around. Francis was only four years old when I first came to France. He was so small, I remember. So delicate and fragile as glass. I instantly felt the need to protect him. The moment I saw him, a fierce love awakened in me. It was a different love than the one I feel now, but just as strong. I was like an older sister to him. He idolised me. He hung on every word I said. I think Francis fell in love much more quickly than I did. The moment he saw me, he was besotted in his own childish way. Do not mistake me; I have always been content with the idea of marrying Francis, but for a long time, I saw him as someone I had to shelter and care for. I felt the need to look after him. To scold him as an older sibling or a parent would. He was a very mischievous child, and I enjoyed putting him in his place. It gave me a sense of authority, I suppose; I am a Queen after all. It is in my blood to be in charge of people. Francis loved to dose off during our lessons or complain that they bored him. "You will be a King one day, Francis." I would remind him. "It is most important that you learn how to rule a kingdom, or you shall be a laughing stock."

He would put his face in his hands and sulk, but you could guarantee that he would not complain for the rest of the day. I believe I was a good influence on him. He liked to follow my lead, and if I was doing well at lessons, he would be too.

Each morning Francis would come to find me, his eyes big and puppylike. "What are we doing today, Mary?" He would ask. I would then list off the itinerary for the day, and

Francis would nod enthusiastically at each suggestion, only screwing his nose up when I mentioned Latin or music lessons. These were his least favourite of them all. He said that it bored him half to death, learning how to play the violin. Francis loved to be free and was only happy when we were outside in the fresh air. The grounds at Fontainebleau were vast, and we could quickly lose ourselves in the gardens. My favourite time was in autumn. The palace seemed to come to life in the autumnal colours. Red, orange, and brown filled the ground. We would put on our warmest furs and race through the leaves. Francis always hated how the autumn sweeps through and kills all of the flowers. He prefers the spring when they are given new life.

When we were young, we saw the palace like a giant playground, and we were often getting into trouble for playing King by Your Leave in one of the vast empty rooms. Francis would hide somewhere in the palace, and it was my job to seek him out. Unfortunately for him, he wasn't particularly good at finding a decent spot and would often choose the same one. I would humour him and spend ages pretending to look for him before finally giving up and winning the game. He would stamp his feet and demand to know how I managed to win every time. Then when it was my turn to hide, I would tuck myself away in one of the most obvious places, perhaps behind a suit of armour with my foot hanging out, or behind one of the enormous curtains. The look on his face when he found me was all the satisfaction I needed, much better than winning the game.

Francis would often tire long before I did. He was a sickly child and was always catching a chill or a fever. Whenever he took to his bed, I was not allowed to see him for fear that I too would become ill. I hated the idea of being parted from him, and I would have to be carried away. It didn't take Catherine long to realise that there was no stopping me. I would sit outside of his bedroom, day and night, and wait for him to recover. I would talk to him through the door, explaining to him that he owed me a game and that he must get better soon, or I would be very upset. I didn't mean it, of course, I just wanted my friend back. He always bounced back. Francis was and is a fighter. No matter how scary it got. No matter how ill he was. I knew that he would pull through.

I believe that it was the last time he was unwell that I began to realise that the way I loved him had changed. I no longer felt like an older sister to him. Instead of sitting outside of his door, I wanted to lay beside him in the bed and hold him until he was well again. It changed in the most subtle of ways. The way I would blush when he addressed me, the way my eyes lingered on his face, the way my heart lept when he brushed my hand. I found that I could not help but look at him. I could not believe how beautiful he was. I would get lost in his eyes, the eyes that are deeper than any ocean. I fixated on the tiny fragment of green so beautifully flecked in the sea of blue. They are the kindest eyes that I have ever looked into. If you can truly see one's soul by staring into their eyes, then you can see that Francis is nothing but purity and goodness. It was so evident that the way I looked at him was different. There was now this spark between us. This aching pull towards him. His smile made my heart leap for joy. His voice calmed and soothed me. We were so at ease with one another, and as we grew, we found that we could sit in absolute silence for hours and still feel at ease. We are content when we sit side by side in the library—a book in my hand and a different one in his. We often read to each other. We sit surrounded by a vast amount of books and read thrilling stories of the world around us—a world we long to see together. There is never a need for words between us. Without speaking, we know exactly what the other wants and needs at that moment. When Francis touched me, his hands felt different on my skin. I started to feel a longing for him to touch me. I never wanted there to be a distance between us. Any space was too great. I longed to see him. The days when he was away were painful. I never feel complete unless we are side by side. I have loved him my whole life. As a brother. As a friend. But that love grew into something utterly beautiful. It expanded and took over my entire being. It was the way he looked at me like there was no one else in the room. The way his eyes lingered on mine. The looks he gave me that were for my eyes only. He knows exactly what I need when I need it. My emotions are his emotions. We feel the same things. We can sense the slightest change in the other. We speak of everything. Share everything. He is more than the love of my life. He is my truest friend in this world. He knows my soul better than I know it. He can see inside my heart and knows the truth that lies there. He has never seen me as 'Mary Queen of Scots'. He sees me as a girl. The girl that he loves. The girl that he adores. I do not see him as the Dauphin of France, next in line to the throne. I see him as the boy that I have loved so well and the man that I now call my own. I have seen him go from a young, fragile boy, to a strong, confident, loving man. A man that puts those he cherishes above anything else. Francis is not like other men. He does not need to be the best at everything. He does not need to be the strongest or the most heroic. He is happy as long as he is good, and he is good. He is the best man that I know. There are few like him in the world. I have not seen much of the world, and yet I know it to be true. He is one of the few with a pure heart and good intentions. Oh, how I love him. I love him. I love him. It feels good to love him. It feels so natural. Our love is never forced. His love completely consumes me. He is beautiful. He is angelic. He speaks with such grace. Every word he says lingers in my mind long after we have parted. He knows how to make me feel better. He is always on hand to comfort me. He makes me a better person. I share parts of my soul with him that I would never give to another person and today, my soul will join with his. Today we will become one.

I awoke this morning with a smile on my face and joy in my heart that I cannot explain. It's a knowledge that everything is going to be alright. That my whole life has been in preparation for this day. Forget Scotland. Forget France. I was made to marry Francis, and today I fulfil that purpose. My Mary's all bustle around me busying themselves with their chores for the day ahead. They are as excited as I am having witnessed the love that Francis and I share first-hand. Each of them has been with me since I was a small child. They travelled to France with me from Scotland when I was just five years old. My mother wanted me to have companions of the same age, so she selected four girls to accompany me. Mary Seton, Mary Beaton, Mary Fleming and Mary Livingston. They are the closest people to me in the world bar Francis. They were with me as a babe in Scotland, travelled with me to France and now will stand witness to the most important day of my life. They are more than my ladies maids; they are my friends. My family. They are the only real family I have ever known. They are all I truly have from the country I rule. Yes. I am the Queen of Scotland. But Scotland is foreign to me. I was sent to France for my protection, and it has been my home since. I succeeded to the throne at just six days old when my father died in battle, leaving my mother and I alone to fend for ourselves. Mother was still recovering from my birth when she had received word that father had perished. My birth had been a stressful one. Mother was worried. Father was away, and she was left with a country at her feet and an heir to the throne growing inside of her. She wished for a boy. A boy would have secured the kingdom. It would have quieted the subjects who would never be content with a woman's rule. But we are dealt the hand we are given, and this is mine. To rule a country I scarcely know. To possess many things yet be kept so far away. It is strange to be the ruler of a country that you can remember so little of. I remember what Scotland looks like. At least the small part of it I have seen. It is green and beautiful with rolling hills and fresh air. It is cold. I will never forget the cold. The rain thunders down unforgivingly, and the air is brisk and cool. I love Scotland with my whole heart, and I am proud of the place that was my first home. Proud of the country that I have been charged to rule over. God chose me for this job, and I believe in his ultimate plan.

It is hard, however, to feel about Scotland in the way I feel about France. France has been my home for so long that I hardly know anything else. There will come a time when I am expected to put the needs of Scotland above the needs of anything else. I dread the day that I have to choose between my home and my kingdom. Between my God-given privilege and my love. As a Queen, I am expected to think of my country before my personal needs. A country I know so little of.

I remember a little of Scotland. I dream about her from time to time, she is green and stunning, with rolling hills and fresh air. She is cold. I will never forget the cold. The rain thunders down unforgivingly, and the air is brisk and biting. I love Scotland, for I may not know her well, but she is mine, and I have been tasked with providing for her. I hope that I am cut out to rule her. I was born a queen. I have been taught my whole life how to act like a queen. I have had tireless lessons on how one should govern a country but have yet to put it into practice. Some day I will be Queen of Scotland and France. I worry that I may not be as good a ruler as my mother. She never asked to rule and yet she has done such an excellent job of looking after Scotland for me.

My mother often writes to tell me of Scotland. She tells me of the strife that continues between the Catholic and Protestant faith. The Protestant's bang at her door like wolves hungry for blood. They want a protestant ruler. They want to be counted. The Catholics want a return to the true faith. They want to feel safe again in their own country. I am a Catholic. I was born into the Catholic religion, and I chose to continue in the Catholic faith. I worship in the faith of my family, of my husband and of the country I adopt. Yet I do not judge those who choose a different journey for I believe that we shall all meet in heaven one way or the other. I do not worry about my mother. She is strong. If anyone can keep my country safe while I am away, it is her. Although I do not know her as I wish I did, I have a deep respect for her. She travelled from France to marry my father and rule Scotland by his side. Yet she was left alone to rule with a small baby in the crib. It cannot have been easy. One day I hope to have

even an ounce of the strength that she holds within her. The picture I have in my mind of my mother is a loving one. It is the last time I saw her. The tears that she held back as she said goodbye. The kiss she planted on my cheek. All I know of my mother is what I can decipher from her letters. I know that she will do anything to protect myself and my country. I know she loves me even if it is not always evident in the way we speak. My father is more of an enigma to me. I never met him. I was so small when he died that instead, I have had to rely on stories to paint a picture of him. From what I can gather, he was a good king with a warriors heart. I hear that I look a lot like him. I have the undeniable Tudor in me. The strong will and auburn hair. I am my fathers daughter through and through with little of my mother about me. I have the heart that my grandmother Margaret Tudor had.
Steely determination and the will power to stand my ground. I am of the Tudor bloodline, and I am of the Stuart bloodline. Combining in me to make royal blood sing in my veins. I lay claim to two thrones—the throne of Scotland and the throne of England. No one can deny my claim. I am the niece of King Henry VIII and the great-granddaughter of Henry VII. I come directly from two great bloodlines. I could succeed to the English throne after Mary. Some believe I have a much better

claim than Elizabeth and that when Queen Mary dies, I should make my play for the throne. Elizabeth was made illegitimate when her mother's marriage to King Henry was annulled. But I do not know what I want. I do not strive to be all-powerful. I want a simple life with my love, but I have to do what is expected of me, and I believe that I will be hearing about England for a long time to come. Francis says he will love me whether I chose to pursue England or not. He is not ambitious. I believe that if he were told he could take me and hide away somewhere, leaving the throne to someone else, he would go and never look back. He only wants me. My mother would like for me to take England. She is a woman of ambition. She would love to see our two countries joined. She would love to see me ruler of a great nation, in control of three countries. I cannot imagine it. I already feel the weight of one country. England is a distant possibility that I shall concern myself with in the future.

***

In just under an hour, I will make my way to Notre Dame Cathedral. To the place where my life begins. I could hardly keep still this morning. My ladies fussed around me, trying to dress me in time for the ceremony. I am almost ready now. My Mary's have dressed me in my wedding gown and adorned me with jewels. My gown flows down me in stunning folds of fabric. It is white and silver, pure and angelic. I shine as I turn, the silver gleaming in the early morning light. Over the dress I wear a mantel of deep purple, a colour befitting my royal blood. It has been tirelessly worked on. Stitched and embroidered with gold. At my breast, I wear diamonds. They drip down from my neck delicately like glass. More diamonds gleam from my ears and on top of my head is a crown of every Jewell you can imagine. Sapphires, rubies, lapis, each colour beautifully accentuating my fair complexion. The blue of the sapphires brings out the deep blue of my eyes. The red of the rubies brings out the fire in my hair, which has been pinned to the top of my head, apart from one loose curl that falls down my face. I look around at my Mary's each of them dressed in gold. Each young and beautiful. Mary Beaton, a classic beauty, with her blond hair and blue eyes. She is the kindest of the four, with her soft and gentle ways. Mary Seton, darker in complexion but just as fair. She is a rare beauty among us. Her hair is black as coal, and her eyes are as dark as night. She has always seemed older than the rest of us. In both character and looks. She is wise for her years. She sees life for what it is. Then we have my dearest, Fleming. Possibly my favourite of the women. She is not afraid of my title. She sees me as her friend before anything else. She often complains about her looks. She doesn't have the delicate features of Mary B or the dark mysteriousness of Mary S, but Fleming holds her own beauty, it is in her composure. She carries herself with grace and poise that many do not possess. Her features are much harder than the rest, with her drawn in cheeks and straight nose. Then we have Mary Livingston. Mary is the sweetest amongst us and the one we often coddle. She is small and pretty, bonny they might say in Scotland. She has a fuller figure and less defined features. Her hair is auburn like mine and her complexion almost as pale. She is the naughtiest of my women, always joking at another's expense or laughing at the wrong time. Beaton has taken it upon herself to keep Levingston in check Today. However, I am confident that she will behave. I feel a great joy to have these women surround me today. These women that I know will be by my side through everything.

As I look into the mirror, I am taken aback by just how beautiful and graceful I look. Usually, I find that I am too quick to compare myself to others. I wish that I had Mary B's blonde hair or Mary L's womanly figure. Often, I feel that I am too lean. Too tall for my own body. I am envious of the other women at court. I have been told by many that I am a great beauty, but I do not always find that easy to believe. However, today I know it to be true. As I look at myself, I do not see a child. I see a woman finally grown into her looks. I cannot wait to see the look on Francis' face when I meet him at the altar.

Finally, Mary Fleming takes hold of my hand and informs me that the carriage is ready to take us to the cathedral. I take a breath to steady myself before making my way out to the courtyard. As the doors of the palace are opened, and we make our way down the curved steps of Fontainebleau, we see before us a stunning, gilded carriage. It shines golden as the early morning sunlight bounces off of it. As we climb in and take our seats, myself and the ladies are almost giddy with excitement. I have never seen the girls smile so much. They have waited as long as I have for this day.

As we make our way through Paris, the streets are lined with people who have come out to get a glimpse of their new Dauphine on her wedding day. Men, women, and children crowed around the carriage, hoping to get a look. The children smile and wave, the women shout words of love to me, and the men cheer as we pass by. The youngest spectators have never seen a royal, much less on their wedding day. They grin at me, some sitting on top their fathers' shoulders to get a better view. I am very well loved here in France. Having been here since I was a small child, the people have adopted me as one of their own. Both the royal family and the common people have been nothing but kind to me. France is more of my home than Scotland. And I love her more dearly than my own country. I cannot help but feel such a great sense of belonging as I look out of the carriage and at the land that I shall someday be the queen of. I look out at the people that will one day be my subjects and am filled with pride. I do not only marry Francis Today. I marry his people. I marry his country. It will be my most tremendous honour to stand beside him and rule. Together we will be a force for both Scotland and France. Today, I not only gain a husband, but I gain a king for Scotland. A king that will stand by my side and support me in all of my endeavours. I praise God for all that he bestows upon me.

As we turn a corner, I finally see Notre Dame before me in all of its beauty. It really is the shining jewel of Paris, with its stunning architecture and fabulous stained-glass windows. I have always enjoyed this cathedral. It was built with such care. With such a love for God in mind. It is the perfect place to solidify my union with Francis as God shines down on us. Outside of the cathedral is a small crowd of nobles and at the head of them stands Henry, Francis' father. He is smiling broadly as we come to a halt at the entrance. I have become accustomed to Henry's usual grimace and am taken by surprise as he happily offers me his hand to step down from the carriage. Henry's reason to be happy. Today is much different from my own. He sees me as a grand prize and hopes that with this marriage, he will gain both Scotland and England. He is a man hungry for power and is never far from a plot to gain more. I have known Henry to be a cold man. A man that is not against striking Francis when it suits him. He tells me that it is character building. That it will teach Francis to be a strong king. I believe it is actually to make Henry feel stronger. He prays on weakness. Today, however, he is in good spirits as he puts his best foot forward for all of the nobles. He looks younger than his years as his usual frown is replaced by a smile. I can see today that he is actually a rather handsome man. He and Francis share the same eyes. Only Francis' are kind and Henry's stern. He is tall and athletic with dark hair and delicate features. He wears a purple Jerkin today and a golden crown on top of his head. He is much bigger in stature to Francis, and that gives him great pleasure. The truth is that Henry is afraid that Francis will be a better king than he is.

Henry then offers me his arm and leads me into Notre Dame. Following close behind us are Francis' younger brothers, Charles and Henry. Little Henry has a look of self-importance today as he follows close behind my train. He is such a kind soul, just like his older brother. As we enter the cathedral, we are met by the glorious sounds of violins. Trumpets begin to blare, making everyone aware of our arrival. The guests turn and gasp as they get a look of me. The first person that I lock eyes with is Catherine. She smiles warmly as she sees me. She looks immaculate today, in a gown of rich silk, her hair pinned up like mine, pearls draped all over her. I am always taken aback by the way she looks. When I smile at her, it is the smile of a child seeking reassurance from their mother. Which is precisely what she is to me. A mother. She looks back at me with complete adoration. She is glad today. She has always known that Francis and I were made for one another and has been our biggest advocate in bringing this wedding to fruition. Then something else catches my eye, and I am lost completely. My mind can no longer focus on anything else as I see him. Finally, I see him. He is waiting for me, and when my eyes meet his, my heart stops. I am frozen at the doors to Notre Dame as his eyes hold me fixed in place. I am rooted to the spot as I am taken away to another world altogether. Suddenly I am soaring above the clouds and no longer attached to my own body. Forget about the jewels and the gowns. Forget about the gathering crowd. Of France or Scotland. This is where I am supposed to be, and in just a few short steps, I will have finally found my true home. The love I feel for him is only matched by the love he feels for me, and in this moment, that love overwhelms me.

Henry whispers my name to wake me from my dreaming, and I suddenly remember my place and the expectant crowd that fills Notre Dame. As we begin our walk down the cathedral aisle, it takes every ounce of strength I have not to forget all protocol and run to my love. The wedding march is unbearably slow and as we near Francis my hand is already outstretched waiting for him. He takes my hand, and his touch instantly warms my whole body. The feeling is like no other as he pulls me into his arms and places a soft kiss on top of my head. We should not be so informal, but it is hard to contain the joy we feel when we are so close to each other. I take in the whole of him, and my heart melts. He looks more handsome today than I have ever seen him. He has dressed in white and silver to match me. He's jerkin is silk. He wears diamonds and rubies around his neck and on his hands. I look up into his eyes, and I am met by the adorable look of a man very much in love. His blue eyes are wide and puppylike as he fixes his eyes on me. His lips, one of his most alluring features, are posed as if he wants to say something but has lost the words. His cheeks blush as he takes in my full figure. He stands a little shorter than me, but that has never bothered either of us. Francis is not athletic like his father. He is slim and small. But today, he looks majestic—more king-like than Henry. I completely lose myself in him.

I am only brought back down to earth by his voice at my ear "Mary, my love. They are waiting for us." He chuckles.

The ceremony begins, and the priest starts with a speech about the sanctity of marriage and the weight of the promise we make today. Today Francis and Mary enter into the unbreakable promise of marriage. Through their love, they will be bonded in a relationship of companionship and unity, for the rest of their lives. As God looks down upon them, they promise never to divide what God has united."

The rest of his words are a blur. All I can think about is how I just want to be alone with Francis, how I long for him to reach up and touch my cheek. To run my hands through his hair. To kiss him. The priest prompts us to repeat his words. Francis goes first, his voice breaking slightly as he speaks, then it is my turn. "I Mary do take Francis to be my lawful wedded husband." I begin. "in sickness and in health." "To honour and obey." And my final, eternal promise. "Till death, we do part." It is the easiest, truest vow that I have ever made. We are bonded until death and beyond.

We take mass, and finally, the priest blesses us under a cloth of silver. The priest announces us as husband and wife and the nobles rise from their seats, cheering with joy. I feel something within me in this moment. Something so final. Something solid. The link between our two souls is finally complete. Francis' eyes meet mine, and it is all so very clear. Our forever has just begun.

Chapter 2

Today has been the best day of my life. I lie now beside the fire, Francis' arms wrapped around me and a smile of contentment on my face as I think back over the day's events. I have so much to be thankful for at this moment. My husband, who at this moment runs his hands through my hair and places gentle kisses on top of my head. My new family, who have always treated me like one of their own. My two countries, which will live harmoniously, ruled by Francis and me.

I could not feel more joy than I do now. I have everything I could ever want in this room with me. I keep thinking about how Francis is truly mine now, that we are indeed each other's. My heart beats a little faster as I realise that I can reach up and kiss him whenever I want, that I can tell him that I love him, just because I feel it in that moment, That I can hold him and love him every moment for the rest of my life. What an honour I have been granted to love this man.

Henry spared no expense today. We have spent the whole day feasting and celebrating. From the lavish ceremony to the great feast that Henry had laid on, every person in the palace was in good spirits. The nobles smiled and danced; every one of them congratulating Francis and I. This was a good day for France. The whole country has watched our love grow and blossom. The people of France have eagerly awaited our union. And they are all genuinely happy to see us finally together.

If I am to be honest, as much as I have enjoyed the day, I am delighted to at last be alone with my sweetheart. All day, I could think of nothing but finally being in his arms. When we are before the kingdom, we have a protocol to follow, which leaves us with only a few stolen moments to enjoy being newlyweds. I am glad that we can finally be ourselves. Usually, at this point in the evening, the bedding ceremony would take place. Thankfully, Henry has allowed us to share our wedding night privately. Throughout the day, I blushed every time I thought about the evening I would share with Francis. Nerves grew in my belly at the idea of sharing my bed with him. And yet, now we are here, I find all nerves have dissipated. Something just feels so right about this. Something deep within me longs for this. I am grateful that I will share this experience with a man who makes me feel so safe. Frankly, this is something that I want to do, something that a part of me has longed to do for a while. I want our relationship to be complete in every way.

When we arrived in his bed chambers, Francis pulled me into a passionate kiss. The kiss of someone who had been denied the touch of their love for so long. It was needy and thirsty, as was the kiss I returned. I was breathless as he pulled away. I ran my hands through his hair and allowed him to place gentle kisses down my neck and along my collarbone. The feeling was like nothing I had ever experienced before. It was as if my skin came to life under his touch. We did not race to jump into bed. Instead, we took our time exploring each other's bodies with our hands. Francis shook as his hand gently glided along my stomach, and I realised that he was nervous. I pulled away and looked at him. I think the look on my face told him all he needed to know about my love for him. I kissed him again, this time wanting to convey all of the emotion that I felt within me. I wanted to say, without words, that it was okay. There was no need for nerves. I slid his jerkin off of his shoulders and began to pull his shirt off, but Francis took my hands to stop me.

"My love, there is no need to rush." His voice shook ever so slightly. "Can we just sit a while . . . Just enjoy being alone?"

Francis walked over to the chair by the fireplace and pulled me onto his knee. I gently placed my head onto his shoulder and allowed the sensation of being held by him to wash over me. We have sat in this spot for ages now, allowing the hours to slip away. I have never felt more contented than I do now in the arms of the man I love. We are entirely alone. If I could have it my way, we would stay this way forever. The world could carry on around us, and I would be happy to stay here with Francis, like statues frozen in time. I need nothing more than his lips on my cheek and his arms around my waist. If only we could be sustained by love alone.

After a long while, Francis breaks the silence. "Mary, today has been wonderful," he begins. "But I am just so happy to be alone with you."

"As am I," I reply.

"Can you believe that we are finally wed?" He chuckles.

"It feels as if my whole life has been leading me up to this point," I confess.

Francis' smile is broad as he answers me. "As if we were made for this purpose alone," he agrees.

"It is the only thing that makes sense to me,"

"I just hope that I am good enough for you. That I am strong enough for Scotland. I worry that I am not enough. Father would have me believe that I am not enough," Francis admits. Tears begin to form in his eyes, and he drops his head as if he is ashamed. I'm taken aback by his confession. I had no idea that he felt this way. I turn to face him and take his face in my hands.

"Francis, you are all I have ever wanted. Never question if you are good enough for me. You are too good for me. And you will be a strong and courageous king to Scotland and France."

"I hope so," he says gently.

"You know that I will never want anyone else. You may not physically be as strong as others, but your strength lies within your heart, and it is the purest heart I have ever known. You are so good. So gentle and loving. How could I ever want anyone else?" I kiss him gently on the lips. "You are the one I adore. I will always want you. You are going to be a wonderful king to Scotland and France. Then one day, you are going to be a wonderful father to our children. I see it already, my love. I see our future so clearly. Never doubt my love, for it is as vast as the ocean, and it's all for you."

Francis pulls me in closer and kisses me. "Mary, your love for me astounds me." He allows the tears to fall now, slowly. "You are an angel sent to me from heaven."

I laugh gently. "No, my love. You are my angel." I wipe the tears from his face.

When we kiss, it is like fire as Francis grows hot under my touch. He begins to get the feel of my whole body as we rise from the chair, and he takes my hand and pulls me to the bed.

"We do not have to do anything tonight, darling. No one will know," I suggest. Francis still appears to shake from nerves, and I do not want to cause him any stress.

To my surprise, Francis is quickly behind me, and he begins to unlace my gown. His mouth is at my ear as he speaks in almost a whisper. "There is nothing I want more than to become one with my wife." He places feather-light kisses down my back as he goes.

I turn in his arms and kiss him on the lips, allowing his hands to graze down my back. "Love, I thought you were nervous about this?" I ask.

"I am," Francis admits. "But nothing will stop me from giving you the whole of me."

"I want you," I confess. We both shake from head to toe as we slowly undress each other. Neither of us has much of an idea about what we are doing, and we both giggle as nervous tension fills the air. All I need to know at this moment is that I love him and that he loves me.

He is so gentle. So tender as he lies me back onto the bed. He moves his hands awkwardly, and I am all limbs as I move to allow him to climb in beside me. At first, we simply kiss. Francis' touch is so soft as he runs his hands all over my body. It feels glorious to be touched by him. He kisses my neck and my thighs. His lips feel so sweet as they graze my thighs. Francis stares into my eyes and, with a slight stutter to his voice, asks if I am comfortable. I kiss him in answer, conveying that everything is as it should be.

And then, suddenly and carefully, Francis is making love to me, and the fear begins to melt away. He is so careful as he moves slowly to keep from causing me too much discomfort. It hurts me at first, but as we continue, it becomes less painful. Every few moments, he stops to make sure that I am comfortable. His lips are always on mine as he whispers that he loves me. His hands are in my hair, and his eyes fixed on mine. I love how close I feel to him at this moment. I feel more connected with him now than I ever have as we experience this for the first time together. He is my first everything. My first friend, my first love, and now, he is the first and last man that I will ever lie with.

For a few short moments, we are entirely lost in each other. We move together in gentle unison as our bodies collide. And to my surprise, it becomes pleasurable. It is like an ache in my bones as Francis keeps a delicate rhythm. He moves back and forth, always touching me, always caressing me. His hands are on my breasts, on my stomach, on my neck. He places sweet kisses along my jaw. I touch him back, allowing my hands to feel all of his body. I touch his chest and feel his beating heart underneath. He takes my hand, and with one final movement, he collapses on top of me. We lie in a contented heap of sweat and exhaustion.

Francis moves so that he may lie beside me and hold me in his arms. We both try to catch our breath as I lie naked next to him. The feel of his skin on mine is indescribable, our skin bare to the other. "How do you feel, my love?" he asks as he runs his finger down my cheek.

I take a breath, trying to gather my composure. I cannot keep the smile from my face. "I feel like I love you more now than I ever have. I did not think it possible," I say as I lie in awe of my incredible husband. "How about you?" I ask breathlessly.

"I could not have said it better myself." Francis kisses my head. "I adore you, Mary. I promise you that nothing will ever part us."

We do not move for the rest of the night. We sleep beside each other, our limbs wrapped around each other, naked. Our hearts full with the love that we feel for the other.

***

We spend the next few days celebrating our marriage. Henry has put on a grand, three-day event filled with feasts and masques to entertain our guests. He is showing the world how magnificent France is and how happy he is to claim the Scottish queen as one of his family. Unfortunately, Francis and I do not spend nearly as much time together as we would like. He has his duties by his father's side as Henry shows his heir off to all the world, and my duties are to sit beside Catherine on our thrones and look pretty. As entertaining as the whole thing is, it can get a bit tiresome sitting and smiling politely. I want to dance with my husband and laugh and make merry. The only time we have is when we steal glances throughout the day or when his hand gently grazes mine in passing. My stomach fills with butterflies every time he walks by me or when I see him standing by Henry's side, tall and proud, just the way he should be.

Then the evening comes, and finally, we may be alone. We talk about our day. We kiss and cuddle. Then we make love and sleep soundly side by side. The next day we eat together, then go about our duties. Francis is very busy. I have little to do at the moment. I long for the day to pass and the night to come, when everything is right in the world again. The moments when we are alone, hands interlocked and my head on his chest, we talk about everything. Of our future. Of the dreams that we have. Of the plans for our countries. Our hearts are the same. Our dreams are the same. We both see a brighter future for our countries. We talk of all the children we want to have: a boy to carry on our line and strong girls like the long line of women before them. I close my eyes, and I see those children—the boys, handsome like their father, the girls with my strength and determination. This dream is so close, I could touch it. For now, I wish to simply enjoy my life with Francis. Responsibility will always be there; our youth will not.

Chapter 3

Being wed to Francis is a breath of fresh air. It is a joy to wake up to him each morning, and to gaze into his eyes each night before I fall to sleep. I love him more now than I ever thought possible. I am not complete unless I am lying in his arms. We stay together every night.

Our days are often spent apart due to the responsibilities we both have. Francis is next in line to be king, and his father is keen to teach him all that he knows so that he may carry on the Valois name with pride. Francis wants to be a good king. He tells me of the future he sees for France, a future where his people never go hungry. Where everyone is treated as equals. I know that with me as his queen, I will do everything I can to make that dream a reality.

Henry is still full of life, and I believe it shall be a long while before Francis and I are called up to do the job. Once that happens, I know that things will change for both of us. We will have to work harder at our relationship. With Scotland pulling me in one direction and France pulling us in another, we will find it harder to steal moments together. Which is why I made Francis promise that even if things get hard, even if we are both busy with delegates and orders of state, every few days, we make time to do the things that we enjoy together. No matter the amount of business we have on our plates, we ensure that we take a few hours just to be Mary and Francis. I do not want to lose the feeling of having him all to myself, even if it is only for a few short hours.

I despair at the thought of him being taken away from my side, but it is part of what it means to be a ruler. Your kingdom comes first, and your marriage second. For now, everything is perfect. For now, my mother rules Scotland in my stead, and I am nothing more than a figurehead. However, this will not be the case forever. The idea that at some point I will be the ruling queen of not just one, but two countries weighs heavy on me these days, and I find myself having doubts as to whether I am ready. Although I have been the Queen of Scotland for almost all of my life, I have not spent a lot of time as acting ruler. Someday I will have to be queen regnant, and the thought scares me. I should be confident in my abilities. After all, I have spent my life learning what it means to be queen—understanding how good rulers should behave.

My grandmother, Antoinette de Bourbon, ensured that I had instilled in me everything I may need to rule and rule well. I stayed with her for quite some time when I first came to France, and over time, we formed an incredible connection. She is a woman of great strength and willpower. I have always looked up to her and the way that she capably looks after the lands owned by my Guise family. She may be a woman, but she is the real head of the family here in France. I hope that I am as resilient as she is when I come into my own. I hold a vast place in my heart for my grandmother. She is the closest real family I have here in France. She was here when my mother was not. Antionette is more responsible for my upbringing than anyone else. She is the person who has shaped my opinions and influenced the way I think and feel about things. She is the reason for my faith in God. For my strength. To her, family is of utmost importance. She puts her kin above anything else.

Antionette is a formidable woman who works hard to ensure that this family has its deserved place in society. She always said that I was destined to be the queen of France. She knew that her kin would rule long before I was born. The Guises do not care much for my Scottish crown. France has always been more important to them. They are an ambitious family who have won their way to the top of the aristocracy. My mother knew what she was doing when she sent me to Antionette. She could not have put me in more capable hands. Under Antoinette's guardianship, I received lessons in all the things that would equip me for my future.

It was not always all hard work, though. We had a lot of fun, and I enjoyed the dance lessons very much. Grandmother would often be a part of these. She loves nothing more than to dance, and whenever she hosted a banquet, she would be the first up on her feet with a young gentleman. Her laugh is one of the most heart-warming things to hear. Often, when I require a bit of comfort, it is her laugh that sounds in my head. She is one of the happiest people I have met, the kind of person you could never be sad around, and her beaming smile is always so contagious.

She is always so quick to praise me, too. Always so encouraging. She couldn't help but tell everyone how proud she was of her pretty little granddaughter. She would write to my mother and express her happiness at being charged with looking after such a graceful little queen. I loved her every bit as much as she loved me, and I enjoyed nothing more than sitting on her knee as she read to me.

She loved telling stories and would often tell me about my history and where I came from. She always told the stories like they were a grand adventure. It is thanks to her that I long to see more of the world. I loved to hear the stories of my grandfather, Claude. He was a general, and an extremely successful one at that. He had been responsible for many victories and had impressed Francis I so much that he had Claude made the first Duke of Guise. Grandfather was a stern man who did not have much time to deal with children. He died when I was only eight years old, so I did not know him as well as my grandmother.

As I think of her now, a smile comes to my face. I am always so taken aback by how beautiful she is. Now I see some of her in my own face. We both have slim faces and slender forms. She is unlike me with raven hair and brown eyes, but we have the same smile. She and my mother both look alike. They are both great beauties. I am more my father, but I see one of their looks cross my face from time to time.

My grandmother is very conservative in her appearance. She dresses in darker colours, with the hems all the way up to her chin. I used to love when she would sit me down on her bed and show me all of her jewels. She would lay them out onto her bed and allow me to pick each one up in wonder. It made me so happy to hear the stories of where she got them from. Some gifts were from my grandfather, some handed down to her.

She is also a deeply religious woman. Her worshipping of God is the most crucial part of her day, and we would never miss an opportunity to pray. It would be the one thing that got me into trouble. If I did not take my prayers seriously, she would scold me, and I would then receive a lengthy lecture on why I should be thankful for all that I have because they are gifts from God. She would tell me how he has chosen me for the role I am in. I am special, and God has given me an important purpose.

It all weighs on me sometimes, the idea that God has deemed me right for this role. I feel as if I have many people watching me. Many people are expecting me to succeed. The fact that I am a Tudor, a Guise, and a Stuart should mean that I have everything I need within me to be a great ruler. I have the essence of two great royal houses running through my veins. I feel like I have a power I do not yet know how to control. After all, I am only fifteen years old. Yet there have been men younger than I to rule alone.

I also worry that Scotland will not accept me. They are so used to being ruled by regents. So used to my mother and her advisers. I believe I must seem foreign to them—a Scottish queen who has been brought up French. I worry that I will not be good enough for them. I am loved in France, and my mother says that Scotland loves me, but I have never known my people. How can I know what they truly feel about their faceless queen? Francis says that soon enough, we shall visit Scotland. He will accompany me home so that we may show the country their new king and queen.

One day, I shall inevitably take over the ruling of Scotland. My mother cannot do it forever. I am coming to an age where I will have to look after my own affairs and my own people. I worry that this will take me away from my husband. Will I have to live in Scotland part of the time? So far away from my Francis. I could not bear to be so far away from him, yet I know that I would have to put my country first. I am unsure how prepared I am to put the needs of my country above the man that I love. I know that if it came down to it, he would need to put France first, and I could not blame him. We are rulers first and lovers second.

I sit today in my rooms. My ladies surround me with books or embroidery. There is nothing that needs my attention, and I am determined to have the afternoon to myself. It has been so busy lately with the wedding and the celebrations that I am worn out. Francis will join me for dinner later, but for now, I enjoy a little bit of my own company.

Today is the first time that I have been able to put my thoughts into some sort of order. I find that when I have a quill and parchment in my hands, I am at peace. Writing about my thoughts and feelings helps me to work through the things that worry me. I put the words down onto paper, and it helps me to organise my busy mind. The thoughts that I have I can tell no one but Francis. No one else understands the pressures that I feel. He is in a similar position to me. Only he has to wait to inherit his crown, and I already possess mine.

He is always so respectful of my feelings. He has an ear for whatever is bothering me. We have had many conversations about the future. I tell him how much I worry for the years ahead and he soothes me. He reminds me that as long as we are together, then nothing else matters. We can get through anything if we work as one.

Things were so much simpler when we were children. When our responsibilities were so far away, those years were all too short. It seems that we went from babes to adults in no time at all. We were never able to be just children in any case. We may not have known it, but we have always been working towards our destinies. It was merely easier when our parents took the brunt of our duties. Now

Francis is in full king training, and my mother is slowly putting more on me. She comes to me for advice now. She wishes me to start making decisions for my country. I believe she is gradually getting ready for me to take over. Her goal is for me to one day have the full responsibility of Scotland on my shoulders. She believes in me. If only I had that belief in myself.

When I think of our childhood, I realise how easy everything was then. When we could just be ourselves. I think of the day we first met, when I was presented to Francis as his betrothed. My grandmother had brought me to Fontainebleau, and once there, we were first introduced to Henry and Catherine. At first, Catherine De' Medici appeared cold. She had a strong look and a furrowed brow. She was beautiful. Intimidatingly so. She sat on her throne looking down on me with a quizzical look on her face at first, as if she were sizing me up. Then her face broke into a smile and she stepped down from her throne to greet me. I remember how she kissed me on both cheeks and said in the most beautiful accent, "Ahh, Marie, jolie petite reine".

Catherine always astounded me when I was young. She always looked immaculate. No matter the occasion, she was always dressed to impress, decked in the most stunning of jewels, constantly dressed in the brightest colours. Exactly the image of a queen.

Catherine is yet another woman who I can credit with shaping me into the person I am today. She had as much of a hand in my upbringing as my grandmother did, and she has become dearer to me than even my own mother. She raised me in exactly the same way she raised her own children. I was never denied a single ounce of love from the Valois. When I had sleepless nights so far away from home, it was Catherine's mothering arms that would enfold me. When I fell and hurt myself, it was Catherine who scooped me up and cradled me.

It is Catherine who I watched and imitated, hoping to rule as she does. Her kindness and love are the reasons that I feel whole and wanted. Where my own mother sent me away, Catherine kept me close. When I think of my future as Queen of France, I think of her and the perfect example she has set for me to follow. I wish to continue with the grace and beauty that Catherine carries with her every day. I have always been in awe of the way she cares for each of her subjects, for the kindness that she bestows upon those lower than her. She has always been a credit to Henry. She is the person who keeps him on the right track, and even when he is too busy running around with his mistress, it is always Catherine who keeps him steady.

Henry was also kind to me when we first met, but there was a coldness to him that I could not understand. He was intimidating in a different way; I was so small then, and Henry towered over me. He was strong and loud. I remember being extremely wary of him at first. I bowed, just as Grandmother had shown me, and he returned my bow politely before calling for Francis. He has not always been so cordial, and now he barely makes note of my presence unless it is somehow beneficial to him. Henry is power hungry and would do anything to add to that which he already has.

Henry can be unkind and has many times taken his frustration out on Francis. He is not happy that the child to succeed him is, in his words, "weak and sickly." He wants France to have a strong leader after he is gone, and he does not believe that Francis is up to the task. I believe that the truth of it is that Henry is jealous. Francis is young and has his whole reign lain out before him. Henry is getting older, and his days as a young king have passed him by.

It is true that Francis was not the healthiest of children. Because of his size and stature, he was vulnerable to any illness. He struggled to breathe when he was a baby, and Catherine was worried that he would not live to see his first year. But as I have said before, Francis is a fighter. He would not give up easily. Francis may be small, but he has never let that stop him. From the first moment I saw him, I knew he was special. The moment he walked in, my face lit up. I could not help but think what a magnificent little thing stood in front of me. He was so small, so fragile, yet so proud and strong. He walked in with his head held high and bowed low to me.

"Queen Marie. It is my honour to meet you," he said in the sweetest of French accents. I was only a year older than him, but the difference was so apparent. I was clearly way ahead for my years, and Francis was small and frail for his age. I towered above him even then. I dipped into a curtsy, and as scripted by my grandmother, said, "Dauphin. I am incredibly pleased to meet you. Votre maison est magnifique."

The next part had not been planned by anyone, but I just remember not being able to help myself. I walked over to Francis and pulled him into a hug. When I stood back, I waited to be scolded by my grandmother for breaking protocol, but to my surprise, Catherine and Henry laughed.

"They like each other already," Henry exclaimed, clapping his hands together.

From that moment, I took hold of Francis' hand and refused to let go. I kept him by my side for the rest of the day. He was such a shy little thing and barely spoke a word to me to begin with. I pulled him out of his shell in no time. After the great feast that Henry had put on in my honour, I broke decorum yet again when I extended my hand to Francis and asked him to dance. Fortunately, everyone was so taken by the little royals that no one cared that I had broken protocol. I took the lead due to the fact that I had had many lessons and Francis, still to this day, is an awkward dancer. We whirled around the room, and the nobles cooed and awed at their future king and queen. We were loved from the very first moment we met. The French people fell in love with the petit couple.

I was sad at first when my grandmother left me in a strange place. It was scary to be left with people I did not know, with no family around me. But soon enough, the Valois became my family. Catherine made me feel welcome from the very beginning, and Henry made sure I wanted for nothing. I was given the best tutors and rooms that befitted my position. I quickly grew to love Francis' sisters—Elisabeth, who was a year younger than Francis, and Claude, who was just a baby. I felt as if they were my own siblings. Elisabeth and I grew up to be great friends. When I was not with Francis, I was gossiping with Elisabeth. In France, I suddenly had something I had never really felt before. And that was a family, siblings, and a home. A permanent home.

I look back on my childhood and see a happy one. I believe I have had a better life here in France than I would have done had I stayed with my mother in Scotland. Here, I had many things to entertain me. I had a big family to enjoy. From the beginning, I was accepted as a new addition to the family. I loved my new friends and playmates. For the first time, I was around children my own age rather than adults. I had other children who I could share my lessons with, other people who shared a great responsibility on young shoulders. I still received visits from my grandmother from time to time and letters from my mother, but I was now a Valois. I think Mother realised this. I do not begrudge my mother for sending me away. I know that it was the best thing for me. She only did it to keep me safe.

I wish I had a better understanding of her. I wish I knew her better, but she is almost a stranger to me. What I know of her I know from the letters I have received over the years. However, they very often complain of the state of Scotland and not so often inquire after me. I believe she loves me, but I also believe she shuns that love in order to protect herself from being hurt by my absence. The problem with becoming queen at just six days old is that you are vulnerable to any threat. Usurpers see an easy way to the throne.

It was important that Mother find me a match that would benefit us and keep me safe. At first, she considered a match with England. England is next door to my little Scotland, and as such would be the perfect protection for a young queen. But Henry VIII was a complicated man, and when he intended for me to wed his young son Edward, he instead acted with force to bully us into agreement instead of coming to us with peace. This pushed my French mother to rethink the match, and she decided that France was the perfect solution. France would not only offer her protection as kin, but it would gain something in us too. It would be getting the queen of Scotland and an heir to the English throne. Henry could not refuse.

Everything my mother did was out of love—love for me and for Scotland. I only wish I could feel the love she has for me. I have a half-brother. He is the result of an affair my father had many years ago. I look forward to seeing him in person once again someday. For now, my family begins and ends with Francis. He is all I need. All I will ever need. And soon enough, we will make our own family, our own line of little royals.

Francis has just come into my rooms, and I am awakened from my reflection. I take a long look at him. He looks tired. His father is asking more and more of him these days, and Francis is so determined to be a good king that he spends hours with Henry, learning from him and taking note of how his father behaves.

I instantly stand and am by his side. His arms are around my waist and my head on his shoulder. He waves a hand and my ladies begin to pack away their things and leave us. We dine in my room tonight, appreciating some alone time together. I cannot help but take note of how lost Francis looks. He is stressed and worn out. He smiles every time I catch his eye, but I can tell that it is forced. We eat in near silence, which is strange for us. Usually, we cannot wait to talk about our days, but the mood is solemn tonight.

As our plates are cleared away, Francis gets up and goes straight to bed. I climb in beside him and rest my head on his chest.

"What is the matter, sweetheart?" I ask as I take hold of his hand and kiss it.

Francis sighs and runs his other hand through his hair. He looks older than his years today. He looks tired. His beautiful eyes are surrounded by dark circles and his jaw is clenched tightly shut. It makes my heart feel heavy. He is trying so hard at the moment to impress his father and the nobles whose backing he needs to ensure that the transition to his rule is smooth.

"I'm fine, love. It's just that my father was particularly hard work today," Francis tells me. "He said that I am no better than a bastard and that if he had it his way, he would make my brother king before me." Tears well in Francis' eyes. His father always knows exactly how to upset him. He has never treated him in the way he deserves. "He said that he is ashamed to have a son as weak as I am. That I do not have the guts to be king."

It makes my blood boil to see how his father affects him so much. Francis is everything that Henry is not. He is gracious and kind. He is good from the inside out. Francis will be a good king for every reason that Henry is not.

"Francis, darling, you must not let your father get to you. He is scared. He knows that one day you shall possess all that he owns, and he is not ready to give that up." I take his hand in mine. "You will be a better king than him by far. So much so that his reign will be left in the dust and yours remembered long after we are gone."

Francis smiles for the first time this evening. He holds me so tightly within his arms. "Do you know what I am always astounded by Mary?" he asks as he cups my face in his hands.

"What's that, my love?"

"Your unwavering and absolute faith in me." Francis' eyes are filled with love as he kisses me. "Whenever I lose confidence in myself, all I have to do is look at you and I know that I am worth something. *You* make me worth something."

"I feel the same. Whenever I feel low, I turn and see you by my side, and then nothing else matters. I will always believe in you, Francis. You are the greatest man I know. Your father knows that you are going to be a better king than he, and he cannot handle the idea that he will lose control to you. He is scared of death, and your presence makes him realise his mortality. You remind him that one day he shall die." My words are harsh but ring true.

Francis looks so much lighter as the worry lifts off his face. It is awful to see him so affected by the words of one bitter man.

"I love you, Mary. More than you could ever know." Francis' lips are soft as he places a kiss on my forehead.

"Not half as much as I love you." I run my hands over the stubble on his face. "Tomorrow, tell your father that you are unwell and spend the day with me," I suggest, needing a day alone with Francis more than anything.

“Father will be mad,” he answers. But he is thoughtful for a moment. “But let him stew. I want to spend the day with my wife.”

Chapter 4

Today, I awoke in the arms of the man I love. Usually, Francis has rushed off to meet his father long before I wake. However, today he has chosen to be with me instead. As far as Henry knows, Francis felt unwell during the night and does not feel able to do any lessons today. Henry will surely come back with some vile words about a sickly king, but we do not care. For once, Francis is choosing to spend the day how he wants to. He is so used to following his father's orders and keeping to his duty that he has rarely had time just to be a young man. Francis will do anything to ensure that he is the best king he can possibly be, even if in doing so, he is unhappy. It is an admirable quality, but I wish for him to enjoy the time he has before he succeeds his father. I wish for us to be young and carefree, even if it is only for a short time.

The morning passes as we snooze soundly beside one another. The early sun shines through the window and gently illuminates the room. We do not move from the bed until lunchtime. We eat in peace, with nothing but silence in the air and the soft breeze that flows from the window. Francis smiles at me from across the table. He looks happy today, I think that the everyday stress is far away from his thoughts. There will be consequences, and we both know it. But for now, we are an average couple, young and in love, sharing a lazy day together. I intend to distract him today. I want him to know that no matter how heavy the crown may weigh on his head, he will always have a sense of peace with me.

After lunch, we decide to take a stroll in the palace grounds. The breeze is fresh, with the subtle warmth of spring hanging in the air. The buzz of the palace fades away as we breathe in the beautiful nature that God has provided for us. We find a space in the palace grounds where we are concealed from view and perch under a tree for the rest of the afternoon. We are both at peace today, as we lie beneath a tree, with the warm sun on our faces and the dewy grass beneath us. It had rained a little this morning, but that did not stop us from sitting a while.

Outside is where Francis comes to life. He smiles contentedly as the bee's hum and the breeze gently ruffles his hair. We love nothing more than being in nature together. The world outside is the perfect example of all the graces that God has given us. The tall, strong trees that have stood in these grounds for hundreds of years. The freshly trimmed grass that is soft under our feet. The daises that return every year. We can completely lose ourselves out here. There is no one bowing to us or serving us. No nobles are vying for our attention. We are entirely alone. Just Mary and Francis, the way we wish it would always be. I feel so complete outside of the crowded palace and surrounded by vast stillness. We can hear ourselves think. We can say what we wish. There is no protocol to follow when there are no eyes on us.

"Do you know what I find fascinating?" Francis asks. He looks quizzically up at the sky as if he cannot quite work it out.

"What is it, my love?" I reply.

Francis is silent for a moment, as if he is trying to find the best way to frame his words. Finally, he turns to me with the strangest look on his face, like he is some distance away from here. "That one day, when everything here ceases to exist—when the palace is gone, when my parents are gone, when you and I are no longer here, and this world is a vastly different place—this will stay constant. The sky will never move. The sea will surround these lands. The air will continue to give life. They will still be here. Never changing. Never leaving. Remaining in a constant cycle of life. Is that not the most extraordinary thing?"

It was a truly extraordinary thing that something could be so permanent. No matter what happens, these things will always remain. And yet the answer was so clear.

"God has made them eternal," I answer softly.

Francis looks at me as if all of the love in the world is bestowed in him to give to me. "You're absolutely right, my love." He beams. "That is how I see our love. Unmoving. Unshakable. Eternal."

I do not give him a chance to say any more; I sweep him into my arms and smother him with kisses. It is funny that I always think I could not love him more. That my heart would quite surely burst should it carry any more of him within it. And then he says something like this, something so true, so real, and it grows within me to make more space for him.

***

We stay in one place for the whole day, only moving when the sun starts to disappear, and the sky darkens. We make our way back to our apartments, we are starving, but not for food. We are hungry to be as one. We can hardly keep our hands off of each other. His hands are in my hair, running down my back, on my breast. His lips are on mine. Francis takes hold of my hand and leads me through the halls. We stop for no one and ignore the bows of the court around us.

Francis is full of passion as he guides me towards the bed. His eyes are fixed on my face, like those of a predator on its prey, as he begins to unlace my bodice and kiss me from head to toe. His lips are hot on mine as he covers me in kisses. He is eager. He is full of barely contained lust as he begins to undress himself.

"I want you, Mary," he says as he takes hold of my hand. "I want to be a part of you."

Even in his haste, Francis is as gentle as ever. He loosens my hair and allows it to fall in waves down my back. He cups his hand against my neck and holds me close to him. His lips are on my throat. They linger over my breasts as he kisses them tenderly, and then they find their way to my thighs, his breath warm on my skin. He does not make any further moves before checking that I want this too. He moves up to kiss me on the lips and I breathe a whispered "yes" in his ear. Within an instant, Francis is making love to me. He makes me feel complete as we become closer and closer together. I am full of love and longing, as the connection that we already have is made even stronger. We are one being as we move together. His lips are always on me, and his eyes never leave mine. This is all I want forever. I never want him to stop joining with me. I want us to become so close that we can scarcely tell who is whom. The love that I feel for him is obsessive, and as he holds me and loves me, I feel that obsession grow. I cannot live without him.

The first time we made love, Francis was nervous, and it was over too quickly. But now, we are both so much surer of ourselves and of each other. Making love to Francis is the single-most pleasurable thing in my life. Being able to have the man that I love become a part of me is a feeling like no other.

We lie in each other's arms for a long while after. We do not say a word as we lie side by side, trying to catch our breath. I am sure that this is exactly what heaven will feel like for me. I cannot think of a time in my life when I have felt so pure, so blissfully happy. This is the way I will feel every day for the rest of my life as long as Francis is beside me.

***

When we finally catch our breath, we realise just how famished we are. The sky outside is completely dark now, and most of the members of court have already had their meal. We send for the cooks and ask that they prepare us some wine and a bite to eat. We ask all of our attendants to make themselves scarce for the evening. I am happy to serve my husband; it is a wife's duty, after all. After our meal, we sit by the fire and play a hand of cards. Francis knows that if we play for money, he will end up owing me. I cannot believe just how perfect today has been. All that is left is to lie in bed, my husband's arm around me, and sleep soundly. If only we could do this every day.

As we prepare to go to bed, there is a banging on the door. Without admittance, Henry opens the door and storms into the room. He is angry,

"I hope that you two have had a lovely day today?" His face is red with anger as he eyes Francis. "You see, I was told that the dauphin was unwell and that he would be spending the day in bed. But it seems that I was lied to, as I was just informed that the lovely young couple spent their day outside."

"I . . . I w-w-was ill, F-f-ather," Francis stutters. "I d-d-did rrrest." His nerves grow. I take his hand and realise that he is shaking. That is the terror that Henry has filled him with.

"I would have thought that if you were too unwell to be with me today, you would have been in bed, not lounging around the palace grounds with your wife."

"Francis needed to take some air, Henry. I thought it best . . ." I begin to explain, hoping to save Francis from answering. Henry, however, is uninterested in our excuses.

"I do not care what you thought. You may be a queen, but you are still only a woman." Henry spits as his temper rises. His true colours shine through as he lets anger get the better of him.

"I may be only a woman, but I deserve your respect, and so does my husband." I remain calm as I reply to Henry.

"Listen here, you silly girl. Put one finger out of line, and I will ruin you." Henry is full of rage as he takes hold of my shoulders.

Francis, who has been silent until now, stands tall as he removes his father's hands from me. "Careful how you speak to my wife."

In an instant, Henry swings his arm and struck Francis on he head. Francis falls to the floor as the blow hits him. I am beside him in a moment.

"Francis. Francis, are you okay?" I ask.

Francis nods but has turned red with embarrassment. He complains that his head throbs as I cradle him in my arms.

"You are a pitiful excuse for a man, Henry. I may only be a woman, but I am Queen of Scotland, and someday, England. You need me. Touch Francis again, and I might find that my interest in the English crown falters." I stand toe to toe with him. He is nothing but a bully—a powerful bully who picks on the weak. I am not weak, and he does not scare me.

"Remember that you are in my country, 'Queen Mary'. Do not push your luck," Henry spits back. "That coward on the floor—that is a pitiful excuse for a man. Now pick him up and nurse him. I want him back in my presence tomorrow morning."

Although Henry does not back down, the fear of my words is apparent. He knows I have him. If he wants England, he will have to keep me happy.

I help Francis up and take him to his bed. He is so sad that my stomach twists as I realise that Henry has ruined a perfect day. Francis tells me that this is a regular thing. If Henry does not get exactly what he wants, then he will often strike Francis. I want to kill him at this moment. The idea that someone could ever hurt such a gentle soul hurts me.

Francis falls into a heavy sleep, and I spend the night watching him.

Chapter 5

Today, the Valois family has been struck by tragedy. As we attended the final day of celebration for the marriage of Elisabeth and King Phillip of Spain, Henry was involved in a catastrophic accident. He had taken part in the jousting, just as he always did, despite Catherine's advice to sit it out. Henry has not been in the best of health of late and seems to be overcome with dizzy spells after any physical exercise. The problem is that Henry is a proud man with no respect for the opinions of others. To him, Catherine is fussing too much; he is in perfect health. He can never sit out when an opportunity arises for him to make a show of strength. However, he is no longer as strong as he thinks he is. Henry is not a young king, and as much as he would love to believe that he is still brawny, young, and athletic, he is ageing and less able to go up against the more youthful men at court.

The whole court was in a wonderful mood today, myself and Francis included. The sun was shining, the wine was flowing, and the entertainment was in full swing. Elisabeth was stunning on her wedding day. It makes me so happy to see her married to a man who will look after her. She was always destined to be a queen. She has a regalness about her that is not natural to everyone. It is sad that she is leaving us, but she is going to become the Queen of Spain, and I could not be happier for her.

Henry did what he did best and poured a ridiculous amount of money into a grand, three-day event. There had been more feasting than any of us could handle, with copious amounts of French wine and delicious cheese. Meats had been specially hunted and cooked for the event; the finest duck and lamb had been prepared for us. We danced long into the night and drank more than we should have. Henry wanted to impress Spain by putting on the best event that money could buy. It was his way of saying no one does it better than France.

It was not just the royal family that beamed today. The court was also delighted to celebrate Elisabeth's wedding. It has been a much-needed break from the typical day-to-day drag of life—a chance to celebrate and be merry. Francis was in much better spirits today. With Henry distracted, he was able to let his guard down and be himself for once. I have always loved the way he looks when surrounded by his family. They bring out such a joy in him, a childlike happiness. He loves to step into the big brother role with Charles and

Henry. He spends as much time with them as he can, playing games with them or reading to them. He adores being beside his mother. They have such a fondness for each other. Catherine always looks at Francis with such pride. It makes me jealous in some way. I would love for my mother to look upon me like that, just once.

As per usual, it was not just the Valois and I who occupied the royal box today. We were joined by Henry's mistress, Diane De Poitiers. Diane is Henry's official mistress, and as always, she is afforded the same respects as a wife. I have never understood how Henry can allow such a woman to sit amongst her betters as she does. It has always astounded me how Catherine holds herself in this situation. She acts with complete poise and grace, even as both Henry and Diane disrespect her so openly. Throughout my whole life here in France, it has always been accepted that although Catherine is Henry's wife, Diane is the woman he truly loves, and he has treated her like a queen. It shocks me, that Henry as a Catholic man, would so openly break the sanctity of marriage with another. Unfortunately, as women, we must accept that our husbands can do whatever they wish, while we must remain true and honourable wives. I am just so thankful that Francis would never treat me in such a way.

I have never much liked Diane. Honestly, her presence disturbs me. I hold such a great love for Catherine that it hurts me to see her cast away. However, if she holds any disdain for the situation, she does not show it herself. She is nothing but courteous to Diane, allowing her to share her husband. Somehow, they manage to coexist with each other. Diane had a hand in the children's upbringing and has even been known to aide Catherine when sick. I could not do it myself. Francis and his siblings have accepted her. They know that it is easier to let Henry do what he thinks is best.

While I am polite to her, I am also very wary. What I dislike most about Diane is her arrogance. She seems to think that her place is rightfully granted. She is calculated. She smiles to your face but sneers behind your back. We have all been witness to it. Anyone can see why Henry was attracted to her. A lot of people say she surpasses Catherine in beauty, but I have to disagree. She is beautiful, with her pale skin, high cheekbones, and delicate features. She is tall, with long legs and a slim waist, but it is her eyes I do not trust. They are dark and cloaked like she is hiding something.

Today, Henry displayed her favour, as he always does. I watched in distaste as he allowed her to tie it to his lance and kiss him on the cheek. Catherine did not move at all. She remained poised as always.

As we sat in the royal box, we watched in horror, fixed on the scene unfolding before our eyes. I still cannot believe what has happened. I close my eyes, and I am taken back to that moment, in my seat like a statue, unable to move, unable to do anything to help. Henry had made his way to the tiltyard ready to take his turn at the joust. The crowd cheered with excitement as he sat tall and confident on horseback. His studded armour was gleaming in the afternoon sun. He looked prouder than ever as he waved to his countrymen, all in awe of their beloved king. He looked majestic in his new tiltyard erected for this celebration.

Henry has always been an excellent jouster. He is used to winning, which is part of the reason he was so confident today. That, and the fact that usually no one would dare beat the King of France. He was sure he would win. He should have won. His opponent, Lord Montgomery, was also one of the best jousters in the kingdom. When up against anyone besides the king, he never lost. However, I think that Lord Montgomery was just as shocked by the unfolding events as anyone else. Earlier today, he nearly unseated Henry. He refused a rematch, but of course, Henry convinced him to take him on again.

As the flag was waved, signalling the riders to begin, it was already clear that Henry was not as stable as he should have been. He wobbled as his horse took off at full speed. Unfortunately, it was clear that Montgomery had not noticed the king's disadvantage. None of us were prepared for what was about to happen. It should never have been possible. Montgomery should have never taken the chance, but for some reason, he decided to make the strike.

As the two riders drew closer together, Henry raised his lance, ready to strike, but was stopped short as Montgomery's lance extended out and hit its target. We all gasped as the lance hit into the king's helmet, sending his head sharply backwards, and splintered all over the tiltyard. Wood from the lance flew everywhere, but it was one piece that caused the most significant distress as it separated from the lance and pierced Henry's eye. Henry wavered and tumbled from his horse. I felt sick to my stomach as I realised exactly what was happening. Diane shrieked, and Catherine flew up from her seat, hand over her mouth in shock. Francis' hand tightened around mine as he was struck frozen in place. At first, I was frozen beside him, not quite sure what I should do. The whole crowd seemed to be stuck to their seats as we all gazed down at the scene, hopeless.

It was Catherine's screaming that finally broke me out of my shock. "Help!" she shouted. "Somebody help the king!"

I ran down to the tiltyard, unsure of what I was doing but knowing that I had to assist in any way possible. A crowd had surrounded Henry. Men lifted him from the ground and carefully took him inside to wait for his doctor to arrive. It was the most horrific thing that I have ever witnessed. Blood poured out from Henry's helmet, covering Catherine, who was gently holding his head. As the doctor removed his helmet, we could see that the lance had not only pierced Henry's eye, but it had also made its way out of the back of his head. The doctor was reluctant to remove the wood for fear that he would do more damage. I had no idea if Henry was alive or dead. He lay so still, so lifeless. I wanted to help, but I did not know how. I had never seen anything like this before. I looked around, hoping to see some way that I could assist, but everyone just stood around watching in horror.

I realised that Francis had not followed us inside, and I went to find him. He was still sitting in the royal box. His face was fixed in a look of horror. I rushed over to him and took him into my arms. He was shaken to the core.

"Francis. Sweetheart." I took his face into my hands. "Darling, let's go inside and help in any way we can."

Francis did not move to answer me. He barely flinched as I knelt beside him. He had gone ice cold and his gaze was transfixed in the space where his father had fallen.

"Francis, I know you are scared. But we must see what we can do to help," I said breathlessly as panic finally began to overtake me.

Again, Francis simply stared. I took hold of his hand and sat beside him. I waited for what seemed like forever for him to speak finally. I realised that he was probably in shock, so I did not want to move him or push him to answer me. Instead, I sat beside him and held his hand. When he did finally speak, he simply said, "There was so much blood, Mary." His eyes never moved from the spot. His whole body had gone rigid as he squeezed my hand more tightly than ever before.

"I know," I said, at a loss for words. "Francis, it might not be so bad . . ."

"This will kill him, Mary." Francis was so far away as he speaks. "All I saw was blood . . . so much blood."

I do not know what I can say to make this better. All I want to do is comfort him, but I'm unsure how. The truth is that yes, Henry may well die, if he has not already. And I just want to shield my love from that painful truth, but I cannot lie to him.

"Darling, all hope is not lost. Your father's doctors are excellent. He may yet pull through. We need to go inside and see your mother. She is probably beside herself. Your siblings are probably scared. You need to be strong for this family," I say, squeezing his hand. "I will be right with you, holding your hand. I will not let go of you so long as you need me. If it all gets too much, squeeze my hand and know that I am beside you."

Francis finally turns to look at me, and I see the tears that now streak his face. For the first time today, the panic subsides, and my heart feels heavy. I know that his relationship with his father is not an easy one, but it is so apparent just how much he loves him.

"You won't let go?"

"I won't let go."

"You are my strength, Mary."

***

The scene in Henry's chambers is horrific. Doctors rush around as they try to stop the blood flow. The fragment has been removed, and now they try to dress the wound. Henry is unconscious as they work. Francis' hand never leaves mine. His forehead is slick with sweat, and he trembles uncontrollably.

Catherine is here. Her hands are clasped over her mouth as she paces back and forth. At first, she does not even realise that we are in the room. She is so focused on Henry that everything else fades out. Francis does not speak but walks straight to his mother and embraces her. She stops pacing long enough to hold her eldest son. The fright is evident on her face as she watches the doctor work.

"Catherine, what can we do?" I ask.

I do everything I can to keep myself calm, but as I look around the room, my stomach flips with nerves. Henry looks grey, not like the proud man I am used to seeing.

"Oh, Mary, dear, there is nothing to be done for now." She briefly takes my hand. "The doctor just needs to stop the blood. Then we will see how serious the situation is. Francis, can you speak to the nobles? Tell them that the doctors are working, and we will have news soon."

Francis nods reluctantly. The last thing he needs now is to face the scrutiny of the court, but he will do anything that Catherine needs. He is still shaking as he clasps my hand tightly. He takes a breath and leaves the room. I cannot help but feel pride as I watch him use every ounce of strength he has to address the waiting court.

Catherine waits for Francis to leave the room, and then she pulls me into her arms. She does not sob. She will not. It is not in her nature to appear weak.

"Mary, I want you to know how grave the situation is. Henry most likely will not pull through this. I need you to help me."

"Anything. You know that Henry is like a father to me."

"I know, my sweet girl." Catherine runs her hand through my hair. "However, I need you to be strong, Mary. I need you to take Francis away from this. I will sit by Henry's side and pass on information, but I cannot have Francis here. He is so fragile. He has never been able to handle trauma like this. Keep him distant for the time being. I will send for you should he be required." Catherine's other hand is on her heart as she looks between her husband and me. She looks older than her years as she uses all of her composure to keep herself together.

"Of course I will, but will you and the boys be all right?"

"Yes. They are being looked after, and my place is by my husband's side. Your duty is to care for your husband."

Before any more is said, Francis returns to the room. With one last look at his father and a goodbye to Catherine, I lead him away from the bloody scene.

***

I spend the night with Francis in my arms. He shakes and shivers as the shock begins to wear off. We do not speak. It is comfort enough to be able to hold each other. Neither one of us knows what to say. He is frightened, more frightened than he has ever been. He needs me now more than ever. I just have to wait for him to be ready to talk. Until then, I will be a force for the man I love. I will protect him.

Once he is finally asleep, the shock of it all finally hits me. At last, I have five minutes to myself. My mind reels with despair. The bloody scene, the shrieks of the crowd, Henry lifeless on the bed. The afternoon goes around and around in my mind as I relive it in sickening horror. I have been so mad with Henry lately and the way he treats Francis, but even in my anger, he is a father to me. I love the man as if he were my own kin. No matter how cross I am, no matter how much he hurts us, I would never wish this upon him.

And what of Francis? If Henry dies, Francis will be forced into kingship long before his time. We were supposed to have years before our reign. Now I feel the time beckoning us. I get out of bed and I fall to my knees and pray that God saves Henry. For this country, for his family, and for myself. I am not ready to lose someone. I do not sleep.

9th July 1559

For the next ten days after Henry's accident, the whole court holds its breath as we hope and pray that the king makes a full recovery. For a moment, we believed that the worst would be the loss of Henry's eye. Now it seems that the injury has caused poisoning in his blood. The doctor has bled him and cleaned the wound, but the fever takes over the king. We have been told that we should prepare for the worst, and Catherine has instructed us to say our goodbyes.

I have been a coward. Instead of sitting with Henry awhile, I went in as he was sleeping and laid a kiss on his head. I did not take his hand or say any words. I did not linger. I left without a look back. I could not bear to say a final farewell to the man who has been in my life since I was just a small child. My heart is much too heavy. I know that I will always regret my weakness at this moment. That I will hate myself for not taking the last opportunity to talk to Henry. But I am scared. I am afraid of saying goodbye. I am terrified of the finality of it all. Something about saying farewell is so permanent, and I find that my heart cannot take it. The idea of seeing a man I thought of as so powerful brought to his knees awakens a fear deep within me. It makes the reality of life a little clearer.

Francis sat with his father awhile. I do not know what he said. I just know that afterwards, he was a broken man. How much of it Henry could make sense of, we are not sure. I am just glad that his children were allowed to see him.

Catherine has informed us that Henry has given Lord Montgomery a full pardon for the terrible accident. Montgomery was granted an audience with Henry where he apologised profusely and asked that the king remove his head for the appalling crime. Henry, in a rare act of kindness, forgave him instantly.

Now we wait. Francis and I have not slept properly for days. We know that it could happen at any moment, and we dare not rest too long. All of the Valois children have surrounded us, and Francis has taken on his role as head of the family wonderfully. I am in awe of the way he comforts his siblings despite the way he feels. Each night, when we are finally alone, I see just how affected he is. He tells me that he feels such a pang of heavy guilt for the disagreements with his father. When we are alone, the cracks appear. He grieves terribly for the man who raised him. I do all I can to comfort him, knowing that I am the only thing holding him together.

Last night, Francis and I sat up late talking. He was angry with himself. Angry that his father lay dying while he worried about his future. He knew any day now, he would become king, and that idea frightened him. He believed that his only concern should be with the loss of his father, of the man that for years he has looked up to and aspired to be, but he could not shake the panic that set in. In these last days, I have never wanted to shelter him more. I wish that I could take all of the pain on my shoulders and hide him away from the pressure that is being placed on him.

I have never experienced a loss like this. I do not know the best way to handle the situation, but I do know that Francis' feelings are valid. I am also afraid of the future. When Francis succeeds the throne, I will become Queen of France, which is a massive responsibility on both our shoulders. I do not for one moment doubt his ability. He is going to be a wonderful king. I know it.

I am not sure that I can stand in Catherine's shoes. I need to be a rock now to my husband and France, but I feel so weak. Yet in my weakness, I know that I am given little choice. I will make this work. I will stand firm for the man I love. I will not only hold Francis' hand, but I will stand hand in hand with France and her people. I cry in private but am strong for the people who need me. I feel like I am standing on the cusp of a new beginning. A beginning that has started with a tragedy.

***

Yesterday, Henry was given his last rites. All we can do now is wait, knowing that at any moment, he will take his last breath. We gather around his bed and watch him sleep. His chest rises and falls, softer by the moment. We are too numb to say anything as we look on while Henry dies. He looks so different from the man I know. His face is covered in blood-soaked gauze that oozes as the infection grows. It is a sorry state for a man who is usually so strong.

Henry keeps himself going for a final few hours, but today, he lost all strength and finally succumbs. I have stayed true to Francis, with one hand in his and the other holding Elisabeth's. As Henry slips away, Francis and the rest of his children weep for their lost father while Catherine and I stand dry eyed. We stand firm in this moment, true to our word to protect those who need us.

Finally, and suddenly, Henry stops moving. His whole body relaxes as the life he was so tentatively clinging to leaves him. It is a struggle to hold myself together as the rest of the room falls to pieces. Francis is on his knees beside his father. Young Henry and Charles are wrapped in his arms. Catherine takes Claude and Lis into her arms and lets them sob onto her shoulder. She looks at me, and our eyes meet. Without saying a word, I know that this is a silent connection. It is a silent oath that we shall piece this family back together. It is a sign of solidarity in our grief, a grief that we will not share with anyone else.

***

The last few days have been hard. Francis was named king on Henry's death, and I his queen. I do not believe that Francis has come to terms with any of this just yet. I know he will. When it comes to it, Francis will rise from this. He has been stricken so hard with the grief of his father, and the most challenging thing is that he cannot grieve in private. He has had to take on the duty of arranging a funeral for Henry.

At night when we are alone, he sobs. Not just for his father but for the significant change that has come into his life. He has never felt the loss of someone so close, and it has been an awakening to him. He suddenly realises how fragile everything truly is, and it is almost too much to bear. He holds me closer now. He holds his mother a little closer, his siblings, his companions.

"Do you really believe that I am ready for this?" he asks me as we lie in each other's arms. He has been silent tonight, lost in his thoughts. "Can I be a good king, Mary?"

"You already are." I smile up at him. "You are leading this country, and your family, through a time of great loss when you yourself are grieving."

Francis smiles down at me. I cannot believe how different he looks lately. Worry lines fill his young face, the strain of the last week exhausting him. "I just want to be good. And fair. And loved," he begins. "I don't want to be feared like Father. He was a good king, but he ruled with fear. I want to rule with love."

"You were born to be loved, Francis," I say. "You are the most honourable, kind, loving man that I know. France does not need to learn to love you; they already do. I believe in you more than I believe in anything else." I speak honestly.

I kiss him, hoping to pass across some of the confidence that I have in him.

"And you will be by my side?" he asks.

"Always."

After constant preparation, today is the day. Today, we finally say goodbye to Henry. We raise him up into the loving hands of our Lord and lay his earthly body to rest. France has cried out for their king. Great masses have been said in all corners of the country, praying for the soul of a king lost much too early. Today, Catherine once again showed her incredible strength and poise as she followed behind her husband. We made our way to the Basilica of Saint-Denis, the traditional burial place of French kings, a great many mourners lining the streets to say farewell to Henry.

After the service, my husband, my wonderful husband, raised his head high and pays respect to his father before the whole of France. France looks at him differently today. It does not see its young, feeble dauphin; instead, it sees a king ready to lead his country out of grief and toward new light.

"My beloved people of France. We have suffered a great loss this week. The death of my dear father and king does not only grieve my family and I, but it grieves all of you, his most wonderful subjects. I know that he loved all of you as deeply as his own kin." He speaks calmly. His voice is controlled and clear. "King Henry would not wish you to weep for him. He would wish you to remember him with great love in your heart. It is a great honour for me to be stepping into a magnificent man's shoes, and I only hope that you, my people, love me half as much as you did him. Together with my beautiful wife and queen, Mary, I promise you to care for France and her people with as much love and grace as my father and mother have. As we all join in mourning, I do hope that each one of you keeps my father in your hearts and prayers."

I look on in pride as Francis comes into his own. He is more prepared for this than he will ever know. It is more than that. He was made for this. It is in his blood, and as he looks out on a sea of mourners today, I believe he feels at one with the people he has been chosen to lead. Catherine and I share in yet another moment of solidarity as we watch the boy we both love turn into a man right before our eyes. I did not realise I had any more love to give to Francis, but it is an endless sea.

Chapter 6

21st September 1559

Today is the day of Francis' coronation, and all around us, the palace is alive with excitement. For the first time in weeks, there is a joyful feeling throughout the court. Since Henry's funeral, there has been a lack of happiness within Fontainebleau. The king's death was so sudden and unexpected that it has left a dark cloud of sadness in its wake. Today, for the first time in weeks, we put away our black mourning wear and adorn something a little more cheerful. Today, we leave the past behind us and allow the new king to lead us into the future.

Francis has been beside himself with nerves for the last few days. He has never liked the idea of big spectacles or of being on display. "This is what it means to be king," I remind him. "You will always be on show, my love."

We both struggled to sleep last night, as he tossed and turned until morning. Then at breakfast, he could hardly eat a scrap of food. I poured him a glass of wine and told him that it would steady his nerves, but it only amplified what he was already feeling.

"How did it feel when you were coronated, Mary?" he asked.

I looked at him, confused, waiting for him to realise his mistake. Instead, he continued to look at me expectantly.

"Well, if only I could remember." I laughed. "You forget, I was nine months old."

Francis looked at me quizzically. "Right," he said. "I forgot."

I could not help but laugh. He is so adorable when he was nervous. Francis' shoulders relaxed, and he began laughing with me.

"And they are going to allow me to rule a country," he chuckled. "I'll forget which county it is."

"You will think you are the king of Spain." I giggled.

"Maybe I should step aside and allow you to do all of the ruling?" he asked. I think he was half-joking and half-serious.

"I never much liked Spain, if I'm honest," I jest.

It felt so wonderful to laugh. Lately, everything has been so serious. We have had so many formalities to follow that it has not left a lot of time for fun. I love the way Francis looks when he is happy, the way his shoulders loosen and his face relaxes. He looks so youthful when he laughs, and I remember just how young we are.

***

The coronation went as smoothly as possible, just as I knew it would. I could have burst with the pride I felt as my husband was sworn in as King Francis II. For someone who was so overcome by nerves just hours before, he pulled the whole thing off spectacularly. He looked poised and calm as he made his way through Reims, dressed in the most beautiful cloth of gold. He held his head high and breathed his way through the ceremony.

Just before the ceremony began, I had gone to wish him luck. He was still nervous but controlling it. He took me into his arms and drew in a deep breath. "You are my strength, Mary."

I took his hand and placed it over my heart. "Then take it all," I said. With a final squeeze of the hand and a kiss on the cheek, I left him to take my place in the cathedral.

The proceedings began, and Francis made his way down the aisle and toward his Uncle Charles, Cardinal of Lorraine, who led the ceremony.

We began the ceremony in prayer as Francis took his place at the head of the cathedral. He looked angelic today; the aura that surrounded him was like a golden halo.

No one could say that God did not handpick him for this purpose.

As per tradition, he was petitioned by the bishops, who asked that he maintain the rights of the church, to which he wholeheartedly agreed. After we sang the Te Deum, the traditional buskins and spurs were placed on Francis' feet. I looked on in absolute pride as my husband was sworn in. I could have burst with adoration for him as he showed France every ounce of strength that he has. He looked confident as they handed him the Joyeuse—the sword of Charlamagne—and then removed his coat and allowed his back and chest to be exposed for the Chrism.

As Francis knelt, the Litany of the Saints was chanted by the choir, and the Archbishop said the prayer of consecration. Charles then anointed Francis with the holy Chrism by marking a cross on his forehead, his breast, his shoulders, and his arms.

"I anoint thee, king, with holy oil in the name of the Father, and of the Son, and of the Holy Spirit."

"Amen," I said in a whisper, as my chest filled and was overcome by joy.

Francis stood, and as Charles closed his shirt, he was draped in the royal blue mantel, which was adorned with fleurs-de-lys of gold. Both his hands were anointed. The blessed gloves and rings were placed on his hands, and he was handed the sceptre.

Then finally, as I was overcome by emotion, the Crown of Charlamagne was placed on top of his head. It was held in place so that the weight of the crown did not topple him. "God crown thee with a crown of glory."

With a look to Catherine, I saw that she too had lost her composure, as she looked on her son with complete joy and faith in him as king. She smiled as I caught her eye, and then the congregation erupted as Francis was named king of France.

"Vive le Roi."

Chapter 7

Francis and I have been King and Queen of France for a few months now. I am still awaiting my coronation, as Francis is planning a spectacular celebration. The first few weeks after Francis' coronation were relatively easy. The country has accepted the transition from Henry to Francis easily, and it is safe to say that Francis is loved. My Guise uncles have made it as easy as possible by helping Francis wherever they can. However, the Guises are not always popular, and there are a few who would rather they were not involved. It has caused a small amount of uproar throughout the country. I know that my uncles are the right men to guide Francis. They have our best interests at heart, after all.

Unfortunately, that is not the only issue we are facing. Protestantism is becoming increasingly popular in France, and it has caused strife throughout. Much like in Scotland, the protestants demand to be counted. They want the same rights as Catholics. Francis has had a hard time finding the right balance. He is a fair man who ideally wants equality for everyone, but France is a Catholic country, and he is a Catholic ruler.

He will side with Catholicism, and the pope, without a doubt. I give him my opinion, of course. I believe that Catholics and Protestants should be able to coexist in the same world. But I know that what we want and how we have to rule are often two very different things. Our personal opinions do not stand up against the needs of the county.

Although Francis does have help, we are still finding that his personal duties have put a strain on our relationship. We never argue or exchange cross words, but it is becoming evident that our new life is wearing us down a little. We no longer have any time to ourselves. We sleep side by side every night, but Francis is so exhausted by the time we sit down to dinner that all he is interested in is sleep. I miss the connection. I miss having someone to talk to. I have my ladies, but I feel as if I am without my closest friend. I know it is not his fault, but I am finding his absence difficult. It does not help that I have few duties of my own. My mother has Scotland taken care of, and there is little for me to do here in France.

We also now have the added pressure of conceiving and ensuring we have a son and heir as quickly as possible. Our lovemaking is no longer about Francis and me. It is no longer about our needs and wants. It is about fulfilling a duty. The court looks on expectantly, hoping that I become with child soon so that our rule is even stronger than it is now. The people look to us to continue the Valois and Stuart line. I find that the pressure has all become a bit too much, and I long for time to reverse and for us to go back to the way it was before Henry died, when we had the possibility of years before our reign began.

Everything has happened so quickly, and I feel as if I am crumbling under responsibility. I have not approached Francis with this. Between the loss of his father and the beginning of his kingship, I have not wanted to put more stress on him, but tonight, as we dine together, it all becomes too much. I find that I cannot hide what is just below the surface, and all it takes is one look from Francis to send me crashing over the edge.

"Mary. You seem troubled lately," Francis begins. "You know you can talk to me about anything. What is it, darling?"

"Nothing. I'm just a little tired," I say, but it is no use; the tears begin to fall.

Francis wipes a stray tear from my cheek. He looks so worried as the floodgates open, and the tears begin to fall uncontrollably. "Please do not cry, sweetheart. Talk to me." He stands from his seat and comes to kneel beside me.

"It is nothing, Francis." I lie again.

"Now Mary, you promised to never keep anything from me," he encourages. "Am I making you unhappy?" he asks with fear in his eyes.

"No, no. You could never make me unhappy," I answer quickly, hoping to reassure him. "I am being silly."

"Tell me."

I take a deep breath as I try to organise my untidy mind. At first, I am unsure of where to start, but I find that it all comes tumbling out in one long breath.

"It is just that I feel like our lives have suddenly become so busy that we do not have time for one another. I know that I am ridiculous, but I miss you. I feel so distant from you, and I feel like now the only reason we spend the night together is so that we can conceive a child. I just want to feel close to you again." I look down at my hands, ashamed by how erratic I am being. We always knew that our marriage would have to come second.

Francis is quiet for a long while. At first, I think that he must think me childish. But that is not what I see when I look up and see that he too is overcome by emotion.

"Oh, Mary, do you not know that this has been eating me up inside? For weeks now, I have wanted to approach you about this, but I too felt I was being silly. I know our duty must come first, but I just want to be with my wife." Francis kisses my hand. "I have neglected you, Mary, and for that, I am sorry. I am tired all of the time. I have my advisors on me constantly to have a son, and I have let that pressure affect our relationship."

I had no idea that Francis was feeling the pressure as much as I was. I assumed that because he was so busy, he was too tired to want to spend time with me. I feel a little better knowing that we both feel the same way.

"I do not blame you, Francis. I know that France must come before me, but I am so used to being spoiled by your attention that without it, I am lost," I say, feeling the shame of my foolishness. "Things will never be the same again, will they?"

"I wish I could say they will be, but I am no longer just a dauphin. And you are no longer just the Queen of Scots. We are everything to France now," Francis says as he holds my hand to his heart. "But I can make you a promise: a promise that I will never leave you."

This is too much for me, as the pressure of the last few months finally crushes me. The tears fall freely now as I lose control of my composure completely.

"I just want us to go back. I wish Henry were still alive. I wish we could have more days like the one in spring. I wish we were simply Francis and Mary." I confess the words that have been on my mind for a long time.

"Darling, I would give up all of my riches, all of my titles. I would even give up my family if it meant we could simply be Francis and Mary. But what kind of person, what kind of king would I be if I abandoned my people? Especially while they still grieve for their king Henry." Francis holds me close. "Mary, I promise you that we will have more days like the one in spring. We will have better days. Our time together will be endless. I just need you to wait for me and to know that no matter how hard life gets or how much pressure the world puts on us I adore you. With my every waking thought, you are in my mind. I love you, above all else, and that includes France, but she needs me right now. She is weak. You are strong. While I hold France together, you hold me together. Never for a moment think that I neglect you out of loss of love. It is because I love you so much that I know you'll stay true." When he speaks, it is like my heart comes to life. He is so good to me. "Mary, I love you forever."

"I would give everything up for you in a heartbeat. I will wait for you, Francis. I just need to be reassured. The last weeks have made me insecure. How could I ever doubt your love for me?" I ask.

"Because you are a silly woman." Francis chuckles. "There is nothing I want more than to end a busy day by finding you in my chambers. Not because I want an heir, but because I want my every spare moment to be with you."

"I will be there," I promise. "Francis?"

"Yes, sweetheart?"

"I love you forever too."

***

Things have changed slightly from that conversation at dinner. Francis is still busy with the challenges of being king, and I receive more and more word from my mother about the affairs in Scotland. She fights to beat back the protestant's daily. They call for a new rule. They want more say in Scotland. I can only advise that she makes peace with them, but it is never so simple. With the protestants in her own country and England, just next door, she feels as if she is drowning in threats and enemies. She calls on France to send help. I pray that my country finds peace soon. I pray that my mother is safe.

Francis and I decide that an heir is not important to us right now. We know that one day we will fill this palace with beautiful babies, but at this time it is not something we are concerned with. We are young. We have all of the time in the world to have children.

For now, all we need to do is focus on one another.

Chapter 8

Today, I feel light as a feather. I awoke this morning with Francis by my side, just like always, but as I turned to face him, he had the biggest grin on his face. It made my heart melt in an instant to see the glow of happiness in his eyes. He was playful as I asked him exactly what he was thinking about. He could barely contain the giggle inside of him, just like a naughty child with a secret. I made to rise from bed, but he pulled me back down.

"Love, we have a busy day ahead," I scolded him as the grin stretched wider across his face. It was infectious, and before I knew it, I was mirroring him.

"Not anymore, we don't," Francis said with glee in his voice.

"Whatever do you mean? We have a lot to look over this morning. You have a privy council meeting this afternoon and then dinner with your mother tonight." I listed each thing off on my hand.

"Cancelled." Francis beamed.

The shock on my face must have been apparent, but Francis just continued to smile.

"Cancelled? Francis, you are king. You cannot cancel." I chuckled. He looked so ridiculous. I cannot remember the last time I saw him smile so much.

"It is because I am king that I can cancel," he said, looking very self-important. "Everything can wait until tomorrow."

"Oh? And what do you suppose we should do instead?" I asked.

Francis' eyes lit up as he took in the whole of me. His hands were on me now, tickling me. "Well, first, I plan to keep you in this bed for as long as possible." He ran his hands all over me.

"Francis, stop." I laughed as he pinned me down and smothered me in kisses.

"Do you submit?" he asked as he took a breath.

"Submit to what?" I said through giggles.

"To doing whatever I want to do today, with no question?" he asked, serious now.

"Hmm . . . I suppose I could never say no to my king." I kissed him on the lips.

"Your king orders you to kiss him again," Francis said in his most regal voice.

Without another word, he kissed me again, and we lost a few hours.

***

Today has been a perfect day. We escaped from the crowded court and enjoyed a little peace of our own. Of course, Francis' guards and my ladies followed us, but it was a much smaller entourage than we have been used to. Being king and queen means never being alone. Our safety is of utmost importance. As frustrating as that is, when it comes to time with Francis, I will take what I can get.

Francis and I took the horses out of the stable and went for a ride around the grounds, something that, for the longest time, we have been unable to do. The air was brisk, and the winter sun shone brightly through the surrounding trees. I felt all of the weight lift off of me as I breathed in the cool, refreshing air. It was as if each breath I drew in drew out a bit of the worry that plagued me.

I love to ride. I love the way it feels, the wind in my hair, the ground steady beneath me. I love the way I relinquish my trust to my horse, knowing she will carry me to safety. I fall into an almost meditation as my horse stays at a trot, watching her ears move up and down before me. I feel a freedom like no other.

I remember when Henry gave me my first horse, Giles. Each day, I would race down to the stable, anxious to saddle Giles up and gallop around the grounds. I adored him. I fell off once or twice, but no cuts or bruises stopped me from jumping back on the next day.

Francis has never been as fond of riding as I am. He finds the whole thing nerve-wracking. He sits comfortably now, but since he was a child, he has always lacked confidence. He let the horse know that he was nervous, so his horse took advantage of that. He is much more in control now. He is calm as he sits on top of his horse. In taking the throne, he has found new confidence in himself. And I find it so attractive.

When we stopped the horses, we found ourselves in a meadow, just out of sight from the Château. Since moving to the Château de Blois after Francis' coronation, we have not done much exploring outside. The grounds here, although beautiful, are no match for Fontainebleau. They are not as vast and much more open and visible, meaning that the places where I can tuck myself away are fewer. Still, stumbling on this meadow has cheered me up. I think this will be my new spot for when I want to escape.

We tied the horses to a tree and laid a blanket out on the ground. Francis had asked his guards to pack a small lunch for us, which we ate while sitting in the meadow. My Marys and Francis' men joined us, and we passed the afternoon merrily. We relaxed and enjoyed a perfect afternoon. My Marys were always at ease around us; they were friends more than anything, and Francis has become close with a couple of his guards. I suppose when you spend so much time with someone, you find things you have in common, which means that there are no awkward formal moments. We shared stories with each other. We laughed. More than anything, we laughed. Not the polite laughter that we would share at court, but the type that splits your sides and leaves you hunched over.

After food, Francis was in a playful mood. He stood up and pulled me to my feet. "Race me," he said.

"Francis, I cannot do that. I'm queen, you know," I teased.

"Oh, don't be so stuffy." He laughed.

"Fine. Where to?" I narrowed my eyes, absolutely determined to beat him.

"The trees at the edge of the clearing."

Then he sped off at full speed towards the trees. I raced after him, kicking my heels up, trying to catch him. He was always slower than I, and I caught up quickly. I blew him a kiss as I ran past, and as I reached the tree, I heard him laugh behind me.

"Okay, you win." He gasped before collapsing into the grass.

I ran over to him. "Francis, are you all right?" I asked, a little panicked.

We were just out of sight of our attendants now, and they had not seemed to have noticed.

"I'm fine." He chuckled, pulling me to the ground next to him. "I just wanted a moment alone."

We lay there as long as we dared before someone would come looking for us. With a final kiss, Francis pulled me to my feet. He ran his fingers through my hair to discard any leaves.

"Thank you," he said.

"What for?" I asked, breathless as I took in my handsome husband.

"For a day I will never forget."

***

Today, I have felt like I could take a breath for the first time in a long time. It is easy to forget that Francis and I are still young. We have been so burdened by responsibility that we have forgotten our duty to ourselves and to each other as husband and wife. We had forgotten how to have fun. We always have had so much fun together. We returned to Francis' chambers after a long day away.

"I want you to know how much I love you, Mary," Francis told me as he held me against him. "I know life has changed, but that's one thing that will never be any different."

"I know just how much you love me, Francis. I see it in your eyes when you watch me from across the room. I hear it as you say my name. I feel it when you touch me." I blushed as his eyes fixed on mine. His gaze was so soft as he watched my lips move.

"Can you feel it when I do this?" he asked before pulling me close and kissing me.

It is so strange to me that after all this time, he still stirs the same reaction within me, that I am just as much in love with him today as I have always been. His every movement, every breath is so precious to me. Tonight, as he stood and held his hand out for me to take, he seemed to glow. His smile gave me that sense of being home. The way his eyes held mine made me belong. I am whole when I am with him. I am the Mary I am supposed to be. I felt like my old self today, the Mary that existed not so long ago. The one that cared much more for Francis than any matter of state. I have been so concerned with looking after the affairs of two nations and not the thing I should be nourishing. The something that will last longer than any country, any nation; it will outlast the world. And that is the love I feel for Francis.

It is now evening and Francis is tired, but I feel more alive than I have felt in as long as I can remember. As we clamber into bed, there are a million things I wish to talk about. Francis' eyes droop, but I beg him to stay awake a little longer. I want to speak with him as we did before, when we did not rely on sleep to get us through the busy days. We ran on whatever energy we had stored. We would sit up all night playing cards or singing songs, only giving in to sleep when the early morning sun crept in and the birds dared to try to wake us.

"Francis . . . sing me a song?" I ask, glee in my eyes. "It has been too long since I've heard you sing."

Francis rolls his eyes in mock frustration "Mary, today has been fun, but life must resume tomorrow. I am tired."

"Please? I promise you can sleep after." I stick out my bottom lip like a spoiled child. I know that he can never refuse me.

"You promise?" Francis asks.

I nod. "Promise."

"Fine. But just the one." Francis giggles. "What would you like me to sing?"

I am thoughtful for a moment before answering. Then a smile creeps across my face. "Sing a song about me."

"I do not know any songs about you, Mary." Francis gives me a quizzical look.

"Well, then you will just have to make it up," I tease.

Again, Francis rolls his eyes. "I'm not very good at that."

"For me?" I plead.

"Fine," he laughs. "How could I ever say no to such a beauty?"

"Um, Mary . . ." he stutters, not sure what to say. "Mary . . . Her hair was red like the evening sun / Her eyes as blue as the sea / Her cheeks blushed rose, and her lips sung a song made just for me.
Her voice like velvet / Her skin as pale as the winter snow / I pray lord that she never lets me go." Francis begins awkwardly.

We both chuckle, but I urge him on. "Keep going."

"The Queen of Scots has stolen my heart, never to set it free. / Little does she know that in turn, her heart now belongs to me. / I will keep it forever, beneath my breast and throw away the key.
Yes, the Queen of Scots has stolen my heart, and I could not be more happy."

We both fall to the bed with laughter as Francis finishes his verse. It was beautiful; the love he felt for me was evident in every word. I will carry it in my heart for all of my days.

"Oh, Francis. I adore it," I exclaim, clapping my hands.

"I tried my best." Francis blushes, suddenly becoming coy.

"I want you to write it down for me. I will keep it forever."

"Oh, I won't remember it tomorrow," Francis jokes.

"Please?"

"Yes, my love. I will try to remember," Francis promises. "Now go to sleep, my beautiful Queen of Scots."

"Oh, but Francis, I am not tired. Sing me another song." I lean over him as he lies down to sleep.

"Mary, you promised," he scolds.

"I know, but your singing is so beautiful. It'll help me sleep." I try to persuade him.

"I know something that will help."

"What's that, sweetheart?" I ask.

Francis suddenly sits up. "Well, if you don't go to sleep soon, I am going to pin you down until you do." He tries to give me a serious look but cannot hold it.

"You'll have to get hold of me first," I cackle as I burst out of the bed and I run over to the ther side of the room in an instant.

"Oh, Mary." Francis shakes his head as he too jumps out of bed.

He chases me around the room. I have always been faster than him, and as he runs for me, I dart to the side. He runs at me again and again, failing each time to catch me in his arms. Finally, after endless loops around the bed, I can run no more. Francis has the upper hand, and when he reaches for me this time, he catches me in his arms and throws me to the bed. We are both out of breath as he pins me down. I squirm for a moment but have no intention of getting away.

"So, are you going to kiss me?" I ask breathlessly.

"Do you admit defeat?" he asks with mischief in his eyes.

"Never."

"Good. My Mary never losses a battle," he says, relieved.

His lips are on me in a moment.

Neither Francis nor I get a wink of sleep, and although we start the next day exhausted, we are both renewed with happiness we have not felt in forever.

Chapter 9

Sometimes, when life gets particularly busy and I find that time alone with my thoughts becomes impossible, I like to sit outside in the gardens with my quill and parchment and sort through my busy mind. I have always found something healing about writing one's feelings. It is freeing to take them from my over-clustered mind and release them to the world. The past few months have been a whirlwind, and there has been absolutely no time for reflection. I find that a weight lies heavy on my chest the past few days. I believe that whether I realised it or not, the stress of the past few months has gotten to me.

I do not believe that I have allowed myself to grieve for Henry, for a start. When he was ill, my mind went straight into protection mode. Rather than stopping to think about how his death affected me, I worried about everyone else. I wanted to shelter Francis and his siblings from the pain of losing their father. Though I was reminded many times by Francis and Elisabeth that I had as much right to grieve as anyone, I just kept telling myself that he was not my father and that it was my job to help his children through this.

It was the first time I had ever felt such a fierce need to protect the whole family and not just Francis. I found that I wanted to hold us all together as tightly as possible and shield them from the loss.

I have not allowed myself to cry for Henry. Yet now I stop to think about it, I realise how much he meant to me. We, of course, had our disagreements. What family does not? Indeed, I was not too fond of the way he treated Francis at times. He was often cruel and unkind to his family. Yet at his heart, Henry was a good man. He took me into his home and raised me just like one of his own when I was a small child. He treated me as well as any of the children that he or Catherine had together.

The truth of it is that Henry was the closest I had to a father, and I loved him. His death brought great sadness to this family and the whole of France. Now I wish that I had the guts to say my goodbyes to him properly. Like a coward, I spoke to him while he was asleep. I thought it best. I had to stay strong for my husband. If I had broken my composure for one moment, I am not sure that I would have been able to regain it.

Even on the day we buried him, I held myself together. I allowed everyone else to grieve while I was a shoulder to cry on. I only hope that Henry knew that despite my cross words with him, I held him in the highest esteem. I pray that Henry has found peace and that one day we shall all meet again. We must take our memories, the good and the bad, with us forward in this life.

I feel myself changing as I grow older. I am changing as I grow into my role as the Queen of France. I find that in some ways, I am becoming a different person. In the last year, a lot has happened to open my eyes to the world. I have now been touched by death. While I have always known that it is an unavoidable part of life, I have never experienced it first-hand. I now know precisely the way it feels to experience loss. I feel as if it is another piece of childhood that has been stripped away from Francis and me.

In the past few months, we have had to grow up at full speed. I feel like I have spent my whole life preparing for this eventuality, and yet it is still a massive adjustment to me. I have had to realise that Francis must put the country before me, and in that, I have learned that I am not prepared to do the same. I have learned in this what I truly value, and that is my family and my husband. My husband above all else, including both kingdoms. The whole thing has made me come to realise how little I care for power, how little the thought of claiming England means to me. I do not need to be all-powerful. I do not begrudge the things I am blessed with, yet I realise that I would be happy without them as long as I had Francis. Death and significant change make you seriously consider the things you can and cannot live without.

Francis has put a lot of trust in me lately, and he always asks me before finalising a vital decision. I realise that yes, I am changing. I am becoming a queen—a real queen, and not just a queen in name. However, yesterday made me realise something hugely important: that I am Mary. I want to stay this Mary for as long as possible. The Mary who is madly in love with her husband. The Mary who values her family above anything else. The Mary who is not power-hungry. The Mary who is not driven by what she does not have but is sustained by what she does have. I know how truly blessed I am, and I always want to remember that. I want to help people who are not in the position I am. I want Francis and me to end poverty in our countries. I want to be driven by charity, art, music, and love. I long to relish the things I have forgotten about. To write poetry. To read books. Focus on my prayers. I want to paint and hear sweet music. I want more days where I lie on the grass with Francis and can hear nothing but our hearts beating next to one another. Most of all, I want to stay this version of myself for the rest of my life.

Chapter 10

Yesterday, we received some sad news. We received word that just a few days ago, my mother had taken to her bed and passed away. She had been struck down with an awful case of dropsy while staying at Edinburgh and had been unable to recover. My mother has for a long time now been the person responsible for Scotland, and I believe that her last effort to defend the country against the English had pushed her frail health over the edge.

I cannot begin to explain how I feel. When Francis first delivered the note into my hands, it was as if I had been punched in the stomach. It was the strangest feeling to be told that my mother had died, and yet I was not instantly stricken with sadness. To me, my mother was never really anything more than words on a page, and although we had exchanged countless letters over the years, I feel like I never really knew her. We never spoke much about our personal lives. Our letters were always straight to the point and concerned the welfare of our country.

I remember so little of her. I was just five years old the last time I saw her, before she sent me away to live in a foreign country without the comfort of home. I have always held that against her. While I thank God every day that I was sent to Francis, I have never been able to understand how she could so easily allow her child to live in another country. I understand that it was for my safety, but I have always felt that if I were in the same situation, I would not do the same. I have always felt, however illogical it is, that my mother did not want me. I guess in a way I shut myself off from her, afraid to feel too much for a woman out of reach.

Above all, I feel sad for Scotland. She fought for my country with her every breath. She may not have raised me, but Scotland has so much to thank her for. Every day of her life, she went above and beyond for a country that she was not born into. She cherished and honoured the memory of my father, and for that, I will be eternally thankful.

Francis was and is a little alarmed by how I have handled the news. He thinks me in shock. Perhaps I am. While it is a great loss, I am not smothered by grief. Maybe I should be. Perhaps there is something wrong with me. The loss of one's mother should be devastating, yet I feel fine. It helps to know that Francis is by my side, to know that my real family surrounds me here in France. While I will respectfully mourn the loss of my mother, I will not allow it to pull me under.

My thoughts now turn to Scotland. She has for so long been under my mother's loving care and now is left without her most avid protector. I have chosen to write to my half-brother James, and with Francis' agreement and blessing, we have decided to install him as regent while I stay here in France. James is a Protestant, and of course, I am Catholic, but I trust him to rule fairly in my steed. I need someone who will put the people first and treat both sides of our faith fairly. If I were to install a Catholic now, it could cause an uproar in my already unsteady country. James has worked for the Protestant cause for several years now, and he has always respected, if not agreed with, my mother's views. He will be the perfect person to ensure peace in Scotland. I could return, of course. Now would be the best time for me to step up and rule Scotland myself, but I refuse to leave Francis behind in France. And at the moment, our rule is too new for us to leave the country in the hands of a regent. Scotland will wait, and we shall visit sometime in the future. For now, my heart is in France, and I know that Scotland will be in capable hands.

Francis has been a little unwell this week and has spent a great majority of it in bed. He began to complain of a headache and pain in his ear on Tuesday and took to his bed, unable to stand it any longer. I have been dealing with his privy council while he rests, but the nobles are happy to wait while he recovers. I have sat with him almost all day, every day. I sit by his bedside, and I read to him, or I sing to him as he rests his head on my chest and allows me to lull him into a gentle sleep with my song. His mother and I are convinced that he has caught a chill from the drastic change in weather we have been experiencing. Still, I do worry. He is so prone to catching chills and fevers.

By Saturday, we are proven right as Francis begins to feel better. If anything, he is in even higher spirits today. He practically jumped out of bed this morning and demanded that we go for a ride. For the first time in days, the sky is clear, and the rain ceases to fall, so reluctantly, I agree on the promise that he wraps up warm.

When we make it outside, I ask the stable boy to ready both our horses, but Francis tells the boy just to bring his. I look at Francis, confused, but he continues to smile. When the horse is brought round and saddled up, Francis climbs on and offers me his hand.

"I want to hold you close today," he says simply.

I take his hand and climb onto the horse, sitting in front of Francis. He wraps his arms around me and takes hold of the reins.

"We will be warmer like this," he says as he rests his head against my hair. I can feel his warm breath on my neck as he holds me tight. We take a short gallop around the surrounding fields before it begins to pour down and we are forced to return to the stables. We head back inside the Château, and it is clear that Francis is exhausted. It has been a long week, and he is not as fully recovered as he would like to think.

"Darling, I know you are feeling better today, but you should take it easy," I suggest.

"I do feel a little dizzy," Francis says.

"Let's go and warm ourselves by the fire. I'll have Mary fetch us something warm to eat." I take hold of his arm and lead him back to his rooms.

Once back, I sit Francis by the fire and wrap him in one of his furs. Mary Fleming brings us some hot soup, and after an hour or so, the colour returns to Francis' face. He falls into a peaceful sleep as I run my hands through his hair. When he awakes, it is only to say, "I adore you, Mary." And then he falls back to sleep. I spend the entire day with his head on my chest, he sleeps more peacefully than an angel.

Chapter 11

16th November 1560

Today has been the singularly most terrifying day of my life. After a couple of weeks of Francis being unwell, we finally believed that he was on the mend. He had begun complaining a few weeks ago about a pain in his ear, but the doctor had put it down to part of his chill. It would pass, he told us He seemed perfectly fine this morning and looked better than he had done in a while. But suddenly, and unexpectedly, the pain in his ear returned, this time worse than ever before.

We were attending a church service when Francis complained of a buzzing noise in his ear and a headache. Then, quickly, he become very distressed; the pain in his head had become agonizing. As Francis gripped his ear, his hands started to shake uncontrollably. The tears were streaming down his face as pain ripped through him. I turned his face towards me, and I was stunned to see the look of him. He had gone as white as snow, his eyes bloodshot.

"Mary . . . I feel so weak," he mumbled, just as he began to sway on his feet. He gripped my arm, hoping to keep his balance, but his legs failed him. They buckled and gave way; Francis fell into a heap on top of me.

"Francis?" A whisper at first. "Francis!" I screamed, panicked. I began to shake him, softly at first, then more violently when he did not respond. "Francis, wake up," I pleaded, but he could not hear me.

Catherine, who was now beside me, helped me lower him onto the floor. "Somebody get a doctor!" she shouted to the gathering crowd. "Now!" she ordered when nobody moved.

We lay Francis on the floor, and I was struck to the core by the look of him. His eyes had rolled into the back of his head, and his breathing was slow and raspy. He looked so weak and fragile. He looked broken. I cradled his head close to my heart and noticed that blood was pouring from his ear. The tears ripped through me as utter helplessness took hold.

The people around us gasped and panicked, but all I could hear was a hum as I held Francis close to me. I rocked back and forth as I held him. I did not think. I do not think I even breathed. My heart was in my mouth as time ticked away slowly and we waited for the doctor to appear. Time seemed to stop moving as I stared down at my helpless husband. My mind repeated the same words again and again. "Please, God, save him."

His face was twisted in pain. He did not look like the man I knew. The agony on his face had changed him. I felt sick to my stomach with fear. I did not know what to do. I wish I had moved. I wish I tried to help him, but I was terrified.

When his doctor finally arrived, he too was in utter shock as he ordered Francis to be carried to his chambers, where the doctor would assess him properly. I could barely stand as I allowed Francis to be lifted away from me. Catherine took hold of me by the arm, and somehow, I managed to make my feet follow behind.

***

"The king has an abscess behind his ear," Doctor Edmond told us after spending an hour with Francis. The grave look on his face was enough to tell us that it was not good.

"An abscess?" Catherine asked when I found that I could not speak.

"It is a lump behind his ear that carries a kind of poison within it," Doctor Edmund explained.

"I am afraid that the poison has made its way into the king's blood."

Catherine's eyes widened; we all knew what a poisoning of the blood could mean. I could not say a thing at all. My mind had been frozen from the moment Francis collapsed, and now the doctor's words made their way into my ears and stopped there. I stood like a statue; my mouth was dry, my palms wet. My heart did not seem to beat at all. In the room were the three of us. Catherine clasped me tightly in her arms, but I felt as if I were totally alone, surrounded by nothingness.

"What do we do?" Catherine asked.

"We wait," Doctor Edmund answered simply.

The moment the doctor left us, Catherine and I rushed into Francis' room and have sat beside him since. He has slipped in and out of consciousness all day, but he has not been awake enough to grasp what is happening. I hold on to his hand tighter than ever before. He is so pale, so frail and delicate. I hate to see him like this. He looks so much older than his sixteen years, as if he has the weight of the world on his shoulders. I wish that I could take the weight away from him. My mind stays completely blank for a long while. The tears fall, but I feel nothing. I think of nothing. I am not here at all.

Now that I have had a moment to allow everything to sink in, I begin to run mad with concern. As he lies sleeping, I have returned to my own rooms. Catherine persuaded me to take a breathe. My constant worry was setting her nerves on edge, and she said that it was not good for me to lose my mind. However, that is exactly what I am doing: I am losing my mind.

As I pace back and forth in my room, my stomach twists and turns with worry. I have this unexplainable and undeniable feeling of dread. This pit in my stomach. A sickness that I cannot shake. He is leaving me. I feel it in my soul. I feel a darkness creeping over us, an uncontrollable cloud of despair. I cannot begin to explain how I know. It is in my bones. A cold trepidation. If Francis is to leave me, then how shall I continue? He is my life. He is my soul.

As I looked down on my husband today, a deep feeling of despair settled on me. A knowing. He was as grey as ash. All of the colour had drained from his cheeks. All of the light that surrounded him was dulled. I know that God intends to take him from me. Why? I cannot say. He is so young. He has so many years ahead. Why would God strike him down now?

"There's one thing I do know," I speak aloud, "that the Devil himself will not part us."

I do not know who I say it to. Do I speak to myself? Or do I speak to God directly? Either way, I intend to keep my promise.

***

I am in my room all of three hours when I am ready to scream with anxiety. I have spent the whole time pacing back and forth, unable to keep still and praying for news. I feel as if I could scratch my own eyes out or pull every hair from my head. Mary F has somehow kept me in check. I should sleep, she tells me. But that will never happen. I cannot sleep unless he is beside me. She tries her hardest to distract me, but my mind is somewhere else completely.

Panic rises in my throat and makes my chest pound uncontrollably. My thoughts race around my head in a muddle of despair. I keep thinking that I cannot lose him, that I cannot live without him. He is my everything. My whole reason for living.

I keep seeing his face, that beautiful face that I adore so much, cold and unmoving. I close my eyes and I see the image of a coffin, draped all in black. It feels so certain. Mary tells me that I am fearing the worst. My mind is doing whatever it can to convince me that this is the end. It is fear that causes me to lose my mind. I pray that she is right. I do not know how to breathe without him.

Finally, I am unable to take anymore. I make the short journey from my room to where Francis lies. I hold my nerve. My legs want to crumble beneath me, but now is not the time to be weak. I do not wait to be announced. I walk into the room and find Catherine asleep in her chair, her hand resting gently on her son. I could cry to look upon them; the bond between them is undeniable. She must be absolutely heartbroken to see Francis like this. She loves him so dearly. Francis is still pale. He looks no different than when I left him. My sweet, sleeping, angel.

All of a sudden, I feel a control fall upon me. I decide that instead of sitting around and waiting for news, I will find out myself. I refuse to feel useless. I cannot sit idly by while my husband weakens.

"Send for the doctor. I expect a full update on the king's condition," I command. A groom bows and scurries off.

As he leaves, Catherine wakes from her light slumber. "Mary, my dear. I thought you were resting?" she asks.

"I was going out of my mind." I sigh. I walk to the other side of Francis and take hold of his hand. "In any case, I cannot sleep. Any change?" I ask.

"I'm afraid not. He has been motionless." She looks tired. I have never seen her look so tired before.

"Can he fight this?" I ask, despite myself.

"Francis is the strongest man I know. He has come through worse than this. He is a survivor," she says with a weak smile. I am unsure that she believes it, but it is comforting to hear her say it at least.

"You should get some rest, Catherine. I will watch over him," I suggest.

Catherine reaches across the bed and takes my hand. "Mary, sweet girl, we are and always will be in this together." She smiles. "We are family."

I allow a single tear to roll down my face. "Together." I nod.

***

We have stayed exactly the same for two days now. We scarcely eat or drink. We take it in turns to have short moments away, but mostly, we are here. The doctor was of no use except to tell us what we already knew: Francis is in grave danger, should his fever rage on. All we can do is pray.

Francis has come around in brief moments. He awakes and smiles at us. Sometimes he even manages a "my love" or "mother." But most of the time, he is comforted by the fact that we are here and then drifts off again. I have had hold of his hand for three days now. I am scared to let go. I fear that he will feel it if I do, and I do not want him to lose that comfort.

I hardly sleep; I am too scared to take my eyes off of him. I watch constantly as his chest rises and falls with each passing breath. I count his breaths, each one more precious than anything else in the world. As much as I want to sink into the ground and cry in utter hopelessness, I cannot. He needs me now more than ever. So I watch, and I wait. I will stay like this forever if that is what it takes.

***

Today, there is hope. Francis is awake. For the first time in three days, he has opened his eyes. Catherine and I practically leaped from our seats when we saw his eyes flutter open. He is still weak, but he is awake and able to talk to us. It feels so wonderful to have him smile at me again. It may be a weak smile, but it is brave and strong. Doctor Edmund says that his fever is slowly subsiding and that for the first time in days, we may feel hopeful. He is still very pale and in a lot of pain, but he has had some food and water, and he manages to sit up in bed.

I thank God for bringing him back to me. The joy I feel in my heart is indescribable. I was sure that I had lost him. It is like all of the air in the room is gone when I am not with him. I need him to keep me going. When he is unwell, I am unwell. I have been sick with grief, but now I can touch him and talk to him again. For the first time in days, I am able to feel optimistic. I can see our future again. Yesterday my life was a blur, but now I can think straight again. He is young and strong. He has so much to live for. He will survive.

Catherine has left us alone for the afternoon, knowing that we needed to spend some time together.

I lie beside Francis on the bed, holding him tighter in my arms than ever before. I try my hardest to hide the worry that I feel, but Francis can see it in my eyes.

"All will be well, my love," he says softly.

"I thought I was going to lose you." I allow the tears to fall now.

"I will be on my feet in no time, darling," he begins. "We have a future to get started on."

Chapter 12

28th November 1560

Francis seems a little better today. He is smiling a lot more, and he is able to stand for a short time. I have returned to sleeping in his bed with him, and for the first time in days, I sleep contentedly beside my husband. We allow ourselves to feel a little hope. He is strong. He will fight this.

He is eating more now, and tonight he has managed to sit down to dinner with me. He seems to be different tonight. He is glowing brighter than ever, and the colour has returned to him. He is in good spirits, and he laughs and jokes just like he used to. I let my guard down, as for a moment, I allow myself to enjoy having my husband back. I am convinced that this is the new beginning we need. That we will go into the future, healthy and happy. Francis has too much to give the world; God knows it, and so do I.

Tonight, I lie beside him, my head on his chest, listening to his heartbeat. He has one hand in my hair and the other clasped tightly around mine. I came close to losing this feeling. I never want that to happen. I never want to be forced to live without him. I will protect him with every last ounce of strength and willpower that I have.

I do not care how long his recovery takes; I will stand beside him through it all. I made a promise a long time ago to always be a rock for him. I intend to always keep that promise.

The fear that I felt when he first became ill has not disappeared. I have never been afraid of losing him before, and the last few weeks have made that seem like a possibility. I realise that this life is a fragile one and we are not granted every day. Tomorrow and all the days that follow are a gift. I intend to appreciate every second I am able to spend with the love of my life. Every smile he gives me is much more beautiful than before. Every time he says my name is far more breath-taking than the last. I will savour every kiss, every touch, and every beat of his heart.

I see us, old and grey, still ruling over our two countries. Our children are grown and living their own lives. Francis and I are still as happy as the day we wed. The love we feel for each other is the love that we share with our children, who have grown up with a mother and father who adore them. And then one day, when we have lived a full and joyful life, we shall lie side by side and pass into the next world together hand in hand, just the way we have always been. Our children will weep, but they will feel a gladness knowing that we were never parted.

***

30th November 1560

Doctor Edmund says that Francis is through the worst. He expects Francis to make a full recovery in no time at all. The fever has completely gone, and the swelling has shrunk significantly. He has gotten out of bed and walked around a little, with me by his side to keep him steady. Every day, he gets stronger and stronger. All in all, everything seems to be slowly returning to normal. Christmas will be here soon enough, and the doctor is sure that Francis will be recovered enough to celebrate. Everything will be perfect again. Catherine and I have begun to work together on a grand celebration to see in the new year. A year that will be full of health and happiness.

Francis is happier than he has been in a long time. He manages to sit with me on an evening now, and we play cards and talk like we used to. His energy is finally coming back. Soon enough, he will be able to meet with his privy council, and life as we know it will resume.

Last night, we made love for the first time in weeks. Francis shook as he led me to the bed; he is still fatigued from his illness. I took control, laying him down and gently climbing on top of him. I kissed him like it was the last kiss I would ever give, and I touched every part of his body so that I could commit it to memory. I traced the line of his jaw, his shoulders, his lips, promising that I would never forget how they felt in that moment. I held his face in my hands and gazed down into his eyes as if I were looking into his soul. I allowed him to consume me all over again. With each movement, I showed him again and again how much I loved him. I pressed my lips to his neck and savoured the feeling of his skin beneath them. I laid my head on his chest and made a note of every beat that his heart made. I never want to forget the way we felt in that moment, the love between us stronger than ever.

***

5th December 1560

I wish I knew that today my life would be ripped a part. I wish that God gave me a chance to prepare for what was coming. I allowed myself to be convinced that all was well. All is not well.

Francis is sick again. He became unwell a few days ago and has not recovered since. At first it was mostly pain that grieved him. His ear was causing him trouble again. He wept with the agony it caused him. As he lay across my lap, the tears streaming from his eyes, I tried my best to comfort him. I rubbed his back and held him tightly, but I was at a loss. Nothing I did seemed to sooth him. Then his ear began to bleed again. The Doctor ordered him to bed which is where he has been since. He looks even worse than the last time. I did not think that possible, but he does. He has no colour to his skin. His beautiful eyes have faded to grey and his hands have grown cold. Yesterday he told Catherine and I that he was going to die. I had tried to quiet him. I could not stand to hear it. It broke my heart then as it does now. I cannot stand to lose him. I could not imagine anything worse in the world. I would give up my own life should it ensure Francis a long happy one. Although I argued and told him he was being silly, he was insistent that we listen.

"Mary. I can feel it happen. I grow weaker by the day." He tried to take my hand, but I had walked away from the bed. "You need to be prepared. I am not scared, Mary."

This made me angry. How could he talk so calmly about his death, like it was nothing?

"I am. I cannot be without you. Do you not think it cruel to leave me behind? In this cold world without you?" I raged. I was angry at him. I felt as if he had given up.

"I promised you that I will never leave you and I will not let a thing like death stand in the way." He said it so calmly, so matter of fact.

"You are not God, Francis. How do you think we will be together after you are gone?" I raged. I did not want to be angry with him, but I did not know how else to feel. He was fine just a few days ago. We had a wonderful week of health and now he says that he is dying. It did not make any sense to me.

"You know as well as I do that our love is strong enough to defy anything."

"Even death?" I demanded.

"Even God himself, my love."

I took a breath, I had to calm myself. It was no good to be angry with him now. Not when we may not have long left.

"Perhaps you will live." I said with little hope in my voice.

"Doctor Edmund says I will not." He replied.

At this I could take no more. I sunk to the ground. Tears falling freely from my eyes now. How could I stand this? I could not lose him. The thought was unbearable. He knew that he was leaving me, and he was giving up. Pain ripped through my chest as sobs broke free. I felt as if the world had come crashing down around me. I could not hold back the agony that poured out of me.

Francis moved to come to me but was too weak to stand. I pulled myself to my feet and forced myself to stand beside him.

"I cannot do this. I cannot face a world without you." I pleaded with him.

"I know." He said simply.

"I wish it were me." I sobbed.

Francis was angry. "Mary, never say that." He said. "You are the strongest woman I know. You have to live."

"It is pointless without you." I cry. "The best part of me is you."

"My love, no matter what happens, I promised that I will never leave you. That promise was eternal, and I will keep it forever. You may think that I am gone but do you think I could ever truly leave you?" tears ran down his eyes now. "Mary, you are my life.

You are my soul. I would claw my way through hell to be with you."

I laid my head against his chest and allowed all of the pain to flow out of me. He wrapped his arms around me for what would be the last time. He was so frail, so weak. They were not the arms I knew. They were skin and bone. He tried to hold me tightly, but he just was not strong enough anymore.

"My love, I am not going anywhere. I will still be with you every last moment of your life. I will take every breath with you. I will feel every beat of your heart. I will hold your hand and share this life with you."

"I don't understand." I said.

"Every time you smell the summer flowers and think of me, I'll be there. Every time you feel a breeze graze your cheek, that will be me kissing you. When you look up to the stars, I will be there beside you. I will be the butterfly that floats through the air. The birds that sing to you in the morning. I will be with you eternally. I need you to believe that our love can do anything, Mary. I need you to believe that I will never find peace until you are lying beside me. I will wait forever for you. I am not scared of death. What is death to us? It is not an end Mary. It is a new beginning. One that will start when you have lived a full and happy life. You will return to me one day and we will begin our eternity. Can you make me that promise?"

I do not answer for a little while. The sobs take over my whole body and I lie in his arms as the tears fall. How can I say that I believe. Death is so final. It is the end of a story not the beginning. I gaze at him, his lips have paled and cracked. The lips that just a few nights ago were soft and warm under my touch. His hands that felt so strong around me now crumble and weaken. His eyes that showed me all of the love in the world have now faded. And yet, he looks so hopeful, as he waits for me to answer. I cannot deny him a thing. I never would.

"I promise." I say weakly.

"Eternity?" He asks. He is fading. His eyes are heavy and his breathing shallow. He needs to rest now.

"Eternity." I repeat.

***

It is evening now. Night has fallen and still I sit with my husband. He has not woken up in a while and when he last did, he did not recognise me at all. He looked around in confusion and when I smiled at him, he met my gaze with tired eyes and lack of recognition. My heart ached as the man who only hours ago had loved me most in the world now had no idea who I was. I do not think he even knew who or where he was. He did not speak but his breathing has become shallower by the moment. It will not be long now until he leaves me for good and I cannot contain the feeling that is eating me up. The feeling of being utterly alone. My heart is no longer in my chest, it is with him. I hold his hand, but they are barely his hands now. They are cold and unloving. They hold nothing of the man that held me just the other night. His face is a blank canvas. All of the worry and stress has faded away. He looks so young. So carefree. The worries of this world are leaving him as he passes into the next. I cannot believe that just few days ago we thought he would live. I believed that we were to have a long happy life together. But now I know Francis will not make it past tonight.

I have to stop a scream from breaking free from my chest as I kneel next to my sleeping husband. I feel numb and in agony all at the same time. It is not just Francis that dies tonight, he takes my soul with him. There is nothing else for me in this world. He takes all of my joy with him. He looks like an angel as he sleeps peacefully. Perhaps that is why God is taking him. Perhaps it is because he needs him in heaven. He is too good for this world. God must know that he is taking the best of the best tonight. Maybe Francis is going home. Maybe heaven is the only place good enough for a soul like his. We are born with the knowledge that someday we will die. Someday, we will lose the ones we love. That is the only definite in this world. I just never thought it would be so soon. I thought we had a whole life to live together. We have only had a moment.

"Please Francis. Please stay." I say as I stroke his hair. "I love you. I cannot live without you."

Catherine, who has just come into the room, takes my hand as she stands beside me. "Doctor Edmund says it won't be long now." She tells me. The tears stream down her face. I have never seen her like this. When Henry died, she did not shed one tear, her heart is broken.

"The time has come for Francis to sleep, Mary." She takes me in her arms. "He has thought a long hard battle in this life. And he would do it all again for the time he had with you. Let him rest."

We both sob as we hold each other in our grief. Catherine lets go of me and walks towards her son. She kisses him softly on the head.

"You have been the joy of my life." She smiles. "I am so thankful that even for a short time, I was your mother."

"Be still now, my son."

Catherine stays for a little while but with a final squeeze of my hand she leaves me alone to say my final goodbye. Once she is out of the door I fall to the floor.

"My love. It is not too late to come back to me." I say softly. And yet even as I plead, I know it is. I know he has been stalked by death since the moment he was born and now it has caught up with him. "I love you. I love you with my whole being and more." My voice shakes. "I cannot survive without you."

As I kneel beside his bed I watch as each breath gets further and further apart. This is it. He fades and, in a moment, I know he is gone. It is so calm. There is no fit of pain. No heart wrenching final goodbye before his eyes slowly close. It is simple. He is breathing one moment and not the next. I watch as his chest falls and does not rise again. I can feel as he finally goes as he takes his very last breath and disappears into darkness. In this moment, Francis has broken his promise to me. He is gone and I cannot feel him anymore.

I stand for a moment, unable to move, unable to feel anything. My breath seems to have stopped with Francis'. I do not know what to do. There is nothing but silence all around me. Francis is motionless before me. My mind is still. I stand and kiss his head. It is still warm, still familiar. His hand, however, is as cold as ice. I hold myself tightly together as I turn and walk from the room. I do not think a thing. I am desperate to escape, desperate to be away from the room where my husband has faded into oblivion. "Goodbye. My love." I say simply. I know that he does not hear me. I know that his soul has already departed. I cannot explain it, all I can say is that I have always known when Francis is close, and he no longer feels close. There is a distance between us now. We are a whole world apart.

There is nothing but dead air all around as I stare down at my husband. I gaze at his lips, longing for them to move. I wait for his chest to rise. I pray for his hand to reach up and stroke my cheek. But he stays perfectly still. It is as if my mind cannot comprehend what is happening. It was so fast. He was breathing one minute and not the next. I have had no time. No chance to arrange my thoughts. There is so much more that I want to say. There are a million things we have left to do. But it is all empty now. I am empty. My future has been stolen from me.

"Francis?" I say, knowing he will not reply. "Francis, darling?" I shake him gently.

"Francis. Come back." I scream. "It is too soon. Come back."

I can no longer contain the scream that rips its way out of my body. It is an agony that tears me apart like nothing I have ever felt before. I cannot breathe. I cannot think. How could this happen? How was this allowed to happen? I cannot stop shaking as scream after scream breaks free from my body. I cannot catch my breath. My heart has been ripped from my chest and now lies next to my sleeping husband. How can I bear this?

We are both so young. We have both been promised so much life, and yet that life has been taken away. I had the promise of years ahead of us when I married Francis. The promise of happy times, of sad times together, of ups and downs. But now the journey that I started with my love just a year ago has abruptly stopped. I am now alone on this path.

I stand, motionless, scarcely breathing. My hand is still linked with my husband's, but it does not hold the comfort that I am so used to. It feels empty. It feels light. As I squeeze his hand, he does not return the comfort. I have never felt as alone as I do now. The only sound I hear is that of my own heart, and in this moment, I find myself willing it to cease to beat. I lay my head next to Francis, and for a moment I pray that I go with him, that God show a little mercy and, in this moment, take us both together, I would rather be floating above the clouds with Francis than weighted down by the misery of this place. I want to be at peace with my love.

Death is the only answer I can think of in this moment. It surrounds me. I can see only it. I can feel the darkness that creeps around my shoulders. Death is a cruel enemy and a friend to me at the same time, for it may have taken my dear love away, but it can also choose to reunite us. It could take me as well. I silently beg that it take me with Francis. I plead and I plead, whispering into the silence of the room. I see little reason for my staying in this place now. I always believed that nothing could part us, and I refuse to believe in this moment that we will be apart. God himself could not come between us, that is what Francis told me. Yet I am here, and he is gone. I lie in silence for a while, hoping that I will be carried away with him.

***

It is as if Francis' voice shakes me awake from the darkness. I hear it so clearly that I almost believe he had spoken to me. I realise that I have not taken a breath and gasp as the air fills my lungs. I look at Francis. His voice was so vivid that for a moment, I expected him to be sat up in bed, waiting for my reply. I feel the shock of pain again as I see that his body is still lifeless, his lips fixed in a peaceful smile. The pain and worry of this world are long gone.

God, my heart aches with how beautiful he is, how wasted. He looks so carefree, so young. Like he did before responsibility and illness weighed him down. It reminds me of when we were children together, when he was so full of life. So full of love. Only he is not full of life anymore. It has been taken from him. I would give anything to return to our wedding day, when anything was possible, when our futures were bright and waiting for us. I saw a world made for Francis and me. Now I see nothing but blackness.

I can hardly control the shakes that reverberate inside of my chest. My legs are weak, and I lack the strength to rise from my knees. How is this possible? How has this happened? Only a few months ago, I was dreaming about the children we would have, about taking Francis to Scotland so that he may see my home. But now he will never leave France. He will never father my children. I have lost our future today. I have lost the only future I had ever wanted. I had thought that it was inevitable, that we were fated to each other. It is clear now that God had a different plan.

I wait. Wait for his chest to rise and fall as he takes a breath, but of course, that does not happen. He will never take another breath. He will never again move from his rest. His hand will not reach up to stroke my hair, and he will never again lay one of his gentle kisses on top of my head. He will never again hear the sweet sounds of the morning as the birds softly sing us awake. He will never feel the grass under his feet or the wind as it brushes gently through his hair. He will no longer know the feeling of being kissed by me, the feeling of awaking in the arms of someone that you love and the softness of their voice in your ear. He will not ever smile or feel the joy of laughter. He won't ever again experience the things he loves.

As I realise this, I realise that I have lost all of that as well. I will not hear Francis whisper in my ear to rouse me each and every day. I will not feel his hand as it glides down my back or the warmth of his arms around me on a cold winter's night. I will not see his eyes stare into mine. I will never in my life feel a love like this again. That too has been lost to me forever. I will search my whole life to find a love like this, all the while knowing that it will never return. Never again will I know what it feels like to be completely a part of another person. A love like ours is only unlocked for the lucky few. We are not allowed another chance at it. Once it is gone, it is gone forever. And mine dies with Francis today.

I need to move. I need to stand. *Stand my love. My sweet Mary. And fight.* I hear his voice so clearly in my mind. I pray that I will always hear it. I pray that I never forget what he sounded like, how he laughed, how he sounded when he was angry with me or worried. I pray I never forget his face, and yet I am consumed by the fear that this is exactly what will happen. That for all the years I live without him, he will fade away.

The door to his room opens and Catherine walks in, holding on to Francis' two younger brothers. Shock fills her face as she sees for the first time her eldest son's lifeless body. But I do not cry with her. I do not join in her grief. I feel a steely determination take over my whole body. I wipe my eyes and I stand. I take a breath and I ask, "What do we do now?"

Catherine looks at me, confusion on her face. "Mary, come to me, my child." She holds her hand out for me. "We must just be here now. The rest can wait."

I cannot bear the idea of sitting with her and crying over Francis. I cannot bear the idea of being in this room. I feel suffocated. I feel like all the air has suddenly left and I need to move. I cannot sit here one moment longer. I cannot think straight. I need to occupy my mind with something.

"I would like to begin funeral arrangements immediately. We will need to make an announcement," I say as I fight to keep the shakiness from my voice.

"Mary . . ." Catherine walks across and puts her arms around me, but I am stiff in her embrace. I do not want to be touched by anyone. "There is much to prepare before we make an announcement. Charles is only a child; we need to consider a regent." It is clear that her heart breaks as she speaks to me. Her voice cracks, and the tears run down her face. I look to Charles for just a moment and watch as he holds tightly on to little Henry. Their faces almost send me over the edge as they weep in despair for their dearly loved older brother and king. Everyone weeps. Even the guards wipe their faces and try to conceal their pain.

I cannot do it. I cannot sit in a room full of grieving people. I have to get away from here, or I do not know what I will be driven to do. I need air. I need space.

"Will you stay and look after Francis a while?" I ask Catherine and the boys. "I do not want to leave him alone."

I do not give them time to answer. I nod for the door to be opened, and I make my escape from the room that now holds all of my joy and pain. It is a place of such happiness and sadness, and while I stand within its walls, I see every second of our lives play out around the scene that is Francis' death.

I need to leave this room. I cannot be in here any longer. I wretch as the bile rises in my throat. I cannot look at his body anymore. It is not Francis that lies here. It is an empty vessel. My Francis is gone from this world.

I break out of the palace, gasping for air as I am hit by the cool breeze. I fall to my knees, as I can hold on no longer. My chest is on fire. My heart cannot take any more. I lie on the grass, lacking the strength to move at all. I do not know where to go from here. I do not know how I am supposed to live. I could not lift myself up if I wanted. My stomach twists as I begin to wretch. The emptiness begins to take over as I close my eyes. On my knees on the palace grounds and I lack the strength or will to do anything about it.

"Mary . . ." I hear a voice. It is faint at first, and for a moment, I believe that Francis has come to save me. I open my eyes, and I actually see him coming towards me. I feel his arms around me as I am carried inside and laid in my bed.

I sleep the rest of the day away and am awoken by the realisation that it was not Francis at all. Catherine was worried and had come to check on me. One of her guards—Arthur, I believe his name is—had lifted me into his arms and carried me back to my room.

I wake to an empty bed chamber and reach my arm across to feel the empty space next to me; again, I am reminded that Francis is no longer here. My ladies busy themselves around me. They are drawing me a bath. I realise that I am still shivering. The cold must have gotten into me when I went outside. Catherine is nowhere to be seen, but Mary Fleming tells me that she sat with me a while before returning to her vigil by Francis' side. She had promised to return later.

I find that all I want to do is sleep. I am exhausted and being awake is agony. At least when I sleep, I can dream of him. While I am awake, I feel his absence so strongly.

It is morning and Mary helps me out of bed. She mentions that I should eat, but I simply shake my head. I cannot stand to eat at the moment. I am helped into the bath while my ladies tend to me. They try their hardest to soothe me, but I am beyond comfort at this point. When I am clean, I am lifted from the bath. They dress me and place a blanket around my shoulders. I am then sat in front of the fire. I sit and stare into the flames, unable to do anything else. Time ticks by slowly. My ladies sit and read. They try to remain cheery, but I know that they too will be grieving tonight. None of them attempt much of a conversation. Each of them has given me their condolences in one way or another—a gentle touch on the shoulder or a kiss on the hand—but I am unmoved by any of it. I sit here as the evening turns to night and the sky outside grows dark, but I do not notice. I can do little but stare into the fire without thinking or feeling. Just staring.

Catherine comes as the hour strikes nine. She sits beside me and holds my hand. We do not talk. We sit in our joint loss, neither of us knowing what to say to the other, neither of us wishing to say the wrong thing. She smiles at me, a false smile that is meant to comfort, but it is lost on me. I see the tears in her eyes, and they are like daggers, each one reminding me of my own pain. She stays with me for an hour, and then she stands and kisses me. She takes my chin in her hand. "We will make it through this, Mary," she says with little hope in her eyes. "Francis will help us."

At this, the tears begin anew. I let them fall now, lacking the strength or will to stop them. "How will he help us? He is gone, Catherine."

Catherine's smile grows wide for the first time in days. This is a genuine smile. This one she means. "He has not gone, Mary; you know as well as I do that he would never leave you." She strokes my cheek and leaves. I cannot believe it for the moment. I cannot think like that for now. I need to survive, and I cannot survive by placing all of my faith in ghosts.

I sit by the fire as night turns to day and day turns to night. I sleep a little, in and out of dreams. But for the most part, I am numb. I allow my ladies to carry on around me. I answer them with a simple nod or a shake of the head. I drink sips of wine and take small bites of food, but I refuse to move. I am safe here, and here is where I will stay. I stay in this same place as the days fall away like dust. I feel nothing.

Chapter 13

Francis has been gone almost a week. My heart could not possibly hurt more than it does right now. I have barely moved from the chair in my room. My ladies bring me everything I need. I have had no reason to leave. Life goes on around me, and I fade into the darkness that is now my life. I feel like I have lost the ability to complete normal tasks. I have to force myself to eat and drink. I have to fight my mind to be able to get a little bit of sleep. The tiredness is wearing me down. I jump at every noise. I fear every person who enters my room. I feel on edge every moment of the day.

I allow no one to touch me. I never want another person to touch me again. I want to forever remember how it felt for Francis to touch me. I do not want to forget his hand in mine. I cannot allow another person to remove the feeling of him.

A small part of me still holds out hope that Francis will come through my door and take me in his arms. This is all a terrible mistake, and he is back to full health. Sometimes when

I drift off to sleep, this is exactly what I see. I see Francis coming over to me and kneeling next to my chair. He will lay his head on my lap and soothe all of the worry and hurt away. He will wipe my face and tell me not to cry. I have had a terrible dream and nothing more.

I hear his voice in my head throughout the day. *I will never leave you, my love.* I will it to be true, but it is my mind trying to find some way to comfort me. For all the times that I have believed myself to be sad before, they hold nothing on how I feel now. I have lost more than a husband, more than my dearest of friends. I have lost the other half of me. It is as if death has taken a dagger and cut me straight down the middle. He has taken the better half of me away. What am I now? I am an incomplete person. How will I ever be able to go on, to walk the rest of my days with such a big hole inside? I no longer have a heart. Francis was my heart.

I will never feel again. This much I know. I will forever be a ghost of the woman I was just a few weeks ago. Before Francis truly became ill. When we lived in the sunshine. Our lives were full of light, and now I see nothing but gloom. The winter brings with it a coldness that is too much to bear. I am frozen to the core with grief. The bleakness of December reflects the way I feel inside. There is no escape from my despair. It is everywhere I look. Even with my eyes closed, it is ever present, just at the edge of my consciousness, waiting to creep up on me once more.

My ladies are continually trying to smother me in blankets. They are always at my side with something to drink or something to eat, but I can only stomach a little. Every now and then, I allow a small sip or little bite of food just to keep them off my back. I do not want any of it. I would happily sit here until I fade into the abyss. I am safe within this room, within this palace which has for so long been my home. This is the most comfort I will get. I have my trusted ladies and I have Catherine, but they will never be enough. They will never fill the void inside of me.

Francis was my everything. He was the only family I truly knew. He has been the only thing I have known since I was five years old. A love like ours was not superficial. It has grown from strength to strength over time. It was just a bud when we were children, but it has blossomed into the most beautiful of flowers as the years have passed.

It is not simply the love of a husband and wife. It is the love of family. The love of my closest friend in this world. The love of a protector. Any type of love that is imaginable is what Francis and I had. It was unconditional and untouchable. The loss of such love is catastrophic. I laid my whole life at his feet. I gave Francis every last inch of me, and he gave me every part of his soul. We were one person. Our minds worked in the same way. We had the same thoughts, fears, and dreams. When we looked to our future, we both saw the same outcome. Now that has been removed. It has drifted off into the smoke. It is nothing more than a dream on the breeze.

Catherine visits me daily. It is of little comfort. She reminds me of all I have lost. She tries to talk to me about Francis, but I do not hear it. I will not hear it. If I am to survive, I must shut him out. I said that I wanted to remember every part of him, but now all I want to do is forget. Today, she brought news with her. News of the funeral. I cringed inwardly as she said the word. It is such a final word. The air around me went dead silent as she listed off the details. My mind was lost, and I only managed to catch parts of what she said.

23rd December . . .

Basilica of Saint-Denis.

Her voice sounded so faded to me, like she was very far away. Pictures flashed through my mind of the funeral scene. I saw myself stood before the mirror, draped in black, my ladies crying around me.

"Mary, my dear . . . are you listening?" she asked after a while. "Mary. There are important details that you must know."

"Quite frankly, Catherine, you can do as you please." I snapped out of my thoughts.

Catherine took a breath and held my hand in hers. "Sweet girl, we need to do this. For Francis."

"You can do it for Francis, Catherine," I replied. "I trust you."

Once she had left, I was left alone to think about the not-so-far-away day where I would have to bury my husband. The day that I would be forced to say a final goodbye to my husband. Only it does not feel like my final goodbye. I do not feel ready for a permanent farewell. If we could go on forever without ever having to say goodbye, it would still be too short a time. And yet the day is fast approaching. I will have to adorn my best clothes and keep my head held high as the country looks to its queen for comfort and guidance. Only I am no longer Queen of France. I am now dowager queen. It may come as a surprise how little this fact affects me. I love France with my whole heart and have enjoyed every last second of being its queen, but it is all empty without him. Nothing matters anymore.

The thought that someday soon Francis will be interred into Basilica of Saint-Denis and I will never again be able to look upon his face kills me inside. He will be gone to me forever, and I am more scared than I have ever been. The idea that his body will be placed in the ground terrifies me, the thought of him being alone, without any comfort.

It has always frightened me, the idea that when we die, we are locked up in a tomb. I am a Catholic woman. I have always believed that when we pass over, we move on to a better place. But now that I stare death so plainly in its face, I find that I am not so confident in the idea of heaven, I worry that Francis ended the moment he drew his last breath. I have night terrors where he is trapped in darkness or trapped within his body. What if we do not leave this world at all? Do we face endless blackness when we die, or do we just stop? Cut short, like a smudge that has been wiped away? I fear that he is not in heaven at all. I fear that I will never see him again, that when I die, I too will be submerged into the dark and unable to find him.

I look down at my hands and see that they begin to shake. The panic is gripping me again, and I do not think I can cope with another attack. I need to reach inside of myself and find that part of me that is strong. I need to find my composure. "Just get through the next few moments," I tell myself.

I find myself wishing that I could just jump ahead a year or two, when I will not feel as I do now. When life will surely be easier. Grief cannot last forever, can it? I just want to skip ahead and see where I am two years from now. Perhaps I will find that I can smile again, or at least wake up and not dread the day ahead.

If only it were possible to see into our future. I wish I could jump ahead to my life in a year's time. Will the wound still be so fresh and raw? Will I still yearn for Francis every single moment of the day? Or will I find that life is a little easier? Will my heart be less heavy? And will I find that I can awake from sleep in the morning without the dreaded pit in my stomach?

I just want it all to stop. I just want the constant ache in my chest to cease. I want the throbbing in my head to stop. I want the world to stop. I want to be swallowed up completely. I want to disappear into the pit that I have made for myself.

I am drawn back to one of my nights with Francis, shortly after we were married. One where we talked about all of the unknown things in this world, when death was nothing to us. We knew that one day it would grip all of us, but we had not as yet experienced it. I had asked him what he thought happens to us after we are gone, and his answer is as clear to me now as it was on that evening.

We lay side by side. I was propped up on my elbow, gazing down at him, and I can remember thinking how awful it would be should death separate us. I have often found that the idea of death sets off a panic within me. It is like a dread in the pit of my stomach.

I was touched by death the moment I was born. My world is the way it is because of my father's death. I lost him before I had ever even known him. Death is the very reason I am the queen of Scotland. It is the reason that Francis and I ruled France. As monarchs we know that our role begins and ends with a death. It is the reason that our lives are so well protected. I was sent here to France to keep me safe. To keep me out of death's grip.

When I asked Francis his opinion on what happens when we die, a warm smile dawned across his face. "I believe that when we die, we are carried away to a distant place up in the sky. Far above the clouds. Far from the world we live in now," he explained.

"Far from the people we love?" I asked.

"I think that although we are no longer in the same world, we can watch our loved ones from above."

I was thoughtful for a moment, mulling over Francis' words. They brought me no comfort, for as peaceful as his paradise sounded, it still separated us from each other. "But you will not be with the people you love?" I asked.

"You can see them whenever you want, I am sure of it. And although we may not be able to feel them, we will know they are there."

"How?"

"You will know when it happens," he said simply.

"And what if we are to be separated? Francis, I could not stand it," I said, allowing my illogical worry to take over.

"Then I would spend no time in heaven and all of my time on Earth with you. And then, when you are ready to join me, we shall live in paradise for all eternity. Hand in hand, just like always." He was so sure of it. Like it was definite and nothing would change his mind. I hoped with all of my heart that he was right.

I smile to myself, as for a moment, I can picture that world, a world where Francis and I are bathed in glorious light forever. The picture of my heaven is slightly different than his. In mine, he and I lay on the grass. The day is perfect. The height of summer. The clouds float by in many different shapes, and the birds and the bees fly by happily. The breeze is cool, and the scent of summer flowers floats through the air. No one disturbs us. There is nothing for us to do. We simply spend our time in peace, our hands interlocked for the rest of time.

How I will for that to be true. How I pray that one day soon, that shall be my reality, that I shall join him not long from now and we may begin our eternity high above the clouds.

It is only the more painful when I come crashing back down to reality. When the image of Francis and me is wiped away as quickly as it came. The ache returns to my chest in one powerful wave as I try my hardest to cling to the peaceful picture that for just a moment soothed me. No matter how hard I try to conjure it up again, it is gone. I just want to live in a beautiful lie for the rest of my life. I know it is a lie and yet I do not care. I would rather a lie than the dreadful truth. Why can I not just live in denial a while longer, just sit a while in my perfect fantasy? When my eyes are closed, I can easily imagine that Francis is lying next to me. I can imagine his hand in mine and his breath on my cheek.

When my eyes are open, I feel the bitterness of his absence. I am forced to face the fact that he is not here. I am not sure how much longer I can go on in this way. I go from being numb to being in total agony. The numbness is at least a short break from the dagger in my heart. I am consumed by vile grief as it drags me under again and again. It does not help that as I sit in this room, all I see is my husband. When I look to the bed, I see the many times we made love. The hundreds of kisses we shared. I look to the fire and see us sitting side by side. I can hear our laughs echo through the room. I can see as we lie naked, wrapped in our furs, the warmth from each other's bodies keeping away the chill on a cold winter's night. I look out the window and see Francis guide me down from my horse. I can feel his hands on my waist. I feel his fingers on my cheek and his gentle kiss on my lips.

When I see Catherine, I see Francis in her features. I see his smile and hear in her voice the same lilt that he had. She is a walking reminder of him, and I find that I cannot look into her eyes, which are the same beautiful colour. It is hard to see the same hope in her eyes when my world has turned to ash around my shoulders. The thought of France holds no happiness for me now. When I think about the country I have loved so dearly, I think about all of the places that hold special memories for Francis and me. Inside these very walls, I think of the great hall where we would play as children. In the garden, I see our spot where we would let the long summer days pass before us. Then I look to Notre Dame, where only a year ago we made our vow to each other. When we promised to love each other for the rest of our lives. Never in our darkest nightmares did we imagine that it would be such a short time. How happy I was then. It is such a huge contrast to the pit of despair I find myself in now. On that day, I was stepping into the beginning of my life. Now I feel as if my life has ended.

I allow the air to fill my chest as I try to level myself. I notice now that Mary has been sitting beside me. She is holding a bowl of soup. I look at it and my stomach twists. I realise that I am hungry, yet I have no will to eat. I have no reason to. I do not want to live. If I died of starvation at this point, I could not care less. My throat dries with thirst and my head pounds, but I refuse to take any sustenance. I am not interested in surviving. I long to die here in this place, the place that was my beginning and now my end. I care little for the life that continues on around me. I am not bothered by the bustle of the castle. It is nothing more than a buzz in the background.

Mary gets up to draw me a bath, and for the first time in days, I allow myself this simple luxury. I must admit that it feels good to remove my gowns and allow the heat from the bath to warm me. I had no idea just how much the chill had gotten to my bones. As I look out of the window, finally breaking my motionless stare at the fire, I realise that the ground is white; heavy snow falls from the sky. I had almost forgotten that it was winter outside. Christmas draws near, and it is painful to think about how everyone else in the world will make merry with their loved ones while I sit alone in my misery.

Chapter 14

23rd December 1560

Today, we laid Francis to rest. I cannot explain how I feel or even work through my thoughts. t was like I watched the whole thing from afar. I walked through the motions like a ghost, feeling as if I were not really there. I woke from a fitful sleep feeling like there was a heavy weight lying across my chest, and it has stayed with me since, crushing me more as the day goes on. I refused breakfast as it was brought to me. I washed and dressed without thought. I remember gazing into the looking glass and trying to remember how I managed to get into my black gown. Black, the colour that filled my world now. The only colour I have donned since the moment Francis left is black.

How miserable I looked as I gazed at my reflection. The picture of a widow, my youth stolen away from me. Just like Francis, whose youth has been taken, so has mine. Only he moved on into the next world and I am chained down to this one. I looked exhausted. My cheeks, which once blushed from happiness, are now gaunt and grey. My eyelids are heavy from exhaustion. I sleep, but I do not rest.

My dreams are haunted these days. I see Francis every night, but it is not the type of dream to bring me comfort. Instead, I am bound to lose him over and over again. He dies in many different ways. Every night as I try to rest, I am crippled by images of Francis' death. Each time, I try to save him. I do anything I can to keep him here, but it is useless. The agony I feel when I awake, soaked through with sweat and chest heavy with panicked palpitations, is indescribable. For a moment, each time I am locked into the dream. I am lost in a world where my Francis is dying in agony without my touch. Without my help.

And then the panic is eased as I let the dream drift away. For a moment, all is still and I feel a solitary second of peace. Then, in a breath, it is gone, and the harsh reality hits again. It is already too late. I have already failed in saving him. He is gone, and now all I have to do is get through the day so that I can watch him die on a loop all over again. So that I may suffer through the endless torment of losing him, both in my waking world and my dreamland.

Now I find that being awake is more bearable than sleep. I have almost given up on sleeping altogether. I would rather be awake with my misery than asleep with my demons. Whichever way, I am plagued by longing. Longing for something that is impossible. Longing for a touch I cannot feel, for a voice I cannot hear. Longing to hear the laugh that would raise my spirits high and mend all the hurt.

I have never felt a worse feeling than wanting something with my whole being, something that is rightfully mine and that for so long I have been granted, only to have that thing refused. Each morning, I wake and touch the space beside me, thinking I will feel the warmth of my love, and find nothing but emptiness as I run my hands through the sheets. I will never get used to the sheer despair of realising I am alone.

Today, when I awoke, I stayed in a sleepy daze, my mind aware of today's event. It did not want to register all of the feelings that were ready to burst from my chest. I felt like I have been completely shut down. My heart seemed to beat in slow motion. My body seemed to move just enough to keep me upright and keep my legs from crumbling. I moved from the bed in a fog. I barely looked to my ladies, who wept around me. I needed to be strong today, and their tears would have only called forth mine. I allowed them to dress me, and I stood as still as a statue while they laced me and pinched my cheeks. Not a tear rolled down my face as they fussed and prodded. They asked repeatedly what they could do for me, but I found that all I could do was shake my head. I did not trust my voice. I needed to stay composed. I could not do so if my voice betrayed me by shaking.

After I was dressed, Catherine came to get me. She smiled weakly as my door opened to her. Her eyes were red from tears. I did not weep at all. My grief was my own, and I did not feel like sharing it with France. Today, all I felt was emptiness, like all of the emotion in my body was gone.

I allowed Catherine to wrap her arms around me but took no comfort in her embrace. I sat on my bed while we waited for the moment to leave, and as I closed my eyes, I made a silent promise to myself. *Be strong. It is just one day.* If I did not know better, I would have sworn that it was Francis who spoke and not myself. I hear a lot of things in his voice these days. I believe it is the one comfort that stops me from toppling over the edge completely.

Outside of the palace was filled with nobles and common people alike. They all looked at me as I stepped out, their eyes full of sympathy and heads down with sorrow. My heart should have been warmed as I looked out at the sea of people come to say goodbye to their beloved king, but the only thing I felt was annoyance. I felt like they did not deserve to grieve. They did not know him like I did. Even his privy council had no idea what the real man behind their king was like. If I could have had it my way, I would have said goodbye to Francis without all of the pomp and ceremony. But as monarchs, we are not granted the luxury of a private goodbye.

As his queen and wife, I was allowed the respect of following him in the carriage. I climbed in with Catherine beside me. She took hold of my hand, but I brushed her away. I did not want any comfort today.

We proceeded through the streets, as was custom for a king's funeral. The people shouted and called out the name of their lost king. The bells tolled to aid Francis on into the afterlife, and the people mourned. Much like the day they lined the streets to see me on my wedding day, only on that day, they shed tears of joy; today, they wept for a young man cut down too early. It is heart-breaking to think that the faces I looked upon today had also been there on that not-so-long-ago day when all of our happiness had come to fruition. They had cheered for their dauphin, who they loved so deeply, and now they said goodbye. How cruel is God to allow such a turn of events as this?

From the moment we reached St Denis, I lost almost all coherence. I remember walking into the cathedral, and I remember Catherine's hand on my shoulder. I can still picture the tears as they rolled down the faces of Francis' siblings, who were still dealing with the grief of losing their father and now their brother. I cannot remember many of the words that were spoken or picture much of the ceremony, but I do remember the feeling that I held within my stomach, a sickness that would not cease.

Words were spoken, but there was nothing in my mind but a constant buzz. I looked about me, and all around were people lost in their own grief. They grieved for a king, for a brother, a friend. And although I am sure that each of them was beside themselves with sadness, none of it compared to mine, and in that moment, I hated them. How dare they sob for my lost love? It is I who has to live the rest of my days in darkness. Their hearts have not been crushed like mine has. They may be sad that they have lost Francis, a boy who for so many years has been a precious jewel to France. But within a number of months, weeks even, they shall have moved on. I will never move on. I do not wish to move on. Francis' heart was taken from his chest and laid in an urn for all of time. Mine is right beside his. I will never take it away from him. They shall lay side by side until I join him.

I spent the day like a shadow. Many wished to speak to me, but I turned each and every one away. I allowed Catherine to take the full brunt of queenship this afternoon, and as I looked at her, my eyes full of apology, she simply smiled and reassured me. She has done all of this before. She will grieve in private.

I scarcely have the strength to stand up. My legs long to buckle beneath me. It took all of my strength to not run back to my room, which has been my only solace in the past weeks. Today was the first day I had left my room since everything had happened. It was the first time that I felt the full effect of the bitter winter that raged around us. The cold did not worry me like it normally did; it was nothing compared to the cold that radiated from within me.

At points today, I had to remind myself to breathe. I had to force my chest to rise and fall. I stood like I was set in stone. I was holding myself so tightly together that I feared the slightest movement would rip me apart at the seams. It was a relief the moment Catherine glided towards me and told me that I should return to my room. The moment she relieved me of my duties, I could have turned and ran. Instead, I took my leave gracefully.

However, once back in my room, I let go of all formality and fell to my knees before my bed. I shut my ladies out and refused to open the door for anyone. I have been here since. On my knees. My head resting on my bed. The tears now freely flowing down my face. The shake that I have kept at bay finally breaking free. I have done nothing but sit here and think back over the day. I kept my feelings in check today, but now that I am alone, it feels as if all of the air has been stolen from my lungs.

I finally register the things that happened today as images begin to flood my mind. I see Francis lowered into the tomb that will eternally hold him. I can see it as it is sealed. I can feel the stab in my chest as I think about his heart being removed. I know that it is tradition, but it is just so brutal. The part I love most about him has been torn away.

I cannot help but think back to the last time I saw him. The last words I spoke to him repeat over and over in my mind. I am bolted down by guilt for not saying enough, for not saying the right things. If I had had any idea that it was to be the last time, I would have said so much more. I would have ripped myself to pieces in order to show him how much I truly love him. I would have torn my heart from my chest just to show him that he was the reason it beats.

Now it is too late. He is cold and in the earth, and I can never speak to him again. I cannot say what I would do just to have one more moment with him. Just one more sentence, or even just a word. The goodbye I had today was not good enough. No goodbye ever will be. There is so much that I have left to say and will never be able to. And yet my heart is telling me that I must try. I must go to him now. While the sky outside is dark and the court sleeps around me, I must try.

In a moment, I am on my feet and running to my door. I order a carriage made ready, and I leave the palace as quietly as possible. I only have one person with me: Fleming. She can be trusted to follow silently. No one else must know where I am going. I want to be alone. I order the carriage driver to take us back to St Denis. The night has fallen now, and we steal away under the cover of darkness. I tell the priest not to ask questions as I demand to be let in. Mary waits outside, and I ensure that I am left totally alone in the cathedral.

Once inside, I lose all sense and throw myself towards the newly built tomb that now holds my sleeping husband within it. This is the closest I am able to get to him, and although it is not nearly good enough, I let out a breath, as I know that his body is close. The idea that the man I love lies encased in a coffin is agony. Is he Francis still? It has not been very long since he left me. I imagine his face still holds the sweetness that I cherish so much. How I would give anything to see that face one last time. A painting will never hold the true beauty that he held within his soul. It will never show the goodness that radiated out of him.

There is an ache deep within my body as I sit beside his tomb and weep for all that I have lost. I came here to say goodbye and that is what I intend to do, but the words evade me. I sit for a while, my mind blank, unsure of what I should say now that I am here. I begin to feel foolish. What good will talking to a tomb do? How can I be sure that Francis will even hear me? My head rings with the words *just speak*. And I know that it does not matter what I say, just that I say it.

"My love. I do not know what I should say or even how to express in words what I feel, but here is the best I can do." I take a breath. "I am angry. Angry at you for leaving me. Angry at God for taking you. Most of all, I am angry that I could not save you. I have never felt so alone. I long for the world to swallow me whole. I long to climb in beside you and leave this world in this moment. How will I ever survive this?"

The words that have sat just below the surface now begin spilling out. I stop for a moment, but of course, there is no reply.

"Do not tell me that I am strong enough. I know if I were gone and you were left alone in this world, you could not cope. Why do I have to walk this world without you? I wish that I were dead and you lived on. You deserve to live, my darling. You are so good. So strong and pure.

"I am a weak shell of a woman. I am not cut out for this world. How will I ever cope without the love that you bestowed upon me? It is like being told that I am never again allowed to bask in the sunlight. Never allowed to breath the clear sea air. Never again allowed to be at peace. I never want to feel the touch of another. I want your touch to linger on me for the rest of time.

"I never want to open my heart again. It is forever closed off. I swear to you that as long as I live, I will never love another. No one will ever touch me as you have. No one will complete me in the way you have. In losing you, I have lost my soul." I cannot hold the tears back. "I am now nothing more than an empty vessel left behind to roam the world. I never want to be more than a vessel. I never want to see the sun again, for it is not the same without you by my side. I never again want to take comfort in the stars, for they are black and dead without you. I wish to remain cold and alone until I can bask in your love again." I try to wipe away the tears, but it is useless.

I let the silence stretch out around me. There is no sound but that of my own breathing. I sit in complete stillness as the thoughts that have weighed me down for weeks fight to burst free. The sobs take over as my worst fears surface.

"Francis? What if this is it? What if the day you died is truly the last time I will see you?" My throat tightens as the panic that I have become accustomed to sets in again. "How can I be sure of anything you have told me? You promised never to leave me, and you did. How can I be confident in the idea that we may meet again? How can I allow that to comfort me?" I place my head in my hands as the sobs become unbearable. My chest heaves with each one. "Francis, I need you. I am not cut out to live alone. Please. Please, come back to me. Francis, I need you more than ever in this moment. I need you to save me.

"I cannot bare this!" I scream. "How could you do this to me?" I spit. "How could you leave me?"

Francis and I never exchanged cross words in life. I was never angry or disappointed in him, but in this moment, I feel a rage like never before. "I hate you!" Do you hear me, my love? I hate you. I hate you." I am still for a moment as I let my words echo around the empty cathedral. Even as I say them, I know in my heart that they are not true. I could never hate him. I am just so angry that he is gone. And while I know it is not his fault, I cannot help but blame him for his absence.

The guilt sets in in an instant. I allow the tears to roll down my cheeks as the weight of my words sets in. I am on my feet and standing over his tomb in a moment, the closest I will ever get to holding him again. "I am sorry." I weep. "Oh, Francis, what have I said? Forgive me. I could never hate you.

"I am just so confused at the moment. I have so many thoughts and feelings, things that I have never felt before. I cannot sort one from the other. I am so angry all of the time. But I should know better than to take it out on you. You would never choose to leave me. I know that. I'm so sorry, my love."

I calm now as the sobs change to silent tears. I fall again to my knees, and I rest my head as close to the tomb as I can. "You know that I love you, don't you? I did not mean the words I said."

It is like an almost silent *yes* echoes through the church. It is quieter than a whisper, and I convince myself that it is just my mind playing tricks on me. Yet it comforts me enough that I close my eyes and fall into a gentle sleep next to my peaceful husband.

***

I am awoken by the gentle winter light as it filters in through the cathedral windows. As I rise, I can hear the birds sweetly singing in the early morning. As I get my bearings, I see Fleming from the corner of my eye. She is curled up in one of the stalls, softly sleeping. I go and rest my hands on her shoulder to gently wake her from her dreaming.

She is alert at once. "Majesty." Mary jumps up from her seat and bows. "Sorry, my lady. I must have fallen asleep."

"It's perfectly alright, Mary." I allow her to stand. "Have you been here all night?"

"When I came in to look for you, I found you sleeping so peacefully that I could not stand to wake you. It has been so long since you have slept so soundly."

I am thoughtful for a moment. "That is because I slept next to my husband."

"I know, my lady." Mary smiles.

We make our way back out to the carriage. I notice that it is still early morning, and if we are lucky, we will make it back to the castle before everyone wakes.

Chapter 15

Although visiting Francis' tomb has brought me a small amount of comfort, it is not enough to fill the gaping void that has opened inside of me. Everything around me now only brings me sadness, and I do not believe I am strong enough to stay here in a country that I have loved so well, a place I have called my home. It has been a place that I have cherished, both as its subject and its queen, but which now only serves as a reminder for all that I have lost.

I hide away in my rooms every day. I have no interest in seeing or talking to anyone. It only elevates my pain to see others suffer and to look into the faces of my family and see Francis. I need to save myself. I need to remove myself from a situation that is tormenting me. So it is with the heaviest of hearts that I have decided it is now time for me to leave France.

I have spoken to my half-brother James, and after much deliberation, we have come to an agreement. I shall return to Scotland and take my place as queen. James was wary at first. I have been away for so long, and he is concerned the people may not accept me. It is a risk I am willing to take. I cannot be in France any longer. Honestly, I do not want to be anywhere. However, if I am to continue on in this life, I may as well put myself to good use. I was born to rule Scotland, and I think that it is high time I get to work. At least by returning to Scotland, I will be going to a place that I already know. I will be taking back what is rightfully mine. I always knew that one day I would take control; I just thought that Francis would be beside me. However, now that he is gone, I see no reason to stay in France.

My Guise uncles, who were such a great help to Francis and me, support my decision. We have had many conversations over the past month, and it became clear that as a widow and a queen, I only had two options: I could remarry and live in another country while my brother continues to look after Scotland, or I could return to my own country and take over. While there are many advantageous suitors, such as Spain, who have shown an interest, I cannot stomach the idea of marrying again. I know that one day I must, but that marriage will be nothing more than a political one. I refuse to disrespect Francis by remarrying so quickly. I know that one day I will need to have an heir, but the thought of another man's hands on me is enough to send me into another fit of panic.

There was another person I had to tell: my cousin Elizabeth. It was important for me to write to her and tell her of my return to Scotland, not only as a courtesy but so that I could obtain her permission to make the journey safely. I have written to her to ask that she grant me a passport through English waters. Alas, she has refused me on both attempts. She is still sore with me because I have not revoked my claim to the English throne. That is not a decision I will take lightly, and I have informed her that I would first like to talk to my advisors in Scotland.

Elizabeth is a very impatient woman and does not like being told no. We have had a few conversations over the years via letter, and if I am honest, she has always come off as if she thinks she is the better woman. I find myself annoyed and shocked by her petty behaviour. I have always tried to be kind and courteous towards her and have reassured her time and time again that I pose no threat to her throne. I simply believe that due to the Tudor blood in my veins, I deserve to have my place in the line of succession, which would mean little in any case if Elizabeth were to have an heir. I can understand her fear. I am Catholic and many of her subjects would prefer a Catholic ruler, but I have no interest in hurting a fellow queen, especially not my own cousin. I would simply like my birth right to be honoured.

I am anxious to return after so long. I do not know what I am going to find. I hope that Scotland will have some sort of comfort for me, that to be in the place of my ancestors may give me back some sort of purpose. At the least, it will help me to stay busy. I have spoken to Catherine and the rest of the family.

However reluctantly, they have agreed that in order for me to begin to heal, I need to move on. They have watched me for months become nothing but a shell of myself. I do not speak. I eat little, and I stay locked away in my room. Catherine says she just wishes to see me smile again. However, I do not believe that I will ever smile again. Not in the way I did with Francis. I am hollow, and nothing in France fulfils me anymore. I need to search for a completely new life for myself. It will be vastly different than the future I once saw, but I will have to make do.

In a couple days, I will set off for Scotland. My things have been ready for weeks, but the weather has not permitted my return. My ladies are excited by the idea of returning home. It has given them a new sense of adventure. It has been so long since any of us have seen home; we are glad to finally be able to see the place where we were all born.

Tonight, I will attend a farewell feast held in my honour. It will be the first time I have attended an event since Francis' funeral. Catherine convinced me to attend, and begrudgingly, I must admit that it will be nice to say a proper goodbye to the Valois family, the people that I owe so much and to say goodbye to my home and my subjects. I do not leave without regrets. There will be a huge hole in my heart where France has been. I will miss my loved ones greatly, and I shall long to look out of my window and see the patch where Francis and I once played. But I also have to set myself free of the grief that bolts me down. I need to find some peace away from here.

I am hesitant to leave Francis behind in France. I will no longer be able to visit his tomb whenever I need a small bit of comfort. It hurts me to know that I will be so far from him, further than I have ever been, yet I know that he would want me to go. He would encourage me to return to Scotland. Since the first night that I went to his tomb, I have returned twice a week. Sometimes I talk to him. I rant and rave about the things weighing me down. Sometimes I sob, when missing him is ripping me apart.

A lot of the time, I sit. I simply sit beside him, and I do not say a word. I remember how Francis and I could sit in blissful silence for ages. There was never a desperate need for words. We never felt the need to fill the air with pointless chatter. We could just be, peacefully in the moment. I would rest my head on his chest and listen to his heartbeat. All other noise faded out as I lay my head on him.

I smile to myself now as I think about the time we had together, yet it is always replaced by deep heartache. It is like I forget for a moment, and then before I know it, I am drowning again. That is all I am doing while I stay in France: drowning. I feel like I am hit again and again, like waves on the ocean, as the grief drags me under. I hope that away from here I will learn to swim again. I do not expect to be the old Mary ever again. She was dead and buried when Francis was. But I do hope that I can at least get through the day without suffocating.

***

I attended the feast on Catherine's orders, but I felt much the same as I did on the day of the funeral. I sat like a ghost while noise and chatter went on around me. In one way, it was wonderful to spend one last evening with the court, surrounded by the many faces I had come to know so well. However, they all looked at me with such sadness and sympathy in their eyes that it made me feel like a different person. They used to smile on us, the sweet royal couple; now they looked at me like half of me was missing. It made me feel hollow.

Each member of the court bid me farewell tonight and wished me happiness. I smiled and thanked them, all the while longing for the moment I could leave.

When Catherine and her children embraced me, for the first time, I allowed the tears to fall freely. I would miss them. I would miss Catherine's motherly warmth and the sense of belonging I feel when surrounded by them all.

For the first time since losing Francis, I allowed Catherine to embrace me, and I embraced her back, holding her tighter than ever and knowing that I will probably never feel so loved again. Knowing that I leave behind the only real kin I have ever had.

I wish that I had the strength to stay, but I just do not. I wish I could stay in a bubble, inside the confines of my world, pretending that Francis is alive and well and that I will see him soon. However, pretending only gets anyone so far. It is a beautiful lie. But it is just that: a lie.

Tonight, Catherine presented me with a ruby necklace, and when I turned it around in my hand, I recognised it instantly. When I was small, I had always admired it. I had loved the way the sun shone through the ruby and danced in the light. It was one of Catherine's favourites, and she had always refused to let me try it on, much to my annoyance. One day, Francis came to my room, his hands tucked behind his back and a big grin on his face. He was so pleased with himself. When I asked him what was so funny, he refused to tell me. As I scolded him, he suddenly sank to his knees in front of me and opened his hands to show me what he was hiding: his mother's ruby necklace.

"Queen Mary, I present you with this jewel." He grinned. We were only about ten and eight years old at the time, but he was full of confidence as he said, “I give this to you as a token of my love.”

I remember laughing so hard that my cheeks hurt, which made Francis turned as red as the ruby from embarrassment.

“You don’t like it?” He hung his head as the tears sprang to his eyes and betrayed him. He wiped them with his hand angrily.

“No. No, I love it.” I pulled him into a hug. “But Francis, it’s your mother’s,” I chuckled.

“I took it for you.” He looked ashamed. “Are you mad with me, Mary?” he asked as he hung his head.

“No, but Catherine will be,” I warned, wiping a stray tear from his eye.

“I just wanted you to have it. Mother has so many jewels. And you love this one.”

“Francis, you are so sweet.” I kissed him on the cheek. “Maybe I should try it on?” I asked. Part of me was excited. I had always loved playing dress-up with different jewels and gowns.

His face lit up in an instant. He gestured for me to turn around and gently tied the necklace around my neck. Then he stood back and crossed his arms. After a quizzical look, he simply said, “My beautiful Mary.

However, at that moment, Catherine burst into my room. One of her maids had seen Francis stuff the necklace into his pocket. Of course, we were both in trouble then. We were banned from seeing each other for three whole days. Francis cried his little heart out. He only meant to do something nice for me. I never saw Catherine wear it again.

Catherine now tied it around my neck. Just like Francis had. As I looked at myself again all these years later, I was taken back to that day. When I had looked at myself in the looking glass then, I was full of youth. Full of happiness. Now my light had dulled, yet this necklace brought a blush back to my face.

"You remembered?" I asked.

"I've been saving it for you, Mary," she said. "You looked so beautiful wearing it that day that I put it away safely for when you were old enough. Now is the perfect time for you to have it. Francis would love for you to have it. I am just surprised that he never attempted to steal it again."

I could not help but smile to myself as I imagined Francis smuggling the necklace into his pocket. He was so pleased with himself that day as he presented it to me. How I miss that genuine innocence he always had about him.

"Thank you," I said as fresh tears rolled down my face.

"I love you, my sweet girl." Catherine took hold of me. "I only pray that you find some peace within yourself in Scotland. It pains me to see such a bright, beautiful young woman so wasted. Now, I know that your life will never be whole again, but do whatever you can to find something worth living for. Learn to laugh again. To have fun. Learn to love again. Have children. Have lovers." Catherine laughed. "Just please be happy. Francis will wait. You know he will. He will wait forever for you to join him, and nothing you do in this life is going to change that."

"I will never love again. Francis is all I will ever want," I said, determined. I needed her to know that he would never be replaced.

"You will never love again. Not in the way you loved him. But you can take comfort in another person. It does not suffice to be cold and alone."

My mind was already made up on the matter; I had nothing else to say about it. Instead, I simply said goodbye. "Thank you for everything, Catherine. You have been so good to me. Francis and I have been so lucky in the family we were given. You are the reason he was the person he was. And I can never thank you enough for allowing me to love him."

"Thank you for coming into our lives and making the short years my son had in this world joyous and full of life. And know that you will always be welcome here in France. You are family, and you will always have a home with us."

***

The feast is over now, and although I am exhausted from the feigned happiness and false smiles, I still have one last thing to do. I must visit my husband one more time. I find that even in death, he is the one person I can confide in and find solace in. He is still the person that I can trust above anyone else, and it is him I seek out when I have a decision to make.

It turns out that deep down, I already knew how he would feel about my return to Scotland. At first, I worried that in some way I was turning my back on him and the life we had built here in France. I believed that if I tried in any way to move on with my life, I would be disrespecting his memory. But I did not give my sweet Francis enough credit. If I just dug a little deeper, I could see that he would urge me to take the next step in my life. He would hate to see me wallowing in my own pity, to be so lost in grief that I could not do a thing. Francis always had such big dreams for our future, and as much as I will hate every moment, I need to try and live my own future for him. I will never forget. My heart will never heal, but I will carry the grief with me instead of lying stagnant in my own pit of misery.

When I arrive, my heart feels heavier than usual. In some way, this really feels like our last goodbye. I have never been so far from him as I will be when I reach Scotland, and the thought is a hard one to bare. Although I cannot be with him, hold him, and love him like I once did, at least the last few weeks I have been able to sit beside his body. It is not good enough, but it is the best I have, and when I return to Scotland, I will not be able to do this every day.

The tears roll freely down my cheeks now as the weight of my decision lies heavy on my chest. Scotland has been a far-off plan for so long, and now that it is only hours away, I feel the true pain of leaving a place that has been such a great joy to me. The place that has been my home. The family I love. The people I have cherished. The husband I have lost. I have questioned my decision since the moment I made it, constantly flipping backwards and forwards in my mind. But I need to be strong. I must be strong. There is a whole country of people expecting me. Waiting for their queen to finally return.

As I take my place beside my husband one last time, I cannot help but feel a stab in my chest. As I run my fingers along the tomb that encases him, I cannot help but wish that it were his face that my fingers traced. The love that I still carry within me longs to burst forth and throw my arms around him. However, the person I talk to now is a stone. It does not hold the warm comfort of my gentle husband. I lay down so that it is almost as if I lay beside him, but it is the bitter cold of his tomb that meets my warm cheek and not the sweet softness that once touched me.

If Francis had lived, I would have never said goodbye to him. Nothing in this world could have ever parted us. Now he is gone, I am forced to move on without him, a fate I had thought I would never have to face. The words all fight to get to the surface now. I have so much to say and no idea where to start. How do I say goodbye to my forever? How do I find the right words? Nothing will ever be good enough. I feel as if this is the last time that I will ever be able to talk to him, that after tonight, Francis will truly be lost to me, and I do not have the strength to face that reality.

I remember the words I heard the first time I visited his tomb, *just speak*, and I think about how easy it was to speak to Francis when he was here. I could say absolutely anything, and even if it were total nonsense, Francis would somehow make sense of it. He knew my thoughts before they even crossed my mind. I just need to imagine that he is here now, sitting across from me and ready to listen.

I close my eyes and I can see him, as beautiful as the day he left me. He sits with one leg crossed over the other. He gestures to me, encouraging me to speak. For a moment, I am completely lost. It seems so real, as if he is really seated across from me. Every detail of him is as I remember it. He smiles so warmly, as if he does not have a care in the world. The aching I feel only deepens with the knowledge that I cannot simply reach out and touch him, although it feels as if I could. I must remember that this is nothing more than a phantom that my mind has conjured up. Yet surely, if I wish it to be real with my everything, then it will become so.

Before I know it, the words begin tumbling out, just as they would if he were alive.

"I have come to say goodbye," I begin sheepishly. I cannot help but feel foolish as I talk out loud to an image that I have conjured in my mind. "You see, I am going away, Francis. I have to leave. I have to go back to Scotland. I cannot stay in France anymore." I let the words sit.

"All I see is you. Wherever I look, you are there, and I am too weak at heart to stand it." I take a deep breath. Francis does not even blink. The warm smile remains on his face. "I do not want you to be mad at me for leaving you. You know that if I could, I would remain with you until the day we are both ground to dust. But Francis, you have already left me behind. I cannot stay here and rot beside you. I know that sounds harsh and unfair, but I need to give myself a fighting chance at making it out the other end. You know that you will be on my mind every second of every day and that the pain of losing you will never dissipate. But if I stay here, I will die. I will let myself die."

Still, he remains unmoved.

"The truth is I long to die. But my faith in God and fear of Hell stop me from joining you now. So I have to do whatever I can to live what small life I may have left. Can you ever forgive me?"

Francis smiles reassuringly, and I decide to plough on. The speech I had practised in my room is completely gone from my mind now. "I do not want to leave you. Heaven knows it has been one of the hardest decisions I have ever made. The day you left, you took all joy with you and left me behind in a cold and empty France. Perhaps Scotland will hold a small bit of peace for me. I need to at least try." I pause for a moment. "You understand, don't you?"

I wait, but Francis does not move to answer me. I remember in this moment that he is an image in my mind and that he cannot speak and move like the living. He is a mirage. His purpose: to stop me from losing my mind completely. In that moment he is gone, and the image of him refuses to return to me. I am left alone again to drown in my own tears, to talk to myself in the darkness that surrounds me. I stand now and kiss the stone that contains my husband's heart.

"I love you, Francis. I will always love you. I swear to you that I will never love another person. You have my heart for eternity, and if I could physically leave it here with you, I would. But hear my promise: my heart remains in the ground with you, my love. It remains in France, and it will never be awoken from the desperate sleep it clings to beside you."

I begin to leave the cathedral. My eyes blur as the tears sting them. I take one look back when I reach the door and say my final words to Francis. "Goodbye, my love. I will see you again. When this is all over and I am finally at peace, we will meet again." My voice breaks on the last word and I slink through the cathedral doors, forcing myself out before I convince myself to stay.

The cold night air is a blissful relief as I finally catch my breath. I release a long sigh as I close the doors behind me and make my way to my carriage. Barring the day Francis died, this is the single hardest thing I have ever had to do. I feel as if I am leaving the best part of me in France. I feel as if I am betraying him.

I replay my whole monologue in my head during the carriage ride home. I convince myself that it does not matter what I said because Francis cannot hear me anyway. He is dead and gone, and I am silly to dwell on words spoken to shadows. Once I arrive back at my rooms I climb into bed and force my eyes to close. Our departure from France is an early one, and I want to be as prepared as I can for my return to Scotland.

Only I do not sleep as I had planned. My sleep tonight has been disturbed by dreams. For the first time in as long as I can remember, I dream in vivid colour and not darkness. For once, I am do not wake in terror from some dreaded nightmare where I am forced to watch Francis die. Instead, I dream up a beautiful place filled with stunning white light. I see clear blue skies all around, and beneath me is a soft floor completely made of clouds. I do not touch the ground. It is as if I am floating. I feel weightless as all of the things that plague my waking life seem to drift off into the distance. I am free. Free as a bird, high in the sky and not a worry in sight.

But that is not all. In a moment, I feel arms wrap themselves around me. I do not know who they belong to, but I know that I feel safe. I feel complete again as the arms pull all of my broken pieces tightly back together. I lean back to look at the person who is holding me, and I see the face that I have yearned for so long to see. It is my husband. Of course it is. No one else could hold me in the way he does. He sits on the ground and pulls me to sit next to him.

In one moment, my soul lifts out of my body, and I am freed from all of the pain I have carried so long. My heart sings as I look into the face of my everything. So many things come to mind, yet I am speechless. What do I say to the love of your life when he is sitting beside me after such a long separation? I begin to speak, but Francis places a gentle finger on my lips.

"My love. It is my turn to talk to you. I have sat and listened to you each time you call out my name, and it has been agony to not be able to reply." Francis' voice is like sweet music to my ears. "I love you so much. So much that it has been agony to watch you these months and not be able to touch or speak to you. We do not have a lot of time, but I needed you to know that."

"Francis, you have no idea how much I love you." I stroke his cheek. I forgot how good such a simple gesture could feel. "You have heard me? I was so afraid that I was talking to myself."

"I hear every word you say, Mary," Francis chuckles. "There is no greater comfort to me than hearing your voice. When you say my name, you pull me back into your world. My only wish is that I could stay with you forever." He pulls me into his arms, and I once again am comforted by the feeling of laying my head on his chest. "Now listen to me. Like I said, dreams do not last long. I only have moments."

"Francis, a moment is not enough. Please don't leave me again," I plead.

"A moment can last forever if we really want it to, Mary." Francis brushes my forehead with his lips. "My Mary," he says, "how I have missed you." The tears fill his eyes now, and I realise that our separation is as painful to him as it is to me.

I kiss him and hold him just like I did when he was alive. My instinct is to comfort him in his sadness. For the first time since the day he left me, he places his lips on mine, and once again my whole being comes to life. He awakens a part of me that I had left to decay, and at this moment, I feel just like the Mary I was last year.

"Mary, I really have to tell you something." Francis pulls away and is serious once again. "When you spoke to me in the cathedral tonight, you were worried that it would be the last time. I could not let you leave France believing that you were leaving me behind. Mary, do you not know by now? Wherever you go, I go. I may not be with you every moment of the day, but when you talk to me, you can be sure that I am listening." Francis is beaming as he speaks to me. The smile on his face is contagious, and for the first time in months, mine is genuine. "My mother was right. Go to Scotland. Live. Do whatever you have to in order to survive. Make bonnie heirs for your throne, and then one day, when you have lived life the best you can, return to me and we shall be together eternally."

"How can you be so sure?"

"Because no matter what, I believe in you and me. Our love can make anything a reality."

"But it can't keep you here," I say as reality begins to hit.

"It can, in a way. I will always be here. And for now, my love, that will have to do."

The dream begins to fade, and I begin to feel weighted down again. I feel my bed beneath me, and consciousness of my room around me begins to seep in. Francis is fading away, and I feel the panic rise as I grasp the edges of the dream,

"Do not fight this, Mary. One day, this shall be our reality," Francis says as his voice disappears into almost nothing.

I wake and catch my breath. Francis lingers before my eyes a moment longer and then is gone. My pillow is soaked as the tears escape from my eyes, but for the first time in a long time, I feel a peacefulness. I know in my heart that what Francis said was true and that God was kind enough to allow him to come to me in my time of need. I feel a small bit of faith has been restored tonight. Francis has given me a renewed strength that I shall take with me tomorrow. Just as he has guided me through life, he will guide me now. He has given me something to fight for, a reason to muddle through and make it to the end of my journey in this world. For the reward at the end will make all of the misery I have felt nothing but a memory.

Chapter 16

I managed to fall into a contented sleep after my dream about Francis and have awoken this morning with a new confidence in my decision. All that is left now is to board the ship that waits for me in Calais.

James has sent a Scottish fleet to escort me across the water to Scotland, with the Earl of Bothwell, James Hepburn, at the head. I have had the privilege of meeting Bothwell once or twice before and have found that he is a kind man intent on protecting Scotland's interests. It will be nice to travel with a familiar face.

Bothwell is an interesting and intelligent man who I find very easy to talk to. He is a lot shorter than me, but what he lacks in stature he makes up for in muscle. His eyes are beady and rather close together, his nose slightly long, his jaw extremely chiselled. Not what you might say is traditionally attractive, but he certainly holds his own charm. He is a very smooth talker with a great amount of finesse to him. I find that I am quite taken with him right away. It will be nice to have a new friend in Scotland.

***

I now stand on the deck of the ship and watch as France begins to fade into the distance. I have been unable to fight the tears as the ship begins to move and the weight of my decision starts to set in. I do not want to take my eyes off of her as the morning fog begins to make her harder and harder to see. Almost my whole life has taken place in France; at least all of the important parts have. After thirteen years, nearly my entire life, I finally have to say goodbye.

This is not the way I ever expected it to happen. I had always thought my departure would be brief, but this feels permanent. I know as I drift away that I will never again look on her beauty. I will never feel the comfort of home again. I have lost so much in such a short amount of time, and now I leave my whole life behind in France to start again.

I grieve deeply this morning, not just for Francis, but for the world we had built around us. For all of the things I will never see again. All the people I have lost. France is not just a country to me; it is the place that gave me everything I had ever wanted. It is the place that took it all away.

I stand on the deck until the very last part of France disappears. My heart breaks as she finally fades from view. I say goodbye to the life I have known and watch as I drift further and further away.

"Farewell, ma chère France," I whisper into the silent morning air.

I wipe the tears from my eyes and make my way below deck. I make a silent vow to myself. I can either go into this afraid of the outcome, or I can find the strength within myself to make the best of this situation. I am a queen, and not just any queen. I am a queen with both Tudor and Stuart blood. I have been raised by the Valois. I am a Guise. If anyone was made for this role, it was me. And if life thinks it has beaten me down, it is about to find out what it's like when Mary Stuart decides to stand up and fight back. I do this for my family, for my people, for Scotland, but most importantly, for Francis. This world has blackened and bruised me, but I refuse to let it win. My heart will beat solely for my people. Mary Stuart the woman is dead. But Mary Stuart the Queen has just begun.

19th August 1951

This morning we landed in Leith, and I must say that our initial welcome was not exactly what we were hoping for. I had expected to find my brother and some of the nobles waiting on the shore, but the closer we got, the clearer it was that no one was there. Unsure of what to do next, Bothwell led my ladies and me to a local merchant's house, where we waited for my court's arrival. The merchant was rather surprised when the queen turned up on his door. He certainly was not prepared for the visit, but he and his wife were very welcoming. They offered us food and wine after our long journey—poor Seaton was still feeling the effects of her sea sickness and could not even stand to look at it—and gave me a room so that my ladies and I could change our clothes.

Thankfully, we did not have too long to wait, and after an hour or so, James finally made an appearance. He apologised profusely, of course; he had expected my arrival to be much later.

"Your Majesty." He bowed low. "I speak for Scotland when I say how happy we are to have you here."

I was instantly taken aback by just how much James looked like the portraits of my father. The same sharp blue eyes and long, straight nose. He too had the height and leanness of the Stuarts. It was as if I were seeing my father in person for the first time. James certainly has more Stuart about him than anything else.

"None of that," I began. "You may call me sister. We are family, after all."

James was honoured. He took hold of my hand and kissed it. "Pleasure, sister," he said. "Now, if you are ready, of course, I will take you to Holyrood, your new home, and introduce you to your new council."

"Lead the way, brother.

There was something about James that struck me. Something I could not quite put my finger on. He seemed loyal enough. However, like most things, time will tell.

***

We made our way through the streets of Edinburgh, and I am pleasantly surprised by the amount of people who line the streets to welcome me home. Much like in France, men, women, and children have come to wave to me on my way to Holyrood. It fills me with confidence to see so many happy faces in the crowd. For most of them, this is the first-ever glimpse they have had of their queen, and this is my first look at my subjects. I feel a warmth in my heart as we make the journey. They love me already for the sake of being their monarch. I know that in time, I will love them too.

The trip to Holyrood is not a long one, and as the palace finally comes into view, I am surprised by the way it looks. It is very different to the palaces that I am used to in France. Something about it instantly seems very forbidding, very unfamiliar. It seems dark and dull, but that could be because the daylight is already beginning to slip away here in Scotland. It is huge, as huge as Fontainebleau. The grounds that surround it are green and luscious, with trees lining the whole estate. I take a breath as I look at it. My new home. I hope that I can find at least a small amount of happiness here.

Once we step inside, I am met by a grand staircase and a spectacular entrance hall lined with golden tapestries. Still, it is very dark in comparison to the well-lit French palaces. I look forward to exploring this place.

Waiting for us inside are my council. Each of the council members bow and introduce themselves. They all seem very happy to welcome me back to Scotland, and of course, they each offer to help me in whatever way they can. They will begin fighting for favouritism shortly, I imagine.

A couple men stand out from the crowd instantly, the first being James Balfour, a small, overweight man with a suspicious look in his eye. He introduces himself to me as a lawyer; on that credit alone, he is one to be watched. I do not like the way he fawns over me so much more than the others. He takes my hand to kiss it, but something about it is slimy and overdone.

The other, Patrick Ruthven, makes little effort to welcome me compared to the rest of them. Instead, he stands back and eyes me strangely, as if he were looking for some flaw. When I catch his eye, he nods and smiles graciously, but there is something about him that looks untrustworthy. He and James seem to have a lot to talk about, as they instantly drift towards each other. Definitely someone to keep my eye on.

After the initial meeting, we then feast in celebration of my return. This is where I am able to get to know some of the other members of court. I meet some of the people who had served my mother. Margaret Beaton was a long-time friend and companion to my mother. She had seen her through everything, had comforted my mother when my father died, and she helped my mother when she had to send me away. She tells me how my mother was very proud of the woman I had become, and although I may not have known it, she was always keeping an eye on me. It brings me comfort to know that she was not alone after losing her husband and her child.

I also meet another woman, named Jane Kennedy, who I grow to like instantly. She is around the same age as me and unbelievably beautiful. I can see the two of us becoming great friends. She has a youthfulness about her that I like, a playfulness, almost. The rest of the court finds it strange when my ladies and I stand to join in the dancing, but Jane joins with us. "It is about time we breathe some life into this court," she chuckles.

I guess it will be an adjustment to realise that the way the Scottish court works is different from the French. Ruthven looks on in disapproval as my ladies and I dance and laugh. Jane tells me that the Scottish lords expect the women to eat silently while they enjoy the celebration. Obviously, they have never met a French queen before.

***

The first week in Scotland is an adjustment, to say the least. Not only is my surrounding so very different to what I am used to, but the people too are strange to me. They all seem to be much colder here. Francis and I had a friendly relationship with all of our advisors in France, yet here, I struggle to find a connection with anyone. James just about humours me, but the rest of them have no interest in anything other than business. I have tried very hard to make conversation with them, especially Ruthven, who I can tell is wary of me. However, all I receive in return is the odd grunt or nod. No one would be so disrespectful to me in France. Likewise, the common people seem uninterested in my return. I had thought that my first week would be busy with audiences, but very few have made themselves known to me. I understand that I am a stranger to most of them, but I had always thought that being their queen would be enough to earn their respect. It is clear that I am going to have to work hard to earn their trust.

Yesterday, I decided to take advantage of the vast grounds that surround Holyrood and lead the court in a hunt. I had hoped that some of the court would feel more at ease away from the palace. James had told me that hunting in Scotland was a much-loved pastime. However, when I made the suggestion, most turned their noses up at the idea. Apparently, hunting is a man's sport.

Thankfully, both my brother and Bothwell were eager to join me, and the rest of the court begrudgingly followed suit.

As we made our way into the woods, it felt

good to breathe in the icy cold air. The wind was blustering, but for the first time in days the rain had ceased, and the fog had cleared. I have been eager to hunt since the first time I had seen the grounds at Holyrood. It has always been something I have enjoyed doing. James has promised that there will be plenty of deer in the forest this time of year.

It seems, however, that I had offended the court from the very start. In France, I always hunted in men's breeches; they were much more flexible, and I found that I could easily move on my horse without being caught up in the skirts of my dress. No one in France had ever mentioned it or complained. It was Francis who first suggested it to me. But of course, this court was scandalised, and so the whispers began. From the outset, I could hear the sniggers from the shocked ladies and the disapproving sighs from the men.

"Men's breeches, sister?" James asked as he rode beside me.

"Is there a problem, James?" I replied with a sigh.

"You certainly like to cause a stir. Between this and the dancing, you are going to make Ruthven ill." James laughed. The smirk on his face told me that he was only teasing.

James was right. There were plenty of deer to hunt, and even a few rabbits. The court was shocked by my skill, as I easily tracked and killed my chosen prey. They will come to learn that I am no weak and helpless woman. I have been hunting since I was a small child.

Francis never had the heart to kill anything, so I would always take over.

It was nice to have Bothwell by my side. He was kind to me while the rest of the court openly laughed behind my back, Ruthven being the worst of them. While the rest of the court were busy hunting, I chose my moment to talk to him.

"Lord Ruthven," I said as I slowed my horse to canter next to him. "I am pleased that you have joined us today." I smiled sweetly.

"Majesty." He nodded curtly. "I could not say no." He said it without a hint of emotion on his face.

"Do you enjoy hunting, my lord?" I asked.

"Sometimes," he said with a small smile. He clearly had no interest in a conversation with me, but I was determined to figure him out.

"It would be nice for us to get to know each other," I suggested. "Perhaps we can become friends?"

Ruthven was thoughtful for a moment. "I am not sure that we will have much in common, Majesty."

I decided to come right out and ask him exactly what his issue was with me. As far as I could tell, I had done nothing to warrant the hostility he held towards me.

"Honestly?" he asked. I nodded my reply. "I do not trust you. You are a foreign queen with foreign ways," he began. He was calm, too calm for someone who so openly disrespected their monarch. "Your mother knew well enough that to rule in Scotland, you must act like a Scot."

"I am a Scot," I said, shocked by his open distaste for me. "Just because I have been away from Scotland does not mean I am not Scottish at heart."

"It means exactly that, Majesty," he replied. "You make no attempt to fit in. You flaunt your French ways openly."

"Perhaps, my lord, it is you who needs to adapt to me," I said as anger began to fill me. "I am the queen, after all, and you my subject."

It was clear that Ruthven did not like my answer; his face changed quickly from disinterest to dislike. "Madame, you may be queen, but that does not give you the right to change Scotland to your liking."

The way he said 'Madame' in the French way was clearly supposed to be a jab.

"Actually, that is exactly what it means," I snapped back. "While I am ruler of this land, you will follow my leadership. If you do not like that, then you are welcome to leave. I will happily take your lands and titles and bestow them on someone more deserving."

Ruthven was shocked. He certainly had not expected that answer. Perhaps my mother let him get away with talking to her like that, but I will never be a ruler who bows down to the whims of men.

"You cannot do that. They have been in my family for generations," he spat.

"I think you will find that I can do as I please, especially when it comes to the ruling of *my* country," I answered calmly. "Now, I wish to continue my hunt in peace. You may excuse yourself and return to the palace. We will talk again. Perhaps next time you will treat me with the respect that my station demands. Consider this a warning."

Without another word, Ruthven turned his horse around and rode back towards Holyrood. I was seething; how dare one of my own subjects treat me with such disrespect. He would not do it again, that was for sure. It is clear that I have a long way to go before my people accept me, but they will need to learn that things are going to change now that I am ruler.

Later in the evening, James came to my room. He was quite furious after speaking to Ruthven, who was livid after our earlier conversation.

"You cannot speak to your advisors like that," he barked. "Ruthven was beside himself."

"And what of the way he spoke to me?" I asked, angry at James' attack. "Is it common for monarchs to be disrespected in this land?"

"Of course not, but Mary, you need to tread carefully. You are a stranger here. You must respect our ways," he said. "Ruthven is an important member of court. You need to apologise."

I could not help but laugh at James' ridiculous suggestion. Why would I apologise to a man who so openly dislikes me?

"I will not apologise for a thing. The fact you suggest it is ridiculous," I said filled with anger. "I am queen here; Ruthven is a lord at my court. He will follow my rule."

"That's not the way it works, Mary, and you know that," he replied. "Rulers are only as strong as the people they surround themselves with. Your mother knew that."

"My mother is no longer here." I raised my voice. "It is time for change."

"You are not a child anymore, Mary," James bellowed. "You do not have Francis or France to shield you. It is time you grow up."

James left the room in a bluster before anything else could be said. I sat shocked for a while, completely taken aback by how my subjects treated me in this place. My own brother was even incapable of following my rule. He was right in one respect: I do not have Francis any longer. What would he make of all this? He would be appalled by the treatment I have received. I wish that he could tell me how I should handle this. I do not know what my next move should be, but I do know that I will have to move carefully.

Chapter 17

I feel cold, cold and alone as I lie here in a bed that is not my own, as I lay in a room that is not familiar to me. I feel a dread. A dread for what is to come. A dread for the unknown. I do not know what awaits me in this country that is so strange to me, a place which so far has made a gloomy impression on me. The days are dull and wet. The nights are dark and noisy as the wind howls around this old palace. Everything is unfamiliar to me. As I lie awake, sleepless for what seems like the third week, I ache for my home. I am tormented by a sickness for the place I love so well. This place holds no comfort for me. I look for Francis everywhere, and yet I realise that I have never been further away from him. He has no imprint in this palace. Holyrood holds no memories for us. I left all of those things behind in France. It was crippling to see Francis wherever I went, but here, I find the lack of his presence even more painful. I long to reach out and touch the space beside me where he once rested his head. I miss the solace I found sitting in our spot, nestled under the tree right outside of my window. I miss the familiar faces. I feel as if I have no friends here. Apart from my ladies, the inhabitants of this palace are strangers to me. Even my own brother is no better than a stranger. I feel alone. I feel as if I have made a grave mistake leaving France and the comfort and security I had there.

It smells different here, as strange a thing as that may be to pick up on. It smells damp. I am so used to the smell of fresh flowers that always seemed to float through Fontainebleau. I lie in my bed and it feels as if the dark walls close in on me. There is no light here. All the corners are dark and full of shadows.

Scotland so far has presented itself as a dreary and unwelcoming place. I realise that I am the stranger. Although I feel that I should have been welcomed with open arms, I feel as if I am on the outside looking in, as if I float around, detached from life here. In the country that I rule, I feel completely on the outside. I am the foreigner here. I may be queen, but I am not yet loved by my people.

In France, I was held in the highest esteem. I was a beloved dauphiness and then an adored queen. Here, I am starting from the bottom. I need to give my people a reason to like me. It is not like other kingdoms, where a title alone grants you allegiance from your subjects. I have been away for thirteen years; some may not even remember me as a child. I had thought that the love they held for my parents would automatically transfer to me, but I am having to prove myself. It is odd to think that I am the one having to try to fit in.

So far, I feel hopeless. I want my people to love me, and yet I do not know how to make them happy. How do I convince a whole country of people that I pose no threat to them and their way of living? I only wish to take my rightful place as their queen without causing any harm.

I have many things weighing on my mind tonight. The thoughts swim through my head and make it impossible to rest. It has been a long month, and the transition has not been easy. As much as the people here need to become used to me, I also need to wrap my mind around the way things work here.

I had thought to make the transition from a Protestant leader to a Catholic as smooth as possible. It was my intention to allow both faiths to coexist in harmony. And yet I find that some people are too small minded to live peacefully. James and I have come to the understanding that should I want to practice my Catholicism in private with my own small group of attendants, then I will not be stopped, so long as I allow my Protestant subjects to continue in the faith they have chosen.

Of course, I agree wholeheartedly. I have never wanted to exert my power over the matter. I would much rather have a peaceful Protestant country than a country at war, divided between the two faiths that worship the same God. My mother fought for the Catholic cause long enough, but with my rule, I wish to usher in a new era of peace between the two. However, some of my "loyal" subjects seem to have a different idea.

When my ladies and I took mass on Sunday we were hounded by angry subjects. We kept to our part of the agreement, making use of my private chapel and using my own priest. Still, it was not good enough. Men and women stood outside of the palace shouting profanities aimed at us. My servant, Charles, who was carrying candles to the service, was stopped and attacked. The candles were knocked from his arms, and he was pushed to the ground. By the time he reached me, he was shaking uncontrollably. The mob outside shouted that they would execute my priest, who was almost too scared to continue with the service. I had promised him protection in this country, and so far, I was failing. James stood his ground outside of the chapel doors, keeping to his word and stopping the mob from coming inside. I dread to think of the outcome had they been able to get inside.

The whole thing was very upsetting and traumatising. It made us feel as if we could no longer practice the religion we were raised in, no matter how accommodating I was to the Protestants. It was a lesson to me. I could not just quietly hope for my people to fall in line with the new way. I would have to declare my stance on the matter publicly. I had hoped that the people of Scotland were capable of being open minded on their own, but sadly, I was mistaken. The next day, I issued a statement telling my subjects that should they wish to interrupt or hound someone for their religious practice, whether they were Protestant or Catholic, they did so on pain of death. I do not like issuing such things, but I will not have anyone suffer for their beliefs.

However, I now face another obstacle: a man named John Knox, who has come to my attention due to a sermon he recently preached against my ruling. It seems that Mr Knox is as bigoted as they come and refuses to accept a woman's rule. Not only that, but he has a great following here in Scotland and is the biggest advocate for Protestantism. James warns me against making him an enemy. Apparently, he was a thorn in my mother's side. But after all, he is only a minister; how much trouble can he cause me? I have decided to take the matter into my own hands and have invited him here to Holyrood this Saturday. I would like to size this John Knox up for myself.

***

Unfortunately, my being Catholic does not simply pose a threat to my subjects. It also poses a threat to my cousin Elizabeth. Elizabeth is a Protestant queen, and she knows only too well that there are many in her country who would prefer a Catholic queen on the throne of England. That and my strong claim to the English throne give Elizabeth reason enough to be wary of me.

However, my intention is not to steal the throne from under her. I would never look to have another queen unseated. As I have told her many times over the past few years, I only wish to be named as her heir. It is only right. Her father, Henry VIII, was my great-uncle, and he made it clear that no Scot was to inherit his throne. I feel that now is the time this was set right. It was never Henry's place to dismiss the Scottish line, and as the great-granddaughter of Henry VII and Elizabeth of York, I have every right to be next in line.

I have always tried my best to keep a friendly manner with my English cousin, and although she refused to give me safe passage through English waters should I have needed it, I do not wish to make such a powerful enemy. I believe in any case she only did so because she was still sore at my adding the

English coat of armour to my own. She would still prefer it if I give up the right altogether, but as much as I need her as a friend, I will never give up my birth right.

Since my return, I have made every effort to show Elizabeth that I pose no threat to her, and so far, our exchanged letters have been nothing but friendly. We have even gone as far as to send each other small gifts. I find it rather enjoyable to converse with a woman in a position similar to mine. However, she knows that I wish to be named her heir, and yet she makes no mention of the matter. At this moment, she is refusing to address the subject at all. Although outwardly I show no annoyance at this, I do worry that she is going to play hard to get.

For now, I choose to be cordial, but I know she is someone I must watch carefully if I am to succeed. If Elizabeth proves to be more like her father than her mother, then she shall be a fearsome enemy to have. I do not fear her, and yet I am well aware of the things she is capable of. She has so far proven herself to be quick to temper. The last thing I want to do is anger her. Yet I know my own worth. Elizabeth naturally thinks that she is better than everyone, but in me I believe she has met her match. I have the bravery of a Scot and the intellect of a Tudor. I will match her at every turn, just like I will match John Knox tomorrow. As unsure as I am about my new setting, the one thing I am sure of is myself and the fire I hold within me.

***

I realise now that tonight is going to be completely sleepless. As I close my eyes, I am too weighed down by my own thoughts to let tiredness take over. I rise from my bed, careful not to wake my ladies, who sleep nearby. I walk over to my window, something I would do many times in France, where I would look out at the beautiful blossom tree that stood beside my window. Here I am greeted by total darkness. It is black outside, and I can scarcely make out the land that surrounds the palace. The stars are my one comfort, as I know that no matter the distance between France and me, these are the same stars that glisten down on my sleeping husband. They are the one thing in Scotland that make me feel close to him, the one thing in this land that we share.

I sit in the chair next to the window and gaze out at the night sky, all the while thinking back to a time when Francis and I would do this together, when we would grab a blanket and sneak around our sleeping servants and out into the grounds. We would lie next to each other and look up to the stars. That was when life would feel endless, when we would feel like anything was possible and this world had a much bigger picture for us to discover. I can still feel his arms around me. Still smell the petals that circled us on the floor. I can still feel the gentle breeze on my cheeks as we wrapped ourselves in each other's arms to stay warm. I wish I could be that content again, when the world made sense and I had everything I needed within touching distance. Oh, how I miss him. I miss him more each day. Time has not been a healer for me; as the days slip away, they only serve to make his absence greater. He lives only in my memory now, in the part of me that still longs for him. He is nothing but an echo, lost in the wind as time ticks away. Just like it did when we were together, the sun comes along and breaks the spell, and I am left feeling empty all over again.

"How do I live without you?" I ask the silent morning. "How do I find the strength?"

Of course, there is no answer.

***

I arose this morning with a reignited fire in my heart. I am unsure of where it came from, but one thing I do know is that I am ready to take on the world. Ready to take on John Knox. I sit in my audience chamber now and await his arrival. Last night, I was concerned that he would best me. Today, I am sure he will not.

When he finally arrives, an hour late, he is cordial as he bows low to me. I had expected him to be disrespectful from the outset, but he is surprisingly polite.

"Pleasure to meet you, Majesty," he says with a thick Scottish accent. Although his demeanour is supposed to charm, I will not be disarmed so easily.

I eye him suspiciously as I gesture for him to take the seat across from me. My expression does not change as I take the full measure of him. He is every bit as gaunt and towering as I have been told. He is a thin man, older by far than I am. His beard is dark grey, and it tumbles down to his waist. His eyes are dark and piercing, as they do not leave mine for even a moment. He is confident. It radiates off of him. My station holds no fear of him. He sees me as a young woman and not as a queen. I am ready to show him just how wrong he is. I give him a moment to sit down before I begin my line of questioning.

"Pleasure to meet you also, Mr Knox." I offer him no hand. "I trust your journey was pleasant?"

"Aye, Majesty. It was pleasant enough," he begins. "I must apologise for my late arrival."

"That's quite all right. These things happen," I respond, a little too sweetly. "You must tell me a little about yourself, sir. It will be nice for us to get better acquainted."

"All due respect, Your Highness, there was a reason you asked me here. Do you not think it better to get to the point?" he asks, almost cutting me off.

I am a little surprised at first. He certainly is as direct as I have been told. Well, if that is the way he wishes to play it, then that is how it will be.

"Fine," I reply with a tight-lipped smile. "Tell me, what issue do you take with my rule, exactly?" I dive straight in.

"I take no issue with you, madam. I only take issue with the Catholic faith," he replies quickly. It is almost as if he has rehearsed his answers.

"My faith has nothing to do with my sex, and yet is it not true that you have written a book denouncing female rulers?" I ask.

I believe he is surprised by my knowledge. Did he really think I would have him here without doing my research first? Yes. I had been asking questions about Knox since before I left France. I knew that he would be a thorn in my side, and I wished to know the enemy I would face.

"All due respect, Majesty, but you should not concern yourself with something that has never affected you." He smiles like the weasel he is. It is a calculated smile, disingenuous and smug.

"Perhaps, then, I should concern myself with the things that have affected me. Like your insistent attack on my mother?" I return the false smile. "Or perhaps the sermon you so easily preached against your queen?"

Knox sits back for a moment. He is thoughtful as he crosses his hands on his lap. He is clearly a very careful man who considers his every word.

"My attack, as you say, was never directly aimed at your mother. My goal has always been to rid this country of the Catholic faith that has for so long been a plague on our nation," he begins. "Scotland has for too long been stuck in the past. If Mary De Guise had her way, we would have stayed there. I see a Scotland that no longer suffers the Pope's judgement. Catholicism is an outdated way of thinking. It is a danger to our soul."

"I did not invite you here to preach to me on my religion, Knox," I interrupt. "You will do well to remember that I am a Catholic and your queen."

"An unfortunate misjudgement on your part," Knox sneers. He is over-confident and brave to talk to me in such a way. He is too clever for his own good. Often, people who are too intelligent end up tripping over their own words.

"You overstep yourself, sir," I warn.

"Pardon my rudeness, Majesty. I am a passionate man." He holds his hand over his heart. His lips smile, but his eyes are full of hate. He hated me before he had ever met me, and nothing I do today will change that. I am already weaker to him by sex alone. If I were a king, he would offer me respect, but as a queen, I am not so deserving.

"Passion is a wonderful asset to have. Only men who allow their passion to run wild sometimes find themselves in sticky situations." I gently remind him of the power I have over him.

Knox remains calm, with tight lips pressed in a straight line. I imagine he is holding back that famous temper of his. He is not fool enough to play into my hands. He knows that I could have him arrested on the spot.

I simply smile and press on. "Now, I understand that you are protective of the Protestant faith. I also understand that this country is just past a huge transition and your faith stands on unsteady grounds. I also know that you are wary of me as a Catholic woman and a near stranger to these lands. However, I would like to make it clear to you that I pose no threat to you or any other Protestant. I may have been brought up in France, but I am Scotland, Knox. Do not forget that. Scotland and I are one and the same. My heart beats for my people. Protestant or not, I love each and every one the same."

"You must know that trust is earned over time. It is not given freely. The simple fact is that you are a Catholic queen raised in a

Catholic country by a Catholic family. Your very existence poses a threat to my faith," Knox replies coolly.

"I have told you that I am no threat, and as your queen, I am owed your trust. If not your trust, then your obedience, sir."

"You will have my obedience, madam, when it is deserved," he says with such vehemence that I am tempted to lose my barely concealed temper. But I know that is how he wins this. He does not lose his temper; he pokes and prods until his opponent does. Instead, I take a breath and compose myself.

The smile on my face is sickeningly sweet as I say, "I am sure we can come to an understanding that suits the both of us and the common people."

"What do you suggest, Majesty?" He returns the smile.

"You have my word that neither I nor any of my attendants shall flaunt our faith to the country. We only wish to be allowed our own ceremonies in private. We shall do so unmolested, and so will anyone who choses Protestantism. I shall be a just ruler, Knox. No one will be punished under my watch for the things that they believe. Now, I need your word that you shall accept me as ruler without question."

Knox is thoughtful for a moment. He opens his mouth a few times to speak, but the words do not seem to form. Finally, he says, "I shall accept your rule, so long as you do nothing to hinder this country. The moment you give me reason to doubt you, I will be a fierce enemy."

I raise an eyebrow to this but let my face settle into a smile as I say with confidence, "As long as you know that should you do anything to hinder my rule, then I too shall be a fierce enemy, Mr Knox."

Knox gives a curt nod. I hold his gaze a moment longer. It is clear that, for now, we understand each other. I know in my heart that this will not be the last time I have to deal with him, but at this time, we will call this a tie.

"Well then, Mr Knox." I rise from my seat. "I appreciate your time."

"Pleasure, Majesty," he says through gritted teeth.

A Love Unkind

Chapter 18

Over the course of the last few weeks, I have exchanged many letters with Elizabeth. I have asked her many to times to reasonably name me as heir to her throne and have been ignored each time. However, now it seems she has come up with a solution. In Elizabeth's most recent letter, she has promised to name me as her successor, on one condition: I marry an English subject of her choosing.

Of course, at first I was appalled by the idea. I was shocked that she would suggest such a thing. For me to agree would be to bow down to Elizabeth and accept her power over me. I know that she only offers this because she thinks she will be able to control me through my husband. It is another way to make her feel safe on her throne. No matter how many times I tell her that I am no threat, she will never believe me. I wish there were some way to prove to her that I am harmless. However, Elizabeth will never feel totally comfortable on her throne. Due to the tragic details of her mother's life and death, she fears even those closest to her. I must say that I do feel for her. She has never been able to trust anyone, and that is a very sad life to live indeed.

My advisors and James have told me that I need to at least humour her proposal. I may not get another opportunity to have my birth right restored. Reluctantly, I agree to write a letter expressing my cooperation. I will at least meet with whatever suitor she chooses.

Deep inside, my heart breaks as I send my reply. The thought of remarrying fills me with dread. I know it has to happen someday. I just wanted to give myself time to heal a little before considering my options. However, the time has come for me to look to the future. I just hope Francis can forgive me.

Marriage is such an important part of a monarch's life, and if I am to have a successful reign then it is something I will have to consider. I know that I will never again marry for love, but for security. This is another of Elizabeth's downfalls, her refusal to pick a suitor. She humours the men that line up before her, hoping to take her hand and her crown, but she will never choose one. Who can blame her? She has seen a dark and dreary image of marriage. I will remarry, however begrudgingly, and that is another reason why my rule will be a stronger one than hers.

***

It has been two weeks since Elizabeth's original letter, and finally, I have received a reply. A laughable one at that. She has suggested that I should marry Robert Dudley, the Earl of Leicester. She must think me a mockery. Every single person around the world knows who Robert Dudley is to her. She is mad for him. He is her closest ally in England, and she knows that he will feed her whatever information she asks for.

I will not stand for it. She has insulted me by suggesting such a match. Does she think me a fool? What would it suggest if I were to marry her toy? It would show the world that I am under her control. How can she so easily offer me the hand of her lover? All it does is prove that Elizabeth cares for no one. She sees everyone as a puppet she may use for her own gain. She will not use me.

I was seething when I first read her suggestion. Elizabeth has always thought that she was better than everyone and that we should all bow down to her. Not wanting to make an enemy, I have bitten my tongue, but now I see no reason to play nice. I am owed my place in the English succession, and I am owed her respect. After all, it is clear to me and to many in her own country that I have the better claim. She is a bastard, and her legitimacy has always been questioned by her people. I have pure blood. I could take her throne if I wanted to. Some of her subjects would prefer a Catholic queen on the throne. James tells me to tread carefully, but I am done with niceties.

I write back to Elizabeth telling her exactly what I think of her suggestion. I do not want her as an enemy, but perhaps she does not want me as an enemy either.

Initially, Elizabeth had suggested that I meet with our shared cousin, Henry Stuart, Lord Darnley. She quickly revoked that suggestion when she realised it would be a mistake to allow me to marry another Stuart. However, he has written to me to suggest that we meet here in Scotland and I have agreed. I have met him once before when he attended my wedding. He was very young at the time, perhaps just fourteen years old. He was a sweet young boy from what I can remember.

His letter says that it may be prosperous for us to get to know each other. After all, we are both of the same bloodline. We share the same grandmother. It is clear from his words that the thought of marriage is on his mind, and I must admit that the prospect is an interesting one to me also. It may be foolish to think like this so quickly, but what a magnificent pairing we would be. With our combined bloodlines, we would be untouchable contenders for the English throne. Our children would have a claim like no other to both Scotland and England.

Henry is an English subject, and one that was presented to me by Elizabeth. I would be fulfilling her demands, which would mean she would have to keep her promise to make me her successor. James warns against my meeting with Henry. He does not like Darnley or his family. He tells me that they are nothing but power-grabbers who are always looking for their next opportunity. Henry's mother, Margaret Douglas, has always felt she was owed a debt. Her mother was my grandmother, Margaret Tudor. She has always felt that her Tudor blood made her destined for greatness, but she was the child of Margaret's second husband, not the king. Now she does all she can to bring power to her son, who is Tudor through her and Stuart through his father, the Earl of Lennox.

I wave James off. I am more than capable of rooting out power-seekers for myself. I see no harm in meeting with Henry. It could prove to be a prosperous opportunity.

Chapter 19

Since being in Scotland, I have found very little to bring me joy. The people are still complete strangers, and the setting is a gloomy one at best. I have felt lonelier here than I have ever felt before. I have no one to confide in. No one to share the highs and lows with. I feel lost. I have my ladies, of course, and they are always such wonderful companions. However, I crave what I had with Francis, the complete and utter trust we had with each other. I long for a friendship where I can bear my soul completely and be totally myself. I want someone who will join me in my darkest moments, who I can confess my deepest thoughts to.

I had thought that when I lost Francis, I lost my only opportunity to feel a connection like that. However, we are blessed with many people in this life who will enrich it in some way, people who will be what we need when we need it. I am not talking about love. I have not fallen for anyone. I talk about friendship, a true and genuine friendship. I did not know how badly I needed this person until I met them just a few weeks ago: David Rizzio. Or as my ladies and I have come to know him, Davey.

Davey is possibly one of the strangest men I have ever met. He is much different from the other men here at court, who are stiff and boring. He is full of life, full of character. He is so bubbly and energetic; it is hard to not smile when he is around. My ladies absolutely adore him, as do I. He has fit into our entourage perfectly.

He came bouncing over to me one day as my ladies and I returned to my rooms from a council meeting. It seemed that he had been working up the courage to speak to me for some time. He had travelled to Scotland in search of new opportunities for himself, but much like the other places he had travelled, he had come up short. I had not even noticed him tucked away with my musicians, but once he presented himself, I had no idea how I could have missed him. David is very handsome with his bright, round eyes and light golden skin. From the very moment he introduced himself to me, I was hooked. It was like being hit with a breath of fresh air. My ladies and I have felt worn down with the constant formality of this place. David's unwavering happiness is contagious. He has brought a much-needed joy back into my life.

David was in a small gathering of musicians in the hall when we walked past. The others bowed politely and went about their business, but David saw his opportunity and made his way over to me. He dipped low into a flawless bow before me.

"Majesty," he said with a roll of the tongue.

I smiled back politely, then made to move away but the stranger had more to say.

"If I may be so bold . . ." he began, but after a moment, he paused, seemingly losing his nerve.

"Yes?" I encouraged him.

"Majesty, I would like to introduce myself," he said, courage returning. "I am David Rizzio. From Italy, Highness."

David seemed to have a childlike way about him. He was nervous, but the grin he held on his face was infectious.

"Lovely to meet you, David," I said. I was ready to go back to my room, but the way he looked at me kept me in my spot. "What is it I can do for you, David?" I asked.

At this, David beamed. "Well, Majesty, you see, I am wasted here with the musicians. No offence," he said quickly, as a few had turned to look at him. "I believe I could be more help to Your Majesty in a different manner."

"Oh, really? What do you think you could help me with?"

David was thoughtful for a second or two.

"It is hard to explain, but if Your Majesty will allow me to try . . ." he began. "You see, I love to make people happy. I would like to make Your Majesty happy again." He must have seen in my face that I was quite shocked by his words. He held up his hands and waved them before him. “No, no, not in that way, Majesty.” He chuckled nervously. “Your Majesty, although beautiful, is not right for me in many ways.”

I should have been offended, but he said it so innocently that I intuitively knew he did not mean it to be rude. I could not help but want to listen to him; he had such a lovely aura about him.

“I just mean Your Majesty is too magnificent a creature for a lowly man like me,” David explained himself. A small bead of sweat had begun to build up on his head. My ladies could not help but chuckle to themselves as David grew more nervous by the second. I hushed them so that he could continue.

“There is no need to be nervous around me. You said your name was David? Would you like to sit with me for a while?” I gestured to the window. David, who had brightened up again, nodded and followed me over to the window. “Now what is it that you would like to talk to me about?” I asked.

“I came here to Scotland in the hopes of finding my way in life, but I only found another dead end,” David began to explain. “But then Your Majesty made her return, and I was struck by just how magnificent and gracious you are. I do not know the words to explain it. But I knew that I had to know you. That you would be the one to help me find my path in life."

"Well, that's truly kind of you, David. I do hope that I can help," I answered, flattered by his admission.

"I also can see that Your Majesty is not happy here. That you miss your home as I miss my home. I would like to be a friend to you, to make you smile." He said it so warmly that I could not help but believe him.

"Scotland is my home," I said simply.

"Ah, yes, but so is France."

I was taken by surprise. He was right, of course, but how could he know what truly lay in my heart? He really was an intriguing man.

"Does Your Majesty like to dance?" he asked. All of a sudden, he rose from his feet and offered me his hand. I was unsure at first. It would not be proper for me to dance with a stranger in the hallway. "I promise I will not bite, Your Majesty," he laughed.

I could not help myself when I rose and allowed a perfect stranger to take me by the waist and whirl me around the room. I giggled as he spun me around and around. He had little skill, but that made it all the funnier. My ladies, who at first had kept to themselves, joined in the laughter as they watched their queen smile for the first time in too long. I knew in that moment that David Rizzio was indeed a man I wanted to have around.

I straightened myself out as I realised that the musicians had stopped to watch us. My cheeks blushed as embarrassment for behaving in such a way sank in, but David, having noticed my resignation, said, "Oh, pay no mind to them. They are just jealous because no woman would dare touch them. From that evening on, David has spent almost every day with me. I should have scolded him for his behaviour. I should have sent him away, but the simple fact of the matter is that David makes me feel happier than I have in a long time. While we were spinning around, I felt carefree for the first time in too long.

He does not want what most men do. He does not see me as a prize to be won. He sees me as a friend, which is something many monarchs are not blessed with. I do not feel as if I am just a project to him or a way for him to garner power. I know he cares for me personally.

For the first time since arriving in Scotland, my chambers are filled with laughter and not sadness. My ladies smile, and so do I. And when I do feel sad, David is there for that too. In the few short weeks that I have known him, I have confessed feelings that I did not even know I had. He is there for the good and the bad. I have never been so happy because of such a rude introduction.

Chapter 20

Today is the day I am due to meet with Henry Stuart. My ladies, Davey, and I have travelled to Wemyss Castle, where I now sit in my audience chamber, ready to meet my cousin. We decided that somewhere away from the ears at court would be best. It is better for us to keep our meeting quiet until we know the outcome.

The nerves build in my stomach as I sit here and wait. We both know going into this that marriage is the question that hangs over our heads. I had never believed that I would be in this position, and now that I am here, the nerves are unbearable.

I dreamt about Francis last night, the first dream I have had about him since being in Scotland. It was not like the dream I had before where we were in some sort of heaven. This time, we were sitting in my room at Holyrood. I lay in bed, and Francis sat in the chair across from me. He did not say a word this time; perhaps he lacked the strength. He looked sad, worried even. The dream only lasted moments, for I was awoken by my maid bringing breakfast. For some reason, the look on Francis' face has stayed with me all day. He was not angry, but something was not right. Today, I cannot shake the anxiety that the dream brought with it.

***

To say I am pleasantly surprised with Henry is an understatement. I do not know what I had expected, but he seems to be the opposite of what James had described when he said Henry was weak and weedy. From the moment he arrives, he emanates charm and sophistication. He is tall, as tall as me, and strong. He is nothing like the young boy that I remember from all those years ago. The moment our eyes meet, he breaks into a stunning smile. He has an instant familiarity about him as he beams at me. I must say that his height is instantly very appealing to me. I have never met anyone as tall as I am.

As he gracefully kneels at my feet and takes my hand, I am able to get a good look at him; he is very pleasing to the eye. He is tall and graceful. His face is still touched by the blush of youth, as it is free of lines and smooth. His round, plump lips part when he smiles to show pearly white teeth. The smile also makes dimples appear on his cheeks. His hair has that same splash of red that comes from his Tudor ancestors.

Only his attractiveness clearly does not simply lie in his looks; there is an obvious confidence that radiates off of him. He holds my gaze without faltering as he bends to kiss my hand. He smiles, subtly biting his lip. I must admit that I am instantly fixed on him. I am surprised by the instant attraction I feel. I have never looked at a man, other than Francis, and felt such a pull towards him. It was something about the way his eyes fixed on me. It made it seem as if we were totally alone, and he had not even spoken yet.

"Your Majesty," he says with a quirk of his lip. "How lovely you are. Much lovelier than I imagined."

I can feel my cheeks burn under his gaze. Something about the way he spoke makes me feel almost giddy.

"Lord Darnley." I return his warm smile. "It is a pleasure to meet you." I straighten up and regain my composure.

"No, Majesty, the pleasure really is all mine." Henry grins. "I must thank Your Majesty for inviting me to meet with her today," he speaks smoothly.

"It is an honour, my lord. I have heard many things about you, and I must admit that I am intrigued," I reply.

Henry smiles knowingly at this. I imagine that he is well aware of his own reputation.

"I am happy to intrigue you. However, I do hope that whatever you have heard hasn't given me too much of a bad name," Henry chuckles.

I think back to what James told me about how Henry is a womaniser and a drunken fool. I had told him that I would make my own mind up, and so far, he appeared perfectly fine to me. Although I can certainly see how he would get his reputation as a womaniser; I suspect he has women falling at his feet.

"I am not one to judge from hearsay, my lord. I prefer to take the measure of a man for myself," I say after a moment.

"Well, here I am, Majesty. Measure whatever you want," Henry replies, sweeping his arm in front of his body. There was a cheek to him, like a naughty child.

My ladies gasped; his meaning was very clear indeed. I chose to take no offence to it. After all, it was rather funny.

"Ah, but my lord, what if you do not measure up?" I tease back. "We would not want to embarrass you."

"I assure Your Highness I measure up in every way." Darnley winks at me.

I have to do all I can to stop my cheeks from blazing red. It is the way he holds my gaze as he speaks. The way he examines me as if I am scrutiny. I have never felt so unsure before, like I cannot quite work him out. He is rude and outspoken, but there is something I like about it. Something refreshing that I am not used to. I like how open he is.

"I must admit, it is refreshing to finally meet someone who shares the same height as me," I say, knowing that I was changing the subject.

"Ah, yes. I have that issue also. No one is ever quite on the same level as me," Henry replies with a playful grin.

"You seem quite sure of yourself, sir," I laugh.

"Well, it seems someone has to be sure of me." Henry shrugs his shoulders. "But in truth, I am only sure of one thing."

"Oh yes? And what is that?"

"That you are the most beautiful queen I have ever seen." Henry is serious all of a sudden as his eyes hold mine.

"And how many queens have you seen?" I chuckle.

"Only a handful. But you far outshine any. I do not need to see the others to know that your beauty far surpasses any other."

Normally, arrogance like Henry's would turn my stomach. The way he is over-sure of himself is not usually a good quality, but the way he owns it, the way he knows himself is intriguing. It has been a long while since someone has called me beautiful not because they want to win my favour, but because they mean it.

"Thank you, Lord Darnley." I cannot conceal the smile that was on my face.

"If I may be so bold, can we drop the formality? I would rather you called me Henry. Darnley is the name used by men who don't really like me." Henry admits.

"I would be happy to call you Henry. And as my cousin, it is only proper that you should call me Mary," I suggest.

Henry smiles warmly. "I would love to call you Mary. You honour me," he says with a gleam in his eye.

We spend the next few moments lost in a look between the two of us. We seem to mirror each other as both of our smiles grow wider. I feel something in this moment that I have not felt since before I lost Francis. I feel a sudden desire for this man. Different than the initial attraction I had felt, it was more like a wanting, a longing for him to touch me. I find myself thinking about how it would feel to kiss Henry. To have someone love me again. To yearn for me. I have been without desire for so long, and this man is striking something deep within me. And then, the guilt begins to set in.

"You said in your letters that you have a proposition for me?" I ask, breaking the silence.

Henry is thoughtful for a moment before answering. "Honestly? I want to marry you," .

I laugh, but it is clear from his face that Henry is deadly serious. His boldness really knows no bounds.

"We do not even know each other," I scold him. "I cannot marry on a whim."

"Then get to know me. I promise, you'll love me." Henry laughed again.

I think for a moment before answering. There is no harm in getting to know him. I knew that this meeting could lead to the question of marriage; I cannot shy away from my duty now.

"Why don't you stay here at Wemyss?" I ask.

"In your room? Agreed." Henry beams.

"You know, you should probably watch how you address your sovereign," I lightly scold. "Would you speak to Elizabeth like this?"

"No. But she is boring and stiff. You are beautiful and interesting," he says with that quirk to his lip again.

"I will have a room made up for you, Lord Darnley," I say pointedly as he leaves.

***

I am readying myself to go to dinner with Lord Darnley, and I find that the nerves I felt this morning are still with me. Only this time it is not just nerves I feel, but guilt, too. I am shocked at myself and the way that I allowed myself to feel this afternoon. I should not allow myself to feel the attraction that I felt for Henry. It is disrespectful to Francis and disrespectful to myself. I intend to stay calm tonight. If I do decide to marry Henry, it will be for my country and nothing else. I am a spoken-for woman. I cannot let myself feel for another man.

When I arrive at my private dining room, Henry is already waiting for me. He bows when I enter and graciously moves my chair for me.

"Mary," he says with a sweet smile on his face.

"Henry." I smile back.

I allow my nerves to get the better of me, and for the first course we eat in total silence. The atmosphere is thick with unspoken words. I know how important it is for me to make a good match, and yet all I can see is Francis. Part of me thinks that I should end this now before it is too late.

"Mary, I have to ask. Is anything troubling you?" Henry asks after a long silence.

"No, I am just a little tired, I think. Perhaps I should retire." I gesture at my maid to take my food.

"I know that we do not know each other yet, but we are family. You can trust me," he says, taking my hand. I pull away quickly. It is too familiar a gesture, and it only adds to the guilt I already feel. Henry takes a breath. "Is this about your previous husband? Francis?"

It is strange to hear him speak about Francis, especially in the past tense. I do not think of Francis as my previous husband; he is my husband still.

"I must admit, I am struggling with the idea of remarrying," I say despite myself. I had not meant to be so open.

"He meant a lot to you, didn't he?" Henry asks.

"I loved him more than anything in this world," I admit.

Henry is thoughtful for a moment, and I feel instantly like I have said too much. No one wants to hear that your intended is still in love with their first husband.

"Mary, I need you to know something," Henry begins. "I will never expect you to forget about Francis. Yes, I wish to marry you, but I do that knowing that your heart belongs to him. I understand how it feels to lose love."

"How can you marry me knowing how I feel about him?" I ask, confused.

"Because I know that one day, you will love me," he says. "I am sure of it."

"I do not know if that's even possible. I am sorry that I may not be the wife you are looking for."

"I am willing to take that chance," Henry answers. "I have been in love with you since I was nothing more than a lad at your wedding."

I had no idea that Henry felt this way, especially back then, when he was just a child.

"Give me a chance?" he asks.

"I will."

Chapter 21

With Henry, life has become easier. He has provided a welcome distraction from the gloom that has filled my world for longer than I can remember. For so long, I have been lost in the agony that has taken over my whole being. I have seen no light in these dark days. Henry has brought a ray of hope into my world. He makes me smile—not the smile that I use for my court, but a real smile. I had forgotten the simple joy of laughter until now, how it puts my spirits at ease. I have become stagnant over time, never for a moment moving away from my grief, and the weight of it has been a hard one to bear.

Henry has found the joy in me that has been buried under mountains of sadness. He offers me a respite from the pain that I have carried every day. With him, I do not need to think or worry. He lives for pleasure alone. He drinks the best wine and eats the best food. He only surrounds himself with people who add to his life. I have never seen him unhappy. He brings out the playful side of me: the Mary who loved to joke and laugh. The Mary who took life in stride. I have missed that part of me, the way I was when I was a young girl, before life opened my eyes to its true colours. Before I faced tragedy. It makes me want to be the Mary I was before I became Queen of France, the girl without a care in the world. When I wake up in the morning full of dread for the day ahead, I am no longer desperate to reach my bed again. Henry gives me hope. Hope for a better life. Hope for the future.

Henry is so sweet and caring. He dotes on me, always complimenting me, always making me feel beautiful. He listens to me and allows me to talk about Francis, about things that are real. We have spent the past week hunting, feasting, and drinking. Away from court, I have been able to be carefree for the first time in forever. It feels nice to allow the formality to drop. Not only am I enjoying my time with Henry, but I have also begun to see a different side of Scotland. Away from court, I have been allowed time to appreciate the vast countryside, the clear air, and the stunning views. She really is rather stunning if you take the time to appreciate her.

Unfortunately, Henry is not completely without his vices. No man ever is, even Francis had his flaws, not that I noticed them. He loves to drink long into the night and never seems to know when to stop. He is an outrageous flirt who fixes his eye on anything. I know it is harmless, though. It is clear from the way he looks at me that he is smitten.

All of his discrepancies are made up for when he turns his charm on me. My attraction to him seems to grow by the day as I watch the way he holds himself when we are hunting, the way he confidently hunts down his prey, like an eagle diving for a rabbit. Or the way he smiles at me, the quirk of his lip and baring of his teeth. He is a magnificent creature to behold.

We allude to our wedding over and over, and still nothing has been set in stone yet. He has been here a little over three weeks, and over the last few days, he has taken to telling me that he loves me. I have to admit that I too feel a love for him. Not in the way that I loved Francis. I will never love him, nor any other man, like I loved Francis. I love him in the only way I can.

He makes my life lighter. He makes me happy. He makes me forget all of my woes for a short time. It is not the deep and meaningful connection that I had with Francis, but it is enough for me. If I can feel even a shard of the happiness I had before, then my life would become bearable. He has awakened a part of me that I had thought long dead and buried. He has allowed me to see a glimmer of light in these dark days. I am thankful that Henry Stuart has come into my life. He has opened my heart again, even if it is only a little bit. And he has brightened up what have been the darkest yeas in my life.

However, when his lips form the question of marriage, he does not receive my instant approval. Is it the smart thing to do? Yes. Will it be prosperous for my country? Yes. Does it put a smile on a face that for so long has been without one? It certainly does.

And yet there is a hesitation in my answer. There is a part of me that longs to agree and allow his energy into my life. A part of me that wants to lie in bed at night and feel the warmth of a man beside me. I miss the feeling of being held. I miss the feeling of being loved. I miss the way Francis looked at me like I was the only thing in the whole universe. I want to feel that love again, the love that for so long I have been denied. Second to losing Francis, the worst thing was losing the unconditional love that he showered on me.

In my heart, I know that there is a part of Henry that only sees me as a means to an end. What I bring to the table is far more than what he brings. However, do I see him any differently? Surely, I too see him as the fix to a situation. It is not fair, but it is the time that we live in. I can never offer him my heart in full. That has been reserved for one man only. However, I can hope that in our marriage, we would share affection.

I feel as if I am falling from a great height with no idea if anyone will be there to catch me at the bottom. But I have to choose whether to take a chance or to live my life in the way that Elizabeth does, to trust no one and never allow myself to move forward. I understand the way she lives. I have considered it myself. But I do not believe it is a viable way to rule a country, not when she is a female ruler and vulnerable to the will of men. It is far better to have a true ally by your side and a son in your belly than it is to live forever as a "virgin" queen.

I chose a different path than my cousin, and with reluctance, I agree to marry again. I must count my blessings and realise that if I have to remarry, at least it will be with a man who makes me smile. I could marry a foreign prince, a cruel man who only wishes to rule Scotland through me. Instead, I have chosen one of my own kin, a man I believe I can trust.

It is bittersweet as I accept Henry's proposal. On the one hand, I am happy to have found someone I feel so open with. On the other, I know that I will never give him my whole being. I feel for him in that way, knowing that he shall never fully possess me. Knowing that every time he touches me, kisses me, or says he loves me, there will be a hesitation from me.

I have spent the last few weeks with Francis at the forefront of my mind. Every time I think about him, a panic rises within me and I feel as if I cannot move or breath at all. I need to do all that I can to keep Francis in the past and face the future head on. I cannot drown any longer. If Francis and I were commoners and not royalty, I would never think of remarrying. However, the past few months have taught me that now is the time to put duty above myself.

Henry is overjoyed when I finally accept his proposal. I do so with a heavy heart.

***

We plan to marry quickly and with little fuss. We would prefer to be married before the rumours begin and find their way to England. We both know that Elizabeth will be unhappy with the match, although I believe that we are only following her wishes. James and my council are unhappy with my decision. They do not trust Henry. However, their concerns fall on deaf ears. I believe I have found the perfect match in Henry. They are simply worried about losing power to my husband.

Chapter 22

28th July 1565

It is the night before my second wedding, and I cannot help but draw comparisons between how I am feeling now and how I felt the night before I married Francis. Back then, I was so youthful and full of hope for the future. I was madly in love and desperate for the day to come when we would be joined. Tonight, my mood is melancholy. I feel a pit of sadness in my stomach as I think of tomorrow.

For one, I do not feel as hopelessly in love tonight as I did then. I was so sure that I was about to marry the man I would be with forever; I was convinced that we had a bright and beautiful future ahead of us. I never envisioned a second marriage for myself, and yet I stand on the cusp of that day. How life has changed so immensely for me in the last few years. Then, I was a young girl who lived in a bubble of happiness unpenetrated by heartache. Now I am a woman of twenty-two with an understanding of what it really means to exist in this world. I was Queen of Scotland then, as I am now, but had so far been untouched by the great responsibility that comes with being a true queen. My heart was light and free. Tonight, it is burdened and heavy.

Tonight, the weight of my decision has finally crushed me as I think about the choice I have made to remarry. I feel the deep cut of betrayal not on myself, but as I inflict it on my darling Francis. The past few days I have experienced moments of panic as the day looms, but for the first time, I let it take over me. I allow the anger and hurt that I am holding back to finally break through. I try to sleep to shake it off and ignore it, but Francis' face is in my mind. He is dressed just as he was the day we married, his face youthful and free of the worry that would later grip him. His eyes are so full of love. He searches my face for the young girl he waits to marry. I look like that Mary, but he will not find that young girl here. I am a fragment of that bright, young, happy girl who stood beside him at the altar. I am not sure that he would recognise me if he were alive now. The very heart of who I was is long gone. I no longer look at the world through youthful, naïve eyes. I see this world in all of its true colours now, and I know that joy and happiness, like everything else, have an expiration date. I need to see tomorrow from a different view, for it is not Francis' Mary who marries Henry tomorrow. It is a different woman altogether, one who knows that true love does not guarantee us happiness and that we must settle for what we are given.

Still, the guilt is heavy on my chest tonight. I long to be the girl who looked into the future with such promise. The girl whose face hurt from grinning. I wish I could look at tomorrow the way I looked at my wedding all that time ago, when I was kept awake by excitement and not dread. When the morning could not come quick enough and I longed to speed head-first into the future with my husband's hand in mine. How changed I am now. Would Francis love this Mary, this cold and hateful person I have become? Or would he find that I am now unlovable? But then, I suppose that if he had never left me, this Mary would not exist, and I would not be facing another wedding day.

I feel Francis' presence tonight. He is here in this room. I know it to be true with every bone in my body. This is not the first time I have felt him, and it will not be the last. He always promised that he would be close, and I believe that to be true. At first, I had thought that he was here to reassure me, to tell me that he understands why I have to do this. I am convinced that Francis would want me to remarry. I know that he would want me to do whatever I have to in order to keep myself and my country safe. But for some reason, I am convinced that he is not happy with my choice. When I ask why he is upset aloud into the chilling night air, all I seem to hear is a snarl and the name "Darnley," spat as if it is a dirty word. The very sound of it opens up a pit in my stomach. The malice behind the name makes me shiver. There is no comfort as the presence of my husband fills my mind. Instead, the warmth that he usually brings is replaced by a cold warning. The hairs on my arms stand up, and a chill fills the air.

At first, my mind tells me that Francis is upset with me, that my decision to remarry has wounded him. However, that does not fit with the man I know so well. The image of him tonight is not as clear. He seems wary, as if he does not want to be here. Perhaps it is nothing more than my own guilt reflecting outwardly. Am I seeing my own worries on Francis' face? Have I conjured him up in an attempt to ease my heavy heart?

When I have time to think about tomorrow and the days that follow, I realise just how difficult the situation may be for me. How will I truly feel when I reach over and find someone in the bed beside me again? Will I feel disappointment as I realise that it is not the person that I really want? How will it feel to allow someone else to make love to me? Will it be the same? Surely, no one will be able to hold me in the way that Francis did. I am happy with Henry, but the idea of standing beside him while we make a vow to each other brings a sickness to my stomach. When I made a vow to Francis, that was supposed to be eternal. That was supposed to be the one and only vow that I would ever make in this life. And yet here I am, readying to make that promise to another. What does that make me? When I so easily take a vow made before God and give it to someone else?

Deep down, it is not the fact that I marry Darnley tomorrow that truly bothers me. It is the fact that I feel for him. That a small part of me loves him. That is where the true betrayal lies. I do not betray Francis with my actions. I betray him with my feelings. I feel a deep guilt begin to grow within me. As I try to sleep tonight, all I can see is Francis' face swimming before my eyes. I can hear his voice telling me that he loves me. I can feel his touch. I will it to be true. With every muscle in my body, I cling to the feeling. How can I agree to be with someone else while my husband is cold in his grave? How can I allow another man into my life so easily? Have I agreed to marry him without thinking about Francis? How can I allow someone else to take his place?

The truth is that I will never let anyone else penetrate my heart. But am I so willing to give my body up to another?

I promised I would never want another man in the physical way that I want Henry. I promised that even in death I would be a true and loyal wife, but I lied. I have broken a vow between Francis and me. I have broken the promise I made to be eternally his. I feel as if I cannot breathe. I feel as if my furs are too thick as they lie on top of me. My chest begins to throb, and the tears that have been mere drops until this point turn into heaving sobs. What am I doing? What would Francis think? Would he hate me for my decision? I fear that I am stabbing him in the back. I feel as if I am pushing him away and putting someone else above him when he is the only man truly engrained in my heart.

"I promise you, Francis, I only love you," I gasp into the silent night.

I know he is listening. I know that he is nearby. I can hear his heartbeat now as clearly as I did when I lay on his chest. I feel him. His hand lingers on my face. It is not the solid form of a man, but a gentle breeze on my cheek, a tingle that runs down my spine as he touches me. I hear his voice in the air. His breath on my neck. I feel his love as deeply as I felt it the day he left me. And yet tonight, I know he does not intend to bring me comfort. He wishes to warn me. I block it out. Again, I am sure that my own fears get the better of me. I close my eyes and he is gone, and I am left alone in the dark again.

As the darkness enfolds me, I am again taken over by panic. It grips me as all of my fear returns to the surface. The room feels so small tonight, the night darker than usual. I am hot, as sweat begins to bead on my head and the sickness returns to my body. I look around me, hopelessly looking for some comfort. I sob into the silent air, catching my breath. My chest aches as each cry breaks free. My ladies do not stir. And if I do wake them, they do not bother to check on me. They have spent many nights like this with me since losing Francis. They have learned that I am best left alone. They know that I will not allow them to be burdened by the pain in my soul.

I cannot be in this room any longer. I need to breathe. The windows are too small. I must get some air. My throat stings and my chest burns as my breathing becomes shallow. I stand, not caring that I am in my night gown, and run from the room. Just outside my door, there is an open window. The cold air on my face revives me a little. I am soothed by the gentle breeze on my face.

And then a voice, one that instantly relaxes me. "My lady, is everything okay?" asked in the thick accent I have come to love. Davey. I turn to face him, and his smile drops as he sees my tear-stained face. "Mary. My queen, what is wrong?" he asks, concern obvious.

"My lady, you are getting married in four hours. You should be resting."

I lower myself onto the ground and sit with my head in my hands. The tears begin again, making new marks on my face. I allow all of the hurt to wash over me, not caring that Davey is here to witness my despair.

"Honestly, Davey? Just that." I sob.

Without another word from me, a realisation dawns on his face. "Ah. Mary, is this about Francis?"

"Yes." I weep. "I'm scared. Scared that I am betraying the man I love."

"You would never betray Francis!" David exclaims. "Oh, Mary. Do not look at it with such gloom."

I have had many talks with David in the past about the grief that still weighs on me so heavily. He knows more than anyone how each and every day, I think about Francis. He knows how my heart breaks over and over for the man I love so deeply. He has sat with me day after day and listened to everything I have to say. He knows just how much it pains me to even think about moving on.

"I feel so lost, David. I feel like I am pushing him away," I confess.

David is thoughtful for a moment. Not one look of judgement or worry crosses his face as he sits beside me on the ground and places his arm comfortingly around me. "Mary, you know that nothing you can do will ever push Francis away. He is with you always," he replies with understanding on his face.

"Does it not make me awful to love him so much and yet so easily marry another?" I ask. "Could I ever forgive him if it were the other way around? I do not think that I would have the strength."

"My darling, Francis is dead. And you are left here to navigate your way through this troubled world," David begins. "If you want to know what I think: live in whatever way you can. Do whatever it takes to make it through this life. If you can steal a little happiness in the meantime, even better. There is nothing you could ever do to turn Francis against you. I know that without ever meeting him. And then, when all is said and done, go to your grave with a smile on your face and a knowledge that your true happiness is just beginning."

David's words bring a tear to my eye. I know in my heart that he is right, that this life is nothing more than a stepping stone on my way back to Francis. I know that one day in the future, God will take me home, and there I shall be reunited with the people I love the most.

"Marry Henry tomorrow. Do it in the knowledge that Francis will be right beside you."

David kisses me on the head and stands to pull me to my feet. I suddenly realises just how tired I am as the panic fades away and is replaced by weariness.

"Thank you, my sweet friend. What would I ever do without you?" I yawn.

"Well, for a start, you would be an absolute mess." Davey laughs. "Let us get you back into bed. We cannot have you looking haggard on your wedding day."

Davey leads me back into my bedroom and tucks me back into my furs. The moment that my head rests on the pillow, I fall into a fitful sleep.

Chapter 23

29th July 1565

I woke this morning, my head foggy and my mind far away. I have been plagued all morning by memories from my first wedding. I awoke on that day full of excitement and eager to begin my new life. Today, I feel a heaviness, and the buzz that I felt back then is replaced by grief. The morning ticks away slowly as my ladies dress me, just as they did all that time ago—only then, I looked the perfect image of a princess in my white gown, adorned with jewels and blushed with happiness. Now, I wear a black gown in respect for my first husband and a solemn look on my face. Black is not usually the colour of choice for a bride on her wedding day, but I must go into this second marriage with respect to my first.

Henry already knows this. At first, he did not take to the idea. He saw it as an insult. He accused me of holding on too tightly to the past. But he soon sang another song when he realised his choice was to marry me in black or not marry me at all. Henry knows that I love him. I tell him enough. But put simply, I love Francis more, and I will not turn my back on him today.

The smile on my face this morning is forced as my ladies prepare me. There is much less for them to do today than before my first wedding. Everything about the ceremony is much more modest. This time, I marry in the confines of my own private chapel at Holyrood. Back then, I married in the grandness of Notre Dame, with the whole of France come out to watch. Now, there will only be my ladies and my brother to stand witness. Then, I was a child of just sixteen years; I was a dauphiness, and a queen only in name. Now, I am a woman grown of twenty-two years, and I am a ruling queen with a country to put first. How my life has changed in just a few short years. Would I have done things differently if I had known my future then? The short answer is no. I would not change a moment of my time with Francis.

I cannot seem to shake the chill that runs through my body. It is the same one that I felt last night. The same one that stayed with me as I slept. It is a feeling of dread that I cannot brush off, a worry that fills my stomach with butterflies. On the surface, I believe it to be nothing more than pre-wedding nerves, but deep down, I cannot help but think that it is something much more unsettling.

***

As time slowly moves towards six, we begin to make our way to the chapel. My ladies follow close behind me and Davey hovers nearby. As we stand outside the doors of the chapel, I stop to take a breath, much like I did when I married Francis. Both intended to calm my nerves, both for very different reasons. I step inside, and I see Henry awaiting me at the altar. It is too late to turn back now.

Once inside, I am joined by joined by the earl of Lennox, the earl of Atholl, and Henry's father who walk me to the altar. As I walk towards Henry, I am again haunted by images from before. When I look up at him, it is Francis' face I see. I look around me and it is as if I am in Notre Dame again. The guests fade away and are replaced by the beaming faces of the Valois. The silence is filled by the cries of the happy people of France. I look around the chapel, and I am met by a warm smile from Catherine. It is as if time has reversed and I have returned to that happy day.

Only when I reach the alter to stand beside Francis, he fades and is replaced by Henry. It is not Francis who smiles across at me; it is Henry. The image conjured in my mind disappears and I am left with the reality. Still,

I hold the smile on my face. My heart breaks as reality hits, but my face shows the look of a woman completely in love with her betrothed.

When I stood side by side with Francis, I towered above him. He looked so small next to me with my uncommon height. Next to Henry, we stand as tall as each other. I must admit that seeing him today reminds me of why I chose him. The way he looks at me, eyes filled with love and excitement, makes me feel a hopefulness for the future. I believe that Henry truly loves me, and it is because of that I feel he will do everything he can to make me happy. That is all I can hope for: a small amount of stolen happiness. I feel that in him, I will find some of the youthfulness that I have lost. He is so young and full of life. How I wish I could return to those days when I was untouched by life's cruelties.

The ceremony goes smoothly and without interruption. Henry is like an excited child as the priest finally announces us as husband and wife. There is a small amount of clapping from the spectators, much different from the roar of happiness in Notre Dame. Henry grins at me as he takes me by the waist and kisses me before our guests.

"You have made me the happiest man today, Mary." He beams. "I love you."

"And I you, Henry." I return the happy smile.

I cannot quite believe that I am now, once again, a married woman. It all seems to have gone so quickly from the moment I met Henry to being stood at the altar. I only hope and pray that I have made the right decision.

***

We spend the rest of the day in celebration, feasting and drinking. My ladies smile, and it makes me feel a little lighter to know that after such a long time of sadness, we finally have a reason to feel joy. Henry has truly come in at the perfect time to lift our spirits. Although my Marys adored Francis and know how much I loved him, they are happy to see me try to move forward with my life. They have spent almost as much time with Henry as I have, and they have grown to like him in such a short time. However, the rest of the court seem to be in a gloomy mood. Ruthven sits with his arms crossed and a grimace on his face. He would not be here at all if it was not his duty. They all make it very clear that they are not happy with my decision, especially James.

"You look as beautiful as ever, sister," he says with a warm smile on his face as he sits next to me.

"Thank you, James." I return the smile.

"I must warn you that your new husband is moments away from drinking Holyrood dry," James comments, distaste obvious on his face.

I look across at Henry, who jokes with his father while gulping down another cup of wine. It is true that he has enjoyed himself today, and I cannot help but wish he tried to stay sober, but I let it go, not wanting to ruin his fun. After all, we are supposed to be celebrating. James is just sore because I did not heed his advice.

"Oh, cheer up, James. It is a happy day. We should be celebrating." I brush him off.

"I wish you could see through him as I do. He is not good enough for you, Mary," James grunts.

"I will have none of that today, James. It was my choice to marry Henry. As I am your sister and queen, you should respect that."

James makes to reply, but from the look I give him, he realises quickly that it is not a good idea to push me any further.

"With your permission, my queen," James begins. "I would like to take my leave. I am weary, and it has been a long day."

At first, I make to fight him; he should be present. He should show solidarity for my decision. However, if he intends to complain all day about my decision, the perhaps it is better that he leave now, before his mood spreads to the rest of the court.

"Of course, James." I nod.

As James stands to leave, he bows low and places a kiss on my head. “Sister.” He abruptly nods at Henry before leaving.

Henry, who sits beside me, gets more intoxicated by the moment. He has been drinking all day, and it is clear from his face that it is beginning to affect him. His face has gone bright red, and his words begin to slur. I tell myself that he is happy and that I should leave him alone, but the rest of the court has begun to chatter.

“Henry, darling. Don’t you think we should go easy on the wine?” I lean over and take his hand.

Henry ignores me and continues to laugh with the men beside him. He has hardly spoken to me at all since the celebration began.

“Henry.” I shake him. He looks round at me sharply, as if annoyed that I am disturbing his conversation. “I really do think that you should slow down.”

Henry is quiet for a moment, as if contemplating what he should say next. I prepare myself for an argument, but to my surprise, he agrees. “You’re right, my love,” he answers. “I’m sorry. I am just so happy today.”

“That’s okay, darling. You enjoy yourself,” I reply, feeling foolish for complaining. I allowed James' judgement to get the better of me.

"I'm done with these imbecile's anyway," he laughs. "Shall we go to bed?" He grins and leans in to give me a sloppy kiss, and I cannot help but laugh as there is a collective gasp around the room. It is not proper for a husband to show such affection so openly.

"It's a bit early," I chuckle.

"Ah, yes. But I cannot wait to have you to myself." Henry falls all over me in his drunken state. One of his hands is in my hair, and with the other he reaches for my chest.

"Henry!" I exclaim. I notice that the whole room has fallen silent and decide that it is probably best that we leave now before he has the chance to do something stupid.

"Yes, my love. I think we should retire now."

I stand to address our guests and the room falls silent. "I wish to thank you all for attending this special day. Henry and I cannot thank you enough for helping us celebrate. It has been absolutely wonderful. However, it is time for us to take our leave now, but please stay and enjoy the food and wine as long as you wish."

I make to leave, taking Henry by the hand and pulling him with me.

"To bed, wife!" He shouts behind us. My face almost turns red with embarrassment, but I chuckle, and the court follows suit.

***

Now we are in my chambers and the day darkens outside. The fire crackles and the candles flicker, filling the room with a warm glow. I sit in a chair by the fire. Henry, who is still inebriated from his day of drinking, snores gently in the chair across from me. My stomach is full of butterflies, and worry fills my mind. We have reached the part of the day that I was most concerned about—the part where I will have to give my body over to another man. The moment when I truly leave behind my past and become tied to Henry. This is a necessary part of a marriage contract. This is the moment we make our vows official.

I am so nervous. I have never lain with anyone other than Francis, and I never thought I would have to. To give yourself over to someone so openly, is to be at your most vulnerable, and I feel that vulnerability tonight. There is a part of me that wishes I did not have to do this, that it was the one thing I could keep sacred. The one thing that I have only given to Francis.

On my first wedding night, I felt confident in this duty. I knew that by joining with Francis, I was only making our bond stronger.

Everything about making love to Francis felt right. The very bones in my body ached for it. Then, once it was over, I could not wait to try it again, to search every part of his body and allow him to fill me up completely.

I do not feel those needs tonight. Tonight, it feels like much more of a task that I must fulfil, something that I have to do. I know that in order for our marriage to be valid I must allow this to happen but lying with Henry makes it seem like the act with Francis was not something we alone shared, but something I easily share with someone else. I cannot avoid this, and yet it feels so wrong. Henry is certainly a handsome man. I do not lack attraction to him. Yet it is not the same attraction that I felt before., the pull I felt towards my previous husband, like our very souls were bonded together. This union is empty in comparison. However, I know that I owe Henry my full self, and however painful it may be, I will give him what he deserves.

I would happily allow Henry to sleep peacefully in his chair all night, but I must be strong. If I don't do this now, I never will. How bad can it be? Henry loves me, and I care for him deeply. I am sure that he will make me feel comfortable. I take a deep, steadying breath before leaning in to wake up my husband.

“Henry, darling.” I say gently. “Wake up, my love.”

Henry stirs but does not wake straight away. I cannot help but chuckle as he shrugs me off and returns to snoring. He looks so handsome even as he sleeps, with his hair in a wavy and tousled mess and his face without a care in the world as he dreams peacefully. Despite myself, I cannot deny the desire that stirs inside me when I look upon him. It goes against everything I have ever promised to Francis, but I cannot help but crave the feeling of being loved again.

“Sweetheart, let’s go to bed,” I say, slightly louder than before.

Henry’s eyes snap open. They are red as he glares at me and then looks about the room, confused.

“Mary?” he asks.

“Yes, my sweet?” I chuckle.

For a moment, I believe that sleep still has hold of him. He looks at me dazed and startled. I smile at him reassuringly, waiting for him to regain his memory, but the look he returns to me is anything but happy. As he rubs the last remnants of sleep from his eyes, he grows angry. Something about the way he looks at me sends a cold shiver running down my spine.

“Why did you wake me?” he asks, sounding irritated. “I was dreaming happily.”

For a moment, I am totally speechless, almost waiting for him to laugh as if he's joking. But when his face does not change, I realise that he is indeed angry that I have woken him.

"Well, it is our wedding night, Henry . . ." I say as Henry continues to stare expectantly. "We have things we need to attend to." I gesture towards the bed.

"Oh, yes," he answers, rubbing the back of his neck. Then, finally, he smiles. It is a broad and beautiful smile, the one I had been hoping to see. He has finally remembered. I let out a sigh of a relief, but it is short lived. "I am king." He beams, taking me by surprise. "King Henry!" he bellows. I cannot keep the shock from my face as his excitement grows. I had thought that his happiness was because of our marriage, but Henry only seems concerned with his new title.

"Well . . . not yet, Henry," I say, breaking through his celebration. I must admit that I am a bit taken aback by his celebration. I always knew that Henry was an ambitious man, but clearly, being king was all he cared about.

"Soon. Then everything will change," he says with the strangest look on his face. It is not the Henry I know. It is calculated and unsettling.

I decide to brush past this, not wanting today to turn sour. Henry is clearly still in a drunken state and has lost all sense of himself. I am sure that in the morning he will return to the man I know.

"That is a matter for another day, my love. For now, we have more important matters to attend to," I say. "Shall we to bed?" I ask, a playful smile on my face.

Henry's face drops again and my stomach flips. He is making me feel uneasy tonight. I have never seen such a look on his face. It is as if he has switched from the loving and happy man I thought I knew to someone else entirely.

"I suppose we have to," he answers gruffly. "Lay down on the bed." There is no warmth in his words. No love. No romance.

Hesitantly, I call for my ladies to unlace my dress, something that I had expected my husband to do. Francis always did. The whole time, Henry stares straight through me. Already, this is completely different than what I was expecting. When they are finished, I dismiss them and lay myself down on the bed. Henry does not move straight away. Instead, he stares down at me. I grow shy under his gaze, but not in a good way. The way he is looking at me is not loving. Instead, he looks at me with contempt. My mind runs through the whole day, searching for something I might have done wrong, but the truth is everything went the way it should have. I have no idea why Henry's personality has changed so dramatically, but it is scaring me.

After a moment, he climbs into the bed beside me. I move to kiss him, but he turns his cheek. I place my hand softly on his face, but he pushes me off. When he turns to look at me, he is angry. He does not look like a man about to lay with his new wife for the first time. I try to push away the worry that builds in my stomach. I try to ignore the niggling feeling in my mind, the voice in the back of my head that tells me I have made a mistake.

Perhaps the reason this feels so wrong is because I know in my heart it is wrong. I know deep down that this is a sin against the man I love. That today I have not only made my vow to another man, but I am now about to give my body away too. Francis lingers in my mind, but he cannot be here for this. Neither of us is strong enough to keep him in my mind's eye while another man takes what is rightfully his. For the first time, I must say goodbye and mean it. I must turn him away tonight, something that I said I would never do.

I frame the words in my mind and hope that Francis understands. "I need to let you go, my love." I begin. "I need to set you free in this life so that we may be together in the next. And yet remember, you will be forever in my heart." A solitary tear drops from my eye, but

I fight to push the sadness away. Francis does not reply. He has already faded away. I look across to my new husband and make a silent promise to give him all of me in this moment.

The longer we lie still, the more anxiety builds within me. Henry is silent apart from his controlled breathing. I can feel the tension build between us—not the sexual tension I had felt before, but a nervous tension. Henry seems to be mad at me. I run through the day's events in my head, but nothing happened that would cause Henry's anger. I open my mouth to ask him what is bothering him, but I barely get a word out before Henry begins to move on top of me. In one swift move, he is pinning me down. He does not kiss me. He does not look me in the face. There are no tender touches. No romance. He does not run his hands through my hair or stroke my cheek. He does not cup my face and kiss me sweetly on the lips. Instead, he is rough. He is rushed and eager. He does not wait or ask me if I am ready like Francis did. He races to lift my shift off. His breath reeks, the scent of alcohol strong on his body. He is scaring me. *This is not assault* I remind myself as he pries my legs apart, although it certainly feels like it. I have given him permission, and as my husband, he has every right to do what he wishes with my body, but this does not feel right. This feels like a violation.

Henry holds me down by the shoulders as he enters me. He moves quickly and without care for me. Again and again, I feel pain as he moves back and forth. His full weight is on me, and he avoids my eyes as they fill with tears. He pushes my face to the side, and his breath is hot on my neck. I squirm underneath him, praying for it to be over. He does not notice me. He moves quickly and pays no mind to me as I gasp with pain. With Francis, he was gentle and sweet. He moved at my pace and always made sure I was comfortable.

Henry is clumsy and forceful. The worst thing is the look of disgust that is evident on his face. He does not seem to enjoy any moment of it as he moves faster and faster to get it done. I grin and bear it, but the whole time, I am desperate to push him off of me. I feel sick as he grips my arms so that I cannot move. I close my eyes and I see Francis. I see his loving face before me. Why is this so different? This used to feel so good, and now I can hardly stand the feeling of Henry on top of me.

Thankfully, it is over quickly, and with one final thrust of his hips, Henry finishes and climbs off of me. He stands from the bed and wraps a fur around his shoulders. Then, without a look in my direction, he walks towards the door.

"Where are you going?" I ask, my voice small and shaken.

I feel disgusting as his cruel eyes turn on me. There is no love in them, only distaste. "To my bed, of course," he answers without looking back as he walks out of the door.

"We are husband and wife now, Henry. We should sleep in the same bed on our wedding night," I try to tell him. "People will talk." I speak, but I have no energy to try to stop him.

"Let them," he says, opening the door and leaving.

Once he is gone, the full effect of what has just happened hits me. I lift my hand to wipe the tears from my eyes and realise that I am shaking terribly. My heart is pounding, and sweat beads on my forehead. My breath catches in my throat as shudders run through me. I feel sick. I feel vile. This was supposed to be a celebration of our love, so why do I feel so detestable? Why do I feel as if I have been violated? Francis never made me feel this way. He was always so gentle. He always made me feel safe and loved. Henry has made me feel ugly and unwanted. The way he looked at me, the way he refused to touch me—it was like he found me abhorrent and couldn't stand to be near me.

I do not understand what just happened. Yesterday, he was loving and kind. Tonight, he could barely stand to look at me. Does he not find me attractive? Or to his liking? If that's the case, then why did he marry me? The niggling voice in my mind is louder than ever now. Was Francis' warning genuine? Has Henry just used me for power? Why am I doubting my husband just a few hours into our marriage? Surely not. He was just drunk and not his usual self. I cannot believe for one moment that tonight I saw Henry's true colours. What I saw tonight was a version of Henry afflicted by wine. It does not bear testament to his true character.

I know Henry . . . or do I? Truly? I suppose it has only been a number of weeks. How much can I really know about someone in such a short time? I married him without knowing anything other than that he likes to have fun and drink. No, no. I do know him. He is kind and warm. He is loving and caring. He will make a great husband. This was just a mistake. I must come to realise that making love to someone will not always be like it was with Francis. Still, I surely should not feel the way I do now. Does every woman feel this way after laying with their husband?

I will sleep tonight. I will not let my ladies into my room. I don't want anyone to know the shame of my husband's absence. I lie awake, still shaken from my experience with Henry. My stomach twists in sickening loops all night long every time I think about the way he pinned me down. Every time I think about how his hands felt on me, how rough he felt as he used my body. My first wedding night, I lay awake thinking about how glorious it was to be complete with the man I loved. Tonight, I feel as if I have been beaten, like what Henry did to me was torture. I feel unclean, like I want to scrub his touch off of my body.

As I lie awake in the dark of the night, I am brought no comfort. Francis is not here to hold me, and Henry feels as far away as possible. There is nothing else for me to do but lie here and feel the coldness of an empty bed and an empty heart.

Chapter 24

This morning, as Henry sat beside me at breakfast, I was forced to conceal the sickness that filled my stomach. Every time I looked his way, I felt nervous. He was back to his usual self, as he returned to smiling charmingly and doting on me. He was not the man from last night, but instead the Henry that I was used to. He was funny and witty, just like normal. No one would for a moment believe the amount of wine he had drank the previous night.

I kept silent throughout the whole meal, my stomach tied in knots the whole time, not knowing what I should say or how I should act. Every time he would reach over to me, I jerked away, not wanting him to touch me. Each time he tried to speak to me, my answer would be no more than a nod or forced smile. I was confused by what I was seeing, not sure which Henry was true: the man I had experienced last night or the one who sat beside me now. Most of all, I felt nervous that he may once again turn back into that man from last night, that once alone, he may show that side of him again.

After we had eaten, Henry leant in to speak to me so that no one else could hear. "Mary, I really do owe you an apology," he began. "My behaviour last night was inexcusable." He looked ashamed as he took hold of my hand. "Can you forgive me?"

I am thoughtful for a moment. On the one hand, Henry was admitting fault in the way he behaved last night, but on the other, he really made me feel worthless. Could I really just brush past the pain Henry caused me? Could I ignore the fear he made me feel? I never thought I would be the type of woman to stay silent while her husband did as he wished. He needed to know that he could not treat me like that and get away with it.

"Henry, the way you behaved last night scared me," I admitted. "I should not have to be afraid of my own husband."

Henry bowed his head in shame. "I know. I know." Tears welled in his eyes. "Mary, I feel so disgusted with myself. You deserve so much better."

I did not know how to answer. I did not wish to convey all of the things he made me feel. I would rather push them to the side and carry on. More than anything, I want this marriage to be a happy one. My mind was telling me to accept Henry's apology and move on. My heart was telling me not to trust him. I stayed silent and allowed Henry to continue.

"Believe me, I am so sorry. I become a different man when I drink. It brings out a darkness in me." His eyes were pleading. He looked genuinely ashamed with his behaviour, and I could not help but soften a little towards him. We all have parts of ourselves that we would rather keep in the dark. He honestly looked so angry with himself. The whole time we were talking, he looked down at his feet. His eyes were full of tears. his voice barely a whisper.

"I get angry and, quite frankly, stupid. It's like I am not myself anymore, but instead am taken over by a demon. I did not wish you to see that side of me. Not one day into our marriage. I feel as if I have ruined things."

With each word, Henry broke me down a little, and I forgave him a little more. He was clearly full of remorse. The sadness in his eyes and the pain in his face convinced me that he knew just how wrong he was. Yes, I was hurt. Yes, I feel violated. However, I need to give this marriage a real chance. I am willing for us to work on this together. In time, I will heal.

"You have not ruined anything, darling," I said, taking his hand. "It was just a mistake." I cup his chin.

Henry smiled broadly, the sadness gone from his face in an instant. "Truly, my love? You forgive me?" he asked full of hope.

I took a breath, hoping that I was making the right decision in trusting him again. "I do. " I said. "As long as you can promise me that I never have to deal with that monster again."

"I promise you that you have seen him for the last time," Henry reassured me.

We kissed and became friends and I decided that I would put my fears to the side for the sake of my marriage and truly give Henry a second chance. Everyone makes mistakes from time to time, and I would allow Henry another chance. Gone was the man I lay with last night. Henry had returned to me, and that man deserved to make up for his actions.

That afternoon, I had Henry proclaimed king of Scotland to the world. He was thrilled with the announcement and celebrated all night long with a cup of wine in hand. When he came to my rooms in the early hours of the morning, I had him barred from entering. He was clearly drunk again, and I wanted to give him no opportunity to make another mistake. He was unhappy and shouted profanities to my guards who held him outside, but eventually, he gave up and crawled back to his room. I only hope that when the celebrations end and life returns to normal, Henry settles down into the life of a king and husband.

The weeks since our marriage have been happy. Henry has proven to be a loving and doting husband. He comes to visit me most evenings, and although our lovemaking is still not perfect, it has become more enjoyable for the both of us. I believe we hit a bump in the beginning, but now, our journey together is becoming clearer.

There are people that are, of course, unhappy with our union. Elizabeth has informed me of her distaste via a letter, to which I replied that I have done only as she has asked and that now I hope the question of my succession be dealt with. Not surprisingly, her response danced around the matter. I am convinced that she is always trying to find fault with me, something that offends her enough to delay her answer.

Henry took her letter from my hand and threw it into the fire. "Ignore her. She is simply jealous that you are far more beautiful than she," he spat.

If only I could ignore her or make her go away. That would certainly remove a noticeably big obstacle from my life. Yet I realised a long time ago that Elizabeth has a big part to play in my life, and I accepted her for what she is. Knox has also expressed his distaste. However, I am not in the least bit surprised. Knox will find a problem with anything. He and my brother are now demanding that I add more Protestants to my privy council. They fear that I am overrun by Catholic influence. Whether they like it or not, it's about time they accepted that their queen is a Catholic woman. However, I am fair, and I have agreed to humour their suggestions. Henry has agreed that we should give the Protestants something to keep them happy for a while at least.

I must admit that although my new marriage is bittersweet in the sense that I leave so much behind me, it does feel wonderful to have the company of a man again, to wake up in the morning without the instant loneliness or to have someone hold my hand under the table and whisper loving words in my ear. I like that I no longer sit alone at the head of the table and that I always have someone beside me in both my personal life and the ruling of Scotland. Henry does not help much with the governing of the country, but he is still learning. He has only been a king for two weeks. He thinks he has grand ideas about the way things should be and how the country should be run, but he has little knowledge to back them up. I think more than anything, he likes to play king, to have power and standing above every other person at court.

He asked me today about the crown matrimonial, which would mean that should anything happen to me, he would rule in my stead. I agreed to think it over, but I must put Scotland first, and I am not so sure that it would be beneficial to myself or the country if I were to make that decision before I know how capable he is. So for now, we have agreed to talk about it at a later time, but I have a feeling this will be something I will have to address eventually. Apart from a few differences in opinion, I am happy to say that I have found contentment in my second marriage, which is something I was not sure I would have. We do not spend huge amounts of time with each other, but it is different to when I was with Francis. Now I am the one who must put my duties first, and that leaves me with little time to dally.

The time we do spend together is lovely. He makes me laugh a lot with his jokes and impressions of the people at court. He absolutely detests Knox and is not quiet about it. He parades around the room, a gruff look on his face and wearing a mock beard made out of a hair piece. "Now listen here, little lady," he says in a thick Scottish accent. "I hate Catholics and I hate women. You are both." He points at me. "But really, I'm just mad that ye won't sleep with me." He cackles. My ladies absolutely love him, and he and Davey seem to have taken a liking to each other. They share the same love for booze and dark humour. For the first time in as long as I can remember, I feel content. Henry is good for me. He looks after me. That is all I could ever want in a husband.

It is true that Henry still likes to drink, but I have accepted it. It is his vice, and I must learn to live with it or fight against it. I choose the easier route. He is young. I am sure that as he matures, he will grow into his new role as king. For now, I allow him to have the youth that was stolen away from me. We are happy. He makes me happy. It is not the same happiness that I have known, but it is better than the despair I have felt for so long. Sometimes, I drink with him. It feels good to forget about my responsibilities and allow myself to be carefree for a short time. Mostly, I go about running the country, and I allow Henry to do whatever pleases Henry. If he is happy, then I am happy.

Chapter 25

I have been gravely mistaken.

I should have listened to Francis. I should have known that all good things must come to an end and that no matter how much I cherish something, it cannot last forever. Henry has reminded me of that. He managed to stay true to his word for just a short time. He promised me that I would never again have to see the demon that lives inside of him, that he only became that person when he had too much to drink. But now, I see more of that demon than I do of Henry. He no longer has to be drunk to turn nasty. He no longer bothers to dote on me or put up any pretence for the way he feels. It is clear now that he does not love me. If he did, he would not hurt me in the way he does.

It began small—a drunken encounter every now and then, the odd argument—mainly because I still do not wish to budge on the crown matrimonial matter. Now, Henry has taken to flying into fits of rage when he is full of drink. He has decided that he hates David, that our relationship is strange and that, of course, something must be going on behind closed doors. He could not be more wrong.

The strange thing is that I am the one who should be jealous. I am the one who must look on as my husband embarrasses me by flirting with the ladies at court and drinking long into the night, every single night. As he makes a fool out of himself before the whole court. To the outside world, we appear to be a happy couple, but inside these walls of Holyrood, a darker truth is known.

He hit me for the first time last night. Before then, our arguments had been just that. We screamed and shouted before one of us stormed off. Henry stamped his feet like a little boy who has been told no and ran away to his own rooms.

Last night was different. Last night, he questioned me again. "Why do you spend all of your time with Rizzio?" he asked as he wobbled on his feet. He was drunk again. It seems he is drunk more often than not these days.

"I will not answer that question again, Henry," I replied, weariness obvious in my voice. This was the third night of such interrogation.

"You will answer me. I am your husband, and I command it," he slurred.

"That you may be, but I am queen of this realm. Do not test my patience." I rolled my eyed. I was sick of the same old tired accusations. It was about time Henry realised his place.

"You will answer me, woman!" he spat. "Why do you entertain Rizzio alone in your room?"

"We are never alone; my ladies are always with me. As I have told you before, you may ask them," I repeated for the third time.

"They would lie for you if you asked. They would do anything to help you. You don't fool me with your lies." His speech grew more slurred with each sentence. He was losing control, just like he always did at that point.

I took a breath, believing that this was about to wind down. It always came to an end when finally, the drink made Henry sleepy. I had assumed that last night would have been no different. I acted as I always did at this point: the doting wife.

"Come now, Henry. Let us get you to bed." I took him by the arm and began to gently guide him to his room. I no longer wanted him to sleep beside me. The stench of alcohol always turned my stomach, and I could take no more nights of being woken up when he finally came to bed.

At first, he let me move him. He nodded his agreement and sleepily shuffled towards the door. But all of a sudden, he got a new burst of energy and threw me off of him. I landed on the floor with a thud, confused and shaken. Henry was even angrier than before, and he was not ready to back down.

He was not sorry for hurting me—quite the opposite, as he shouted in my face. "See what you make me do?"

However, Henry, realising that he had gone too far, quickly changed his whole demeanour, which was the same as every night. He switched between calm and nasty in an instant. He ran a hand through his hair and took a breath. "Mary, my love, I just want to know the truth. I won't be angry anymore. Just be honest," he said, changing tact. His whole mood shifted suddenly as he plastered a sweet smile on his face. I knew his game, though. He had tried this approach many times before.

"I have told you, Darnley. There is nothing between David and I," I replied through gritted teeth.

This made him angry again. He hated being called Darnley, said that it was what people who did not like him called him. He ran at me, pulled me from my feet, and pinned me against the wall. He banged his fist against the wall behind me and shouted inches away from my face. "I asked you to tell me the truth, damn it!" he bellowed. "If you want this to stop, then be honest," he said with bared teeth. His breath was vile; he stank of stale ale and vomit.

"Get out of my room!" I shouted back at him. "I am your queen, and I command you to go," I said with every ounce of strength I had.

"And I am king. You will pay me the respect I am owed."

"You are not and will not ever be a king. Kings are strong and fierce. You are weak and pathetic," I said out of spite. As I said it, my whole body went ice cold and a fear took over me. It was that warning feeling again. I get it every time we are about to have an argument now, like something is preparing me for what is about to happen.

Henry's face turned red with rage. He looked like an animal ready to pounce on its prey. Then, out of the corner of my eye, I caught a glance of his fist as it came flying towards me and struck me on the side of my head. I fell to the ground as the blow hit me.

In total shock and fear, I lay on the ground for what seemed like forever, unable to move as the truth of my situation finally hit me. I had married a monster. Henry's drunken games and vicious arguments were one thing, but this was something totally different. The pain in my head was nothing to the pain I felt inside at making a grave mistake.

Henry stood over me. I think for a moment, he was in shock at what he had done. But then he left the room without a second glance in my direction. My mind could not comprehend what had just happened. My husband had just struck me. When he left, my ladies came into the room. They found me balled up on the floor, too afraid to move.

"Majesty?" Fleming sounded panicked. "Majesty. What happened?"

I could not answer. I could not even find the words to say. I simply allowed them to pick me up off of the floor and carry me to the bed. They wrapped me up and each of them sat around, patiently waiting for me to tell them what had happened. It was only when Davey entered the room that I found my voice again. I had not even realised that Mary Beaton had disappeared to go and find him.

"Mary." He rushed over to the bed. "Mary, my queen. What has happened?"

David sat down on the edge of my bed and pulled me toward him. My ladies left us alone, but I knew that they were all close by, listening in. Deep down, I did not want anyone to know. It was shameful that I had allowed this to happen.

"He hit me," I said simply.

Davey was taken aback. At first, he was speechless. He too was in shock.

"Who did? Henry?" he asked, panicked.

"Yes!" I wept.

"Oh, Mary," Davey said sympathetically. "I am so sorry. I know he has a temper. But to strike you? I never would have thought it possible."

"He thinks that you and I have been sleeping together."

Davey laughed nervously. I imagine the notion really was so ridiculous that he had no idea how he should react.

"Why would he think that? We would never . . . I do not know what to say, Mary." David's face turned grey with shock.

"I know. I know," was all I said.

"I hate that man!" Davey burst out. "Where is he?"

"I don't know. Probably gone to find some more wine."

"Let me go and talk to him." David was on his feet and heading towards the door.

"That's very sweet, Davey. But stay with me. I need you here," I said, not wanting David to find himself in a fist fight with Henry.

David wrapped his arms back around me and held me as I wept and told him all about the arguments that Henry and I had been having lately. I admitted that he had had an issue with David for a while but that I had kept it a secret because I thought it would blow over. I admitted to David that it was the reason I had been more distant lately, more for his sake than mine. He understood, of course, but he was livid with Henry's behaviour. Much like the first night me and Henry spent together, I spent last night shaking, scared, and confused, wondering where the Henry I thought I knew had gone.

***

Today, Henry slept until mid-afternoon, bumbling into court and making no excuses for his lateness. He looked a mess. His hair was all over the place, his shirt displaced, his face seemingly unwashed and unshaven. The court seemed to give a collective gasp as he waltzed in without a care in the world. Here he was, a man who was supposed to be king in this country, looking no better than a pauper begging for food outside of the palace.

When he caught a glimpse of me talking to Jane, he wandered over and bowed in a huge, mock gesture. "My queen," he said, taking my hand and kissing it. I allowed him to greet me cordially, not wanting the court to know that anything was wrong.

"Husband," I said with suspicion clear on my face.

"If it pleases Your Majesty, I would like to speak to her in private." Henry smiled a little too sweetly.

"I am busy at the moment. We will talk later," I said, not wanting to get into another altercation.

"Of course," Henry said before turning on his heel and leaving me to my business.

In one way, I was lucky not to face any embarrassment. Henry had struck me on the side of my head, and the bruising was easy enough to cover. Still, I felt shamed by what had happened. I was sure someone would notice, and it would be confirmed in the eyes of my brother and other nobles at court that my husband was no good. All day, I have carried on full of dread for the moment I would be alone with Henry. David offered to be present, but I do not want to put him in the middle of this. Nor do I wish for my ladies to witness any disagreement.

It would turn out, though, that once again, and now sober, Henry would come to me with his tail between his legs, full of apology and self-pity. He again begged me to forgive him, promising that it was the drink that made him nasty, that were he in his right mind, he would never strike me or put me in any harm, that there was a demon that lived inside of him. The same thing he has said over and over again. The same excuses have been made before.

For one foolish moment, I allowed myself to feel sorry for him again as he wept at my feet. I felt my anger lessen slightly as he told me how much he loved me and needed me. I allowed his manipulation to get the better of me again. I held him and let him cry on my shoulder. I soothed him and told him that we would work through this and that things were going to be fine. When I kissed him, and a small part of me forgave him.

I let myself down by allowing Henry to get the better of me again. I had no idea how dangerous his charm and quick wit could actually be. He had won me over, even as my head throbbed from the bruise that had formed there. I allowed this man to convince me that it was my fault that I wound him up and pushed him to get angry. I did not argue back when he accused me of pushing him to drink. Instead, I found that I was the one to apologise. I said that I was sorry for mocking him and that I should spend less time with David and more time with him. I am not a weak woman, and yet I found it easier to agree and patch things up than to face the truth.

We have had a peaceful night. I knew we would. After a major argument, Henry is on his best behaviour for a short while. I know this, and yet I tell myself that this time will be different. This time, he will stay true to his word.

We sat and talked for a while. We ate together. We laughed, and I remembered why I care for this man. I convinced myself that his good qualities far outweigh the bad. I led in his arms and let his embrace comfort me. I allowed him to make love to me again. We fell asleep in each other's arms, and I sleep peacefully, fooling myself into a false reality where Henry may yet prove to be a good husband.

It is early in the morning, just before dawn, and I have just woken to the sound of my door slamming. I had been sleeping so soundly that I had not noticed Henry sneaking out of bed earlier in the night. He had tried to sneak back in but was louder than he intended to be. It is clear to me straight away that he is blind drunk.

"Sorry," he whispers while chuckling. He climbs into bed and wraps his arms around me. I push him away, not wanting him anywhere near me.

"Where have you been?" I demand.

Henry, who is too drunk to make much sense, continues to giggle like a child. His eyes roll and his head sways back and forth as the drink makes his head heavy.

"You'll be mad," is all he says. He is right. In fact, I am already mad. Just hours ago, he promised me that things were going to be different, and I allowed him to fool me again. How could I believe him so easily?

"Tell me," I say simply, not allowing my true feelings to show.

Henry is beside himself with laughter. Whatever he has done, he clearly finds it hilarious. Of course, I believe he means the fact that he snuck off to drink. I do not for one minute think that it could be anything else.

"I've given you a taste of your own medicine." His laugh is now more of a cackle. His eyes seem to turn evil, his smile that of the demon I have come to know so well.

"Darnley, I have no time or patience for your games," I say, absolutely lacking the energy to care about him anymore. His face changes as I call him Darnley. I know how much he detests it.

"This is no game, Mary." He sneers. There's that look again, the one that I know will lead to no good. It is sickeningly evil, and it makes the panic rise in my chest. My stomach drops, and I suddenly feel a pit open up in my stomach. A dread begins to fill my mind. There is something about Henry tonight, something more twisted than normal. "I thought it was about time you learned a lesson," he says, his voice low and taunting.

My heart begins to pound in my chest as anxiety gets the better of me. Henry looks like a mad man. I am scared, scared that he might hurt me, or worse. I do not know the extent of what he will do to hurt me. Or take my crown.

"What have you done?" I ask, voice shaking.

"I have taken something that you wanted all to yourself. I have taken the man you love and made him my own."

My head swims with confusion. I cannot think what he means. He is the man I love. If not him, then Francis. And he cannot hurt Francis. So who is he talking about? Could he mean David? Has he done something to my dear Rizzio? Panic takes over my whole body as I think of all the things he might have done. He has threatened David in the past. Please, dear God, tell me he has not hurt my friend.

"Henry . . . have you done something to David? Have you hurt Rizzio?" I ask nervously, dreading the answer.

"No. I have not hurt your darling David," he spits. "I have done to you what you have done to me."

"Henry, you need to tell me what you have done," I plead. I long to escape from the room and find David. He says he hasn't hurt Davey, but what else could he have done?

Darnley is quiet for a moment, considering his answer. He makes me wait, I could sense that he was seeing the pain in my eyes and relishing every last second of it.

"Think about it, Mary. What did you do with him behind my back?" he laughs. "I have slept with him, of course."

Henry's words bring my whole world crashing around my shoulders. Suddenly, the floor seems to disappear from under my feet and the whole room begins to spin. He has slept with David. They have made love to each other. That is what he is saying, at least. But can I believe it? Can I trust the word of a drunken, crazy fool like Henry Stuart?

"David would never do that to me!" I scream. The evilness of this man truly knows no bounds. He would ruin the purest of things.

"Oh, but he has." Darnley grabs hold of me. "He has, and what was yours is now mine." He holds me at arm's length. "How does it feel to have me take what you love? First Rizzio, and next, your precious crown. Mark my words, Mary. You'll lose everything you love to me." Henry throws me to the floor. "I will see you tomorrow, wife. We have an heir to make, and it's about time you do your duty and give me the crown matrimonial." Darnley walks towards the stairs.

"Never!" I shout after him. "You will never have my crown or my love."

"I do not want your love. I never did," he shouts. "You have always been a means to an end. Nothing more."

He is gone before I can answer, and once again, I am left alone and shaking on the floor because of this man who is supposed to be my husband. I am not hurt because he does not love me. I am not surprised that he only wants me for the crown. Honestly, I knew it all along. The pain that fills my body now, the betrayal I feel, the aching in my chest—they are down to David, a man I thought I could trust above anyone else. He knows what Henry has put me through. He has sat by my side while I cry, and still, he has betrayed me tonight. Why would he do it? What would make him sleep with Henry? He detests him. That is what he told me, at least.

I cannot seem to move from the floor as I pray once again that the world swallows me whole. Once again, I have thought to find myself a little piece of happiness, and once again, I have had that ray of hope ripped away from me. The betrayal from Darnley hurts. He is the man who swore to love me in the eyes of God. The man who was supposed to put me first in everything. But I now know that I have married an illusion. Henry was just the idea of a man. He was everything he needed to be to get where he is today. He is clever and conniving. He knew that to get a crown, he had to win the love of a queen.

And he did it so effortlessly. He allowed me to believe that he was in love with me so that I would give him my world. His only mistake was failing to keep the ruse going long enough for me to give him full power. The thing that scares me now is that I believe if I had given him the crown matrimonial, he would have had me killed and taken Scotland for himself. I see so clearly now that Henry lives for nothing but his own gain.

The real agony I feel tonight has been inflicted by David, my sweet Rizzio. My first true friend in this world since Francis, or at least that is what I thought. I had thought that Francis had guided him to me so that he may be a comfort to me in this life. I had thought him an angel come to sit on my shoulder and ease my suffering. Yet he too has committed a great deception on me, for he made me believe that he genuinely cared for me while his true intentions were much more malicious.

The agony that rips through me is unbearable. The questions that race through my mind weigh me down. I am stunned by the complete treachery of the people closest to me. I had not thought Rizzio capable of such wickedness. I thought I knew him better than anyone else, but clearly, I am too easy to fool. Obviously, I am not the strong, fearless woman I had thought. I am weak-minded and easy to manipulate. I cannot bear the thought of Darnley and Rizzio entwined together in the thralls of passion. I cannot stand the idea that someone I love so much could so easily hurt me like this.

I try to move, to do something, anything, but each time, I am bolted down by a new wave of betrayal. It is like sharp shocks hitting me again and again as images of them together flood my mind. My blood begins to boil as anger takes over my mind. I keep thinking that perhaps they planned this. Perhaps this was malicious and calculated. Yet I see no reason for Rizzio's part in this. He could not stand Darnley after what he had done to me, so why would he wish to go anywhere near him?

I cannot stand this. I cannot sit here and stew in my own misery. I will go and find Rizzio and get to the bottom of this. I do not know that I will be able to look him in the face without my stomach turning, but I have to know his side of the story. I have to know what Darnley is not telling me. The cold prickles me again, and I am forced to take a breath. I must hear from David's own mouth the truth of this. All I can do is pray that Darnley has lied to me.

I storm from the room, giving my attendants no chance to ask me any questions. I head straight to Rizzio's room. The halls are empty at this early time of day. Most of the court are still asleep in their beds, unaware of the heartache unfolding. Every step I take towards his room, a voice in my head tells me to walk away, that I do not want to lay my eyes on the wretch. Every one of my heartbeats is a thud in my chest. My palms sweat, and my thoughts blur as nerves get the better of me. I know I need answers, and yet a part of me longs to turn around and hide from this. I am so angry, but that is nothing more than a mask for the deep agony I now feel. I do not know what I will find when I get to David's room. Perhaps they are together. The images make the bile rise in my throat.

Before I know it, I stand in front of his door. I fight to compose myself. I do not want my emotions to get the better of me. I knock. No answer. I knock again, and then a third time. Still, there is no answer. I decide to press on. I gather my nerve, then open his door and walk inside. I look around his room. There is broken glass on the floor, Rizzio's things are strewn all over the place, and the whole room is a mess. What I am most surprised to see is Rizzio cowering in the corner. He is lying on the ground, curled up in a ball, shaking and weeping.

My initial reaction is to run to my friend, to comfort him and soothe him. But then I remember why I am here, and my sympathy dwindles. I walk over to him, that same pit in my stomach that I have had all morning. Rizzio, whose eyes have been slammed shut, peeks up at me. Relief dawns on his face.

"Oh Mary, Mary!" he rejoices. "Thank God!"

"God is not present for this." I answer as rage fills me. I am so ashamed to see him like this: weak and trembling on the floor after his betrayal. It is I who should fall apart. Not him.

For the first time, Rizzio really looks at me. He gulps as he sees the fury on my face. "Mary?" he asks meekly. "I'm sorry, Mary. I had thought you were Darnley, come back to finish the job," he confesses.

Rizzio's words confuse me. What does he mean 'come back to finish the job'? Does he expect Darnley back? Do they plan on sinning again? I feel the anger rise in me once more.

"You will address me as Your Majesty from now on," I say with spite in my voice.

Rizzio is taken aback. His face drops and tears begin to fall from his eyes. I think that it has now dawned on him exactly how much I know because he falls onto his knees and weeps at my feet.

"Oh, my darling queen. No, no, you must forgive me," he begs. "It is not what you think."

I do not want to hear any of it. I came here for a simple explanation from my supposed friend as to what had happened this night. I do not wish to listen to his pleas for forgiveness. His tears only make me feel angrier. It is obvious that something terrible has happened here but all I can think in this moment is 'why should he cower and cry before me when I am the victim?'

"I am the one who should be crying, Rizzio. Not you." My voice is full of hatred. "I want a simple answer. Did you or did you not sleep with my husband?"

Rizzio begins sobbing so loudly that I can barely make out what he is saying. "It's not what you think," he says over and over again. "I was not myself."

"Answer the question," I demand. I am cold. I can feel it. All the love I have felt for him is being held down by the great betrayal I feel.

Rizzio pulls himself to his feet and wipes the tears from his eyes. After a deep breath, he composes himself and tells me what happened. David's truth is different than the picture Darnley had painted me. Darnley had come looking for Rizzio. He had been drinking and wanted someone to pick a fight with. Rizzio instead had thought back and demanded to know why Darnley had struck me. Darnley played his usual trick on Rizzio and broke down into tears. He told him all of the lies he had told me about how he cannot control himself when he drinks, or how his anger gets the better of him after a few glasses of wine. He apparently confessed to Rizzio his deep affection and love for me. He hated himself for hurting me and wanted Rizzio's help to make things better. Of course, Rizzio thought he was helping me by agreeing. So

Darnley began plying him with drink after drink. Every time Rizzio finished cup, Darnley was next to him with another.

"It got to the point where I could barely stand, I was so drunk." David continues. I remember Darnley taking me by the arm and offering to help me to bed. Next thing I know is we are in bed together and Darnley is undressing me. I had no power to say no to him. I had no strength to stop him as he began to make love to me . . ." Rizzio drops his head into his hands and begins to weep uncontrollably again. "Mary, how I have betrayed you. I am so ashamed."

I soften towards him as he recounts his story. I know how it feels to have Darnley on top of you. He leaves you no room to get away. I can see that he has also been controlled by a man skilled in master manipulation. As my anger towards David eases, my anger for Darnley reaches new heights. I despise him for what he has done to me and my friend. He truly is vile.

"I must have fallen to sleep, because the next thing I remember is Darnley's fist in my face and a threat that if I told you anything, he would kill me. I thought for sure he would not tell you himself."

I cannot believe how skilfully he had planned and played both of us. My friend and

I have been pitted against each other for the benefit of one man.

"I believe that we have both been used here, David. Darnley has used you and abused you for his own petty whim," I tell David, who is clearly weighed down by the guilt of the situation. "I wish he were dead. I wish that I would never have to see him again. Not only has he hurt me, but he has destroyed someone I love. He has soured our affection for each other. He is a wicked man with a wicked agenda, and we have been played like pawns."

David reaches over to me. "He has not ruined us completely?" he asks softly.

I am thoughtful for a moment. Can I really turn my back on someone who means so much to me? I am still hurt and angry. David was attacked and violated by Darnley. I cannot be mad at Rizzio for this, he is a victim. Darnley has taken advantage of his kind nature just to hurt me. I will not hold David accountable for what has happened tonight. However, I do need a bit of time to arrange my thoughts.

"Give it time, David." I pat him on the hand. "Time heals all."

"Well, at the very least, you stopped calling me Rizzio." He smiles shyly.

I say my goodbyes and leave. I cannot stand to be in that room any longer, knowing what had happened there. I will hire extra guards for David; I don't want Darnley to attempt to hurt him in any way. For now, the morning is in full swing, and courtiers are beginning to leave their rooms, ready for the day ahead. I must plaster a smile on my face, a convincing one, and pretend that I am the happiest queen in the world, even if I feel like I am crumbling on the inside.

Chapter 26

Over the past few weeks, things have fallen into a miserable routine. Any humanity or goodness that was in Darnley has been completely erased now, and we are left with the monster. There is not one single bit of kindness left in him. His face has lost its youthful beauty and is now replaced with a constant, twisted look of hate. His every word is full of venom and spite. His voice, which was once soft and sweet, now sounds like that of the devil himself. He snarls and barks orders at me. He talks to me as if I am scum under his foot and not his wife.

Whenever he is near, my stomach twists in uncomfortable knots. A voice sounds in my head over and over again: *what have I done?* I have married a mad man, a man so full of hatred and loathing, so blinded by rage that he cannot see anything bar the next drink. And now I must live with my decision. I cannot divorce him. My Catholic faith prevents me from truly considering the idea. I cannot send him away and admit to my nobles that I have made a mistake. I cannot flee and escape to safety. I cannot abandon Scotland and all that I have sworn to protect. I must face the fact that I am in a loveless, abusive marriage, and there is nothing at all that I can do to escape. My only hope is that Darnley drinks himself to death. That will be the day I am finally free of him. Finally free of the constant attacks. The constant bruises left on my body. The constant sound of his vile words ringing in my ears. "You're nothing, Mary," he taunts daily. "France didn't want you. Scotland does not want you. And I don't want you."

I no longer feel the cut that his words are meant to inflict. I no longer feel the pain as his fist bears down on me. I no longer feel much of anything. I have totally given up on trying to make him better or trying to change the person he is at his core. I do not talk sweetly to him anymore or bother to say much of anything. When he first started changing, I hopelessly looked for glimpses of the man I thought I loved. I desperately wanted to find in him a saving grace.

Now, I realise that he has none. He is pure evil through and through. He was born wrong. He was not created by God but by Satan, put on this Earth to bring misery to everything he touches. Morning and night, I sit in my chapel and pray that God sends me an answer. I pray that he shows me a way out of this marriage. I hope at the very least, he gives me some guidance on how to make my life more bearable.

Darnley has stayed true to his word about wanting to make an heir with me. The only time I see him now is when he creeps up the hidden staircase and into my room every other night, the slow, clumsy descent from his room to mine. I have begun to loathe that staircase, with its winding darkness and creaky steps that signal Darnley's approaching. I hate him. God, how I hate him. I never thought that I could hold so much distain for a person, but the burning rage I feel every time he is close to me is undeniable. His voice makes the hair stand up on the back of my neck. His presence makes me feel sick. The hate I feel for him is as strong as the love I felt for Francis. It is undeniable and eternal.

He climbs the staircase from his bedroom, which is below mine, and into mine, unsteady on his feet and mischief in his mind. When he enters the room, the way he looks at me is enough to knock me dead on the spot. He is so full of anger and bitterness. It is unnatural the way he climbs on top of me and expects me to give into him, the way he takes what he wants from me again and again. I have gotten to the point now where I let him have whatever he wants. I no longer argue or plead to be left alone. The easier I give in to him, the quicker he is slinking back down to his bedroom. I am not sure if he even enjoys the act or if he simply enjoys the control he holds over me.

As he uses me again and again, I close my eyes and picture a time when I was unbelievably happy. I think back to a time when Francis and I made love and it was the singularly most spectacular experience I have ever had. With Darnley, it is rough. It is rushed. With Francis, he took time to worship the whole of me. He kissed me and touched me softly. Darnley pins me down and refuses to look me in the eye. Francis would whisper sweet words of love into my ear. He would tell me how much he loved and adored me. Darnley has taken to calling me a whore.

I feel no better than a whore when I am with him. I live for his pleasure alone. He hits me on occasion. When I make up my mind to tell him no. When, for the briefest moment, I regain my confidence and tell him to leave me alone. When I have had enough of his breath, pungent and stinking of alcohol, on my face. When I cannot stand his hands being on me one moment longer. Or when the very thought of his being on top of me makes me want to vomit.

I had news for him earlier tonight. I thought it would make him happy. I thought it was what he wanted. It does not make me happy at all. It makes me even more fearful. It scares me that I am carrying something created by a monster. If it were with Francis, I would weep with joy. But with Darnley, I simply have more to fear. I have more to protect now. It is not simply my life Darnley's violence will threaten, but that of the life that grows within me. I found out just days ago that I am with child, and I have been waiting for the right moment to tell Darnley, hoping that it would stave off one of his attacks on my body. I had expected a little relief from him, but instead, it made him red with rage.

"So now I have to share you with someone else?" he fumed. "I have another to compete with for your affection?"

His answer caught me by surprise. He has visited me every night so that we may create a child, and now he does not want it. If he thinks the way we treat each other is affectionate, then he is more deranged than I realised.

"This is a good thing, Darnley. We will have an heir." I smiled weakly.

"You will have an heir, and I still do not have the crown I want." He practically stamped his feet like a spoiled child.

"You are king. What more do you want?" I asked, already knowing the answer.

"I want an obedient wife," he fumed. "I want to be given what is rightfully mine."

"You have already taken all of my joy from me. Do you now suppose I should give you my life? Do you expect I am foolish enough to grant you the one thing that would secure my end?" I asked, not having the strength to argue any longer.

"No, wife. I expect you to be clever and give Scotland over to someone more capable of ruling."

"So you do not deny that you want rid of me?" I spat, anger rising in me.

"Nothing would make me happier," Darnley growled.

"Get out!!" I screamed at him, anger finally taking over. "You know that I could have your head? The words you speak are no better than treason."

"Careful, wife. We don't want any harm coming to the bairn you carry within you." Darnley smirked as he left the room.

Something about the last thing he said has stuck with me. It was said like a warning. It was not said out of care for the life within me; it was said as a threat. The way his face twisted into a grimace, the way his voice became low and taunting—Darnley wanted to scare me, and he has succeeded.

***

I should feel overjoyed. I should be at my happiest. Finally, my belly grows as it holds my unborn son. Finally, I will have an heir for Scotland and England. Finally, I am stronger than Elizabeth. However, it is not joy that I feel. It is sadness. I should be bringing my child into a world filled with happiness, a world where he has a father who loves him. I should be carrying Francis' child within me. Instead, I carry the child of a man who beats me for sport, the child of a man who sleeps with my friends for revenge, a man who is so twisted and insane that he cannot tell what is real and what is not.

There is a part of me that does not want this baby at all, a part of me that wishes I were not pregnant. This little life inside of me has no idea of the hate he was conceived in. I worry that I will not be able to love this baby as much as I would were he mine and Francis, that I shall look at him and regret his existence. He did not ask for any of this, to be placed in the womb of a woman so broken inside. I want to feel the happiness of having my own child. I want to feel the joy that women who is pregnant often feel, but I am filled with dread. I do not know the extent of Darnley's jealousy. My son is in danger before he is even born.

I had thought that my pregnancy would stop Darnley from visiting me at night. I had also hoped that he would treat me with a bit more care now that I am carrying his child. However, I have been proven wrong again. His abuse and nasty behaviour only seem to get worse. I must admit that I believe he would be happy if I lost the baby. As my bump grows, his distaste grows. I am lucky that the baby I hold within my body is still safe and sound.

***

I am now five months pregnant, and my stomach bulges beneath my gown. I have had to have all of my corsets loosened so that they now accommodate my growing size. I have heard from many other women that pregnancy was a joy to them. They loved every moment of having their child grow inside of them. I, however, have found it to be troublesome. My back aches day and night, keeping me awake till morning. My feet and ankles swell and complain if I stand for too long. My chest burns at night as the baby moves restlessly inside of me. The sickness has been unbearable, as I have been able to keep very little down. I have stopped enjoying some of my favourite dishes and instead find that I fancy sweet treats all of the time. My cooks are constantly busy making pies and pastries to sate my appetite. I am tired all of the time and find I have lost the patience for things like council meetings and state occasions. Whenever we dine as a court, I am usually forced to retire early when the tiredness becomes too much.

I am a little over halfway through this pregnancy, and already I find I cannot bear the idea of another four months. I am happy in one way: happy that I shall soon have an heir that I hope will not only inherit Scotland from me but will also take his rightful place on the English throne. No matter the distaste and hate that I feel for Darnley, he has, at the very least, provided me with the one thing I need to ensure the success of my rule here and in England. I have spoken to Elizabeth a lot of late. She seems to have forgiven me for my marriage and now wishes us to pursue a sisterly relationship. I know that she cannot be happy with the news of my pregnancy. Although she offers me nothing but congratulations and appears to be pleased for me, I know just how scared she must be. A son born of mine and Darnley's combined bloodline is a threat to her and her rule. When my son is born, there will be no question of his claim to the English throne. She knows now that my stake is strengthened, and as soon as my son is born, I will have more to give to the English people than she does at this moment. I believe that her nicety is a ruse, meant to keep me on her side if I should have a healthy child. For now, I keep her sweet, knowing that I hold all the cards in my hands.

I see Darnley very little now. While I am bed bound with our child, he does as he pleases. I hear many rumours of the many women he has lain with, and of his drunken escapades. I care little for any of them. He may sleep with whoever he chooses; there is no marital love between us, and I am incapable of feeling jealousy towards him.

Davey quickly returned to my good graces. He was so ashamed of the incident, and I found that I could not stay mad at him for very long. Davey was as in control of what Darnley did to him as I am. Besides, he has been a great help during my pregnancy. He keeps me company when I am bound to my room and always brings cakes from the kitchen with him. Darnley is still jealous, of course, but I no longer hear a word he says.

Chapter 27

9th March 1566

I am still shaken to my core after the events of the last twenty-four hours. I can still see the crimson blood drip from my hands, which have not stopped shaking since this nightmare began. I can still hear the shrieks as they escaped my friend, still hear my ladies' cries for mercy. I can still feel the ache in my chest as my own screams broke free. I am alone for the moment, bar the guard that they have put on my door to stop me from leaving. I sit on the edge of my bed. At my feet, a puddle of dried blood. In the corner, a discarded dagger. Clutched in my hand is a small piece of fabric torn from the shirt of a man who thought I could save him. A man who mistakenly put his trust in me. I have held this little piece of fabric since the moment he was viciously pulled away from me, his arms around my waist, his eyes pleading for my help. All I could do was look back at him, knowing that, for once, I was powerless. The fact that I am queen meant less than nothing. When I close my eyes, I can see the face of each and every man who was in my room last night, their cruel, taunting faces as they dared to defy me.

Ruthven. He was the leader of this group of assassins. He relished the fact that I was defenceless. Raulet. Cowering behind the others as if he were ashamed of his part. The Douglases. The brothers, the two Williams. Heads held high and gleam in their eyes. I cannot name them all—there were too many to count—but I shall remember each and every one of their faces.

Although the guilty stood before me, I cannot help but blame myself for this. I could have done more. I could have saved him. Elizabeth would never allow her subjects to control her as mine have. They would not have dared test me were I a king and not simply a weak woman. My sex has let me down once again. I cannot tell you why when they thrust their daggers into my dearest friend, I stood frozen on the spot, unable to move in his defence. Why I did not fight my way out of Darnley's grip. Perhaps I realised in that moment that I had a choice to make. I could risk my own life to jump to David's defence, or I could save the life of my unborn child. As Darnley held his pistol to me, I had to choose myself and my child's lives over that of a man I have come to think of as family.

Darnley's is the face that haunts me the most. He would have me believe that he was nothing but a pawn in someone else's game, that he was forced into playing his part. But I know the truth. I could see the wickedness in his eyes. I could see the sick joy on his face as the life slipped from David. I have known for a long time that he is a monster, but I had little idea of the extent of his sickness. Last night, I saw exactly how far he will go in his quest for power. As he held me in his arms, his mouth to my ear, whispering for me to stay calm, I could hear the happiness in his voice. He knew that he had won and that I would not fight back. He is evil in its truest form. He will pay. They all will. But if I swear one thing in this life, it is that Henry Stuart will pay for what he has done.

Last night, as I sat down to dinner with Davey and my ladies, Darnley and the other conspirators climbed that vile staircase that has brought me so much agony over the last year. None of us had any idea what was happening until we saw Darnley come through the door of my private supper room. The music and laughter were so loud that we had not heard the footsteps on the stairs. At first, he was the only one I saw. He stood in the doorway, grin on his face and arms open for an embrace.

"Mary, come to me," he said with a smile that would have once charmed me. Of course, he was drunk. That much was obvious from the way he slumped in the doorway. When I made no move to go to him, he stepped into the room, and that was when I noticed there were others gathering in my room. "Everything is going to be all right," he told me. "Just do as you're told."

A collective gasp broke from my ladies and me as we realised that there were close to one-hundred men now gathering in my bed chamber. Ruthven, at the head, stood in full armour and looked self-important, with parchment in his hand. To begin with, I believed that they had come for me. That Darnley had finally swayed the nobles to his cause. My heart began to pound. My head spun, as I was sure in that moment that they were here to murder me, to dispose of me and put Darnley in my place. They wanted to remove me and my unborn child. Darnley would have no competition if we were gone. I stood ready to order them from my sight. Ready to fight back. But I was quickly hushed by Ruthven.

"Majesty, I must apologise for the lateness of the hour and the darkness of our task. However, there is a snake amongst us that must be rooted out." He betrayed himself, as his voice shook ever so slightly.

"My Lord Ruthven. Nothing must be done that I have not ordered." I tried to keep my voice level, but on the inside, I was terrified. These men had clearly come here to try to harm me in some way. They had banded together and come up with some terrible plan to hurt their pregnant and defenceless queen.

"All due respect, Majesty, we could not trust you with this," he continued, full to the brim with pompous pride. "I have an order in my hand, one that has been scrutinized and signed by each man in this room." Ruthven handed me the parchment. "As you can see, my lady, we are here for David. It has been decided that he has offended your honour, and it is because of this that we must remove him."

David, who had been silent until then, moved to stand behind me. I could feel him shake as he placed a hand on my shoulder.

"Remove me? Mary, what do they mean?" David asked, panic rising in his voice.

I could do nothing but stare hopelessly at my friend as I read the order on the document in front of me. They meant to kill him. This parchment was a death warrant signed by everyone, including my husband. I tried to remain calm, not wanting to scare him. "David, I will handle this," I said simply. "David has done nothing to offend my honour. He is a dear friend to me. I will not allow this," I ordered.

"You have no choice, Mary," Darnley finally spoke. "It is done." A smirk played at the corner of his mouth.

I felt anger rise in me like bile, a sickness in my stomach as I turned to look at my wretch of a husband. I have never felt rage like it as I saw his smug face.

"And I suppose this is your doing, Darnley?" I demanded. "Has jealousy gotten the better of you again? Are you still worried that you are not man enough for me?"

Darnley was seething as his face turned red with rage. "My doing, Mary? My doing?" He took hold of me. "Make no mistake, my love, this is your doing. You sealed his fate the moment you conceived his child."

I was too stunned to answer as Darnley's accusation hit me with full force. Pregnant with David's child? So that was the extent of his madness. He was deluded, and he had deluded these men into believing him. I do not know what I could have done to change his mind at that point. He was so convinced that I had lain with David that nothing could have swayed him. I am not even sure that he believed it the first time he accused me. I think he has made the story in his head and said it so many times that to him, it seems real. He really is a confused young man suffering from many hallucinations. I would almost pity him, did I not hate him so much.

"Henry. You and I both know that this is not true," I said as my anger rose. "Perhaps it is your relationship with David that you would rather keep quiet." I held his gaze.

"Mary . . . please don't . . ." David whispered from behind me. It would be just as damaging to him if word got out about their liaison, however much choice David had at the time.

"Madam, I am sorry, but nothing you say will change what we have come here to do," Ruthven pressed on. "Now please hand over the accused."

I hated the way that he spoke to me. All respect and formality had been removed and I was treated like a commoner holding a fugitive. I knew for certain that the moment I had my chance, Ruthven would find himself locked in a cell. I hated all of them. Each one of them forcing their way into my bedroom to threaten one of my friends—it was unheard of, and I would not stand for it. They looked to ignore my crown and take advantage of my sex.

"Ruthven, I do not know what exactly has empowered you to talk to me in the way you are, but I will not stand for it," I said. "As for David, he is under my protection."

"Majesty, we will take him with or without your permission," Ruthven replied.

"Mary, come to me. It will all be over in a moment." Darnley moved closer.

"No! No. You will not do this," I practically cried. David, who was still stood beside me, shook and wept with fear. "David, I swear to you that I will protect you. These men will not hurt you." I took his hand. I knew I was wrong as I saw the shadows of the men who were drawing closer around me. I held David's gaze, trying for a moment to give him even the smallest amount of comfort.

And they lunged at me. It all happened so fast. One moment I was clinging to David, and the next, they grabbed him. Darnley pulled me into his arms. He stroked my hair and kissed my head. His touch made me feel unclean.

"It's okay, darling. Everything will be fine," he said through bared teeth.

"Get off of me!" I screamed. "Darnley, I swear, you will pay if you do not let me go now."

My ladies shrieked around me as each of them was roughly handled by the men in my room, all of them held back and defenceless.

"Mary, help him!" Fleming cried.

Ruthven and his men dragged poor David into my bed chamber, and it was there that they read out the document to him. He never looked away from me for one moment. I smiled weakly. I wanted to reassure him that everything would be all right, although I already knew that it wouldn't be.

"David Rizzio, you are accused of the sin of besmirching our queen's honour. As such, we in this room have decided that you must be sentenced to die." At that moment, each man in the room pulled out a concealed dagger.

Panic took over me in a sickening wave. My eyes blurred, and my body began to shake.

"Does he not deserve a trial?" Mary Seaton demanded.

"Not today," Darnley answered.

With that, Ruthven plunged his dagger deep into a wailing Rizzio's side. "Mary, help me," he pleaded.

"No!" I screamed. I wriggled in Darnley's arms, trying to get away from him and to my injured friend. "Unhand me now!"

A second dagger was then stuck into David as he screamed from the impact. This blow was delivered by Raulet.

"Stop. Please stop," I cried. I tried to fight Darnley off. I kicked him and tried to claw my way out of his arms. I caught him by surprise for just a moment and was able to run to my friend. Where David lay, blood started to spill out, leaving a puddle on the floor. There was still life in him yet, and he clung on to me. His eyes were filled with such sadness and betrayal. Some of the men in that room were his friends. Some had just recently had dinner with us.

I placed my hand on his wound, not knowing what to do but hoping to stop some of the bleeding. "David. My dear friend, I am so sorry." The tears fell freely down my face. "What have they done to you?"

David did not speak. I only managed to steal a brief few seconds before Darnley was behind me and pulling me to my feet. I stood but did not let him hold me. I tried to form a barrier between myself and David. I tried, uselessly, to protect him.

"Darnley, come near me and I swear I will kill you," I screeched. But as I looked at him, I realised that he was holding a gun pointed directly at me. "Darnley?" I asked, confused. Was he truly foolish enough to threaten my life?

"Come now, Mary. Unless you want the life of your unborn child to end here," he said wickedly.

I realised in that moment that my fight was over. I looked at David, who stared up at me from the ground, pleading for me to save him, and my voice dried up. How could I tell him that I had to give up? I reached down and took his hand. "Forgive me, my friend."

I allowed Darnley to take me. He held the gun against my chest, but I did not fight anymore. I could not choose any life over that of my child, even one I love so dearly. I closed my eyes and was surrounded by the screams of agony.

Each man then took it in turn to thrust their daggers into David. The Douglas brothers stabbed him multiple times in unison. The joy on their faces was unbearable. I turned around, unable to look any longer at the scene before me. My ladies continued to kick and scream, but I knew that it was too late. It was too late after the fourth wound. David had since lain motionless on the floor as the men continued to plunge their daggers into him.

"Darnley, quick. It is your turn. You must deliver the final blow." I heard shouted behind me.

Darnley, who held me in his arms, shook like a coward. The scene was too much for him, and he had to close his eyes. He is a pathetic, weak, and vile little man who could not go through with the task he started.

"Go on, Darnley. Do it," I spit. "Finish the deed you started."

"I . . . I ca-can't do it." He shook uncontrollably.

"If you will not, then I will." Ruthven snatched Darnley's dagger and made the final stab, straight into David's heart. "There. It is done," Ruthven said. "Darnley is as guilty as the rest of us."

I finally broke free from Darnley, who was reduced to tears like a little child.

"I swear I shall have you all killed for this," I screamed. "Get out! Now!"

They did not argue with me anymore. They just left dragging David's body with them. I just could not stand to look at them after what had just happened. Each of them reminded me how I had just failed in the worst way. Darnley hovered nearby. He made no attempt to speak to me at first. I stood and walked over to him. He was shaken and nervous, the weight of his part heavy on him.

"You are truly the most vile, wicked man that I have ever had to suffer." I spat at him. Before I knew what I was doing, I raised my hand and slapped him hard round the face. The shock on his face was indescribable. He was white as a sheet and shook from head to toe. He cowered away and went slinking from the room like the snake he is.

Alone, I fell to the floor where David had lain, the tears escaping from me in great heaves, the images of the last hour repeating over and over in my mind, the image of David's lifeless body at the forefront. The room seemed so small now. There was no air. No life. I opened my door, wanting to escape, wanting to find some solace away from there. However, I was stopped on my way out. These men, now fearing for their lives, had placed a guard at my door. One of my own men, Jeremy, who had served me for the last few years, refused to allow me to leave my room. In this moment, I realised how little it meant to be a queen. It would not save me now, not when I was surrounded by disloyalty.

***

It is now the next morning, and I have sat in the same place on my bed for the last six hours. I cannot bring myself to move. I sit and stare at the floor, the image of David still so clear in my mind, his blood beginning to stain the wood of my floor. In the last few hours, I have seen our friendship play out in moments in my mind: from the moment he introduced himself to me, the times he made me laugh, to the nights he would sit up with me until morning, talking of Francis and all of the heaviness in my heart.

How have I gotten to this point? How has God been so unkind to bless me with the light of two angels, only to rip them away from me? He has taken my light and left me down here to fight off the demons. I am so weary. I feel as if I have finally lost any will to carry on or to try to make any light of my life. I feel as if my race to the end has now begun. The quicker I get to my last day on this Earth, the better. I will never again meet another person who compares to the two of them. I have had my joy, and I have been unable to hold onto it.

I feel just like I did when Francis left me: utter emptiness and despair, the longing to see someone who is no longer here.

I honestly believe that Francis sent me David. I believe that he was a gift from heaven, that Francis wanted me to have some comfort in this world. He was my twin flame, just as Francis was, but in a different way. Whatever their souls were made of, they were cut from the same beautiful cloth. I am truly alone in this world now, forced to walk this path by myself. I am not strong enough to do that, to survive alone. No one should have to survive alone.

I feel so cold. I feel scared. What if these men decide to finish the job? What if they realise the only way to ensure their safety is to now remove me? I look down at my hands that still shake uncontrollably, and I ask God why. Why has he put me in this position, only to torment me throughout my life? Why was I born to be miserable, sat in a room where someone I love was just murdered before my eyes? I wretch and fight to hold back the sickness that rises in me as the images of David's murder play out before me. The great sadness in his eyes and the look of betrayal as I left him to the wolves.

Did Darnley ever intend to hurt me? Or was it a game to fool me into giving in? I could have saved David? If I had just listened and spent time away from him, then Darnley would have never been angry enough to kill him. But those other men? How did he convince them to join him? What other lies did he make up? I do not believe that, however wicked Darnley is, he is clever enough to have concocted this whole thing on his own. I could see in his eyes the way it made him feel. He has no taste for murder. He may have thought he did, but when it came down to the gruesome task, it was all too much for him.

When Darnley came to my room in the middle of the night, head hung in shame and mouth full of false apologies, I did not even flinch. A deep pit of anger raged inside of me, but I stayed silent. I want him burned at the stake. I want his head. I want him to suffer the most agonising death imaginable. And it is the hate I feel for him that keeps a small fire burning within me. I will make him pay for this. It will not be today. Or tomorrow. Or even a month for now. But the day will come when he will feel my wrath. Today, he took the one good thing from my life. Francis was taken from me by God. That I could not control. David was taken by the devil, and I will have my revenge. And that revenge will be sweet. I will continue to live on the promise that I will one day ruin Darnley.

My mind must now focus on one thing: survival. If I sit here and allow the numbness to take over, then I may find myself at the wrong end of their daggers. I have to fight through the pain and the agony so that I may live for my child. My ladies have been allowed to return to me, and I have told them what I intend to do. I may despise Darnley, but in this moment, he must be an ally to me. I need him. He is the only person who can save me now, whether I like it or not.

I wait patiently for him to come slinking back to my room. For once, I am happy to see that he is drunk. He will be easier to control this way.

"Henry, love, sit down. You must be weary," I say, walking over to him and taking him into my arms. My whole body practically convulses as I touch him.

Darnley is confused. He looks at me with suspicion as I smile and play the part of the doting wife.

"Mary? I came to beg your forgiveness again," he slurs.

"Oh, no." I smile. "You don't need to apologise," I say through gritted teeth, trying to conceal my hate.

"I don't?" Darnley asks, startled.

"No, sweetheart," I say, fighting back the bile in my throat. "I know that you had no choice. Those cruel men forced you to hurt David."

Darnley is thoughtful for a moment. I can practically see the cogs turn in his mind.

"You know I would never do a thing to hurt you . . ." he begins, sheepishly. "And Ruthven has had an issue with David for a long time now."

Coward. This man is an absolutely repulsive coward. He has seen a way out of trouble and has leaped at it. I play along, knowing that one day I will see him pay for all of his deeds.

"You are just as much a victim in this as I was," I say, holding back the words I truly want to say.

"You mean it, Mary? You do not blame me?" Darnley asks. He is like a small child seeking praise after misbehaving. "I am sorry that I held you back. I did not want you to be hurt."

"I understand," I answer. "Of course I do not blame you. It is the others that will pay for this," I lie again. "However, I do worry, my love . . ."

"What about?" Darnley asks.

"Well, Henry, I think we may both be in danger," I explain. "You see, they fear me because they know I have grounds to execute them. And they may fear you because you know too much."

Darnley thinks about it for a moment. He is so pompous that I do not think he even humoured the thought that they may turn against him.

"Even if they do not harm you, they will certainly harm me . . . and our son. Without me, you will never be king," I say. Each word is calculated. Each word I know will affect him.

"They would never hurt you. You are queen, Mary. That guarantees your safety."

"Does it?" I ask, losing patience. "Think about it, Henry. If they keep me alive, then they sign their own death warrants. Perhaps they wish to place Elizabeth on the throne of Scotland. She is Protestant, after all."

Darnley practically falls in a chair, his head in his hands. He takes a breath before answering. He is now realising exactly how dangerous the situation is. I have hit the mark finally.

"You're right," he answers. "Jesus, Mary. What have I gotten us into?" He begins to weep.

I hate to see him cry. It reminds me exactly how weak and pathetic he really is. He has gotten us into this, and he will be the one to save us.

"There is a way you can get us out of this," I bait him. "It may be dangerous. But I think if anyone can do it, you can."

"I will do anything, Mary."

“We need to get out of Holyrood, Henry,” I begin, “as soon as possible.”

“I can get us out of here. Give me some time, and I will arrange everything.”

Chapter 28

After our escape from Holyrood, with the help of Arthur Erskine and Anthony Standen, two men who have been loyal throughout my reign, we first rested in Seton Palace for a few days before moving on to Dunbar castle. It was clear from the moment we arrived at Dunbar that we had the support of many. It took us no time at all to round up enough forces to take Holyrood back. It has not been easy playing the docile wife in order to keep Darnley sweet, but it has paid off. The rest of the conspirators have fled, fearing for their lives. Quite rightly so. I would murder them myself given half the chance. However, I have had to be clever. It would do me no good to put to death half of my privy council, and with Ruthven in hiding, I am just glad that I do not have to put up with him any longer. Darnley is foolish, I have allowed him to share my bed with me. I have allowed him to eat at my table, all the while knowing that I simply wait for the right time.

He behaves himself for the time being. I can tell that he is afraid of what may happen to him if I decide to be less forgiving. Now that most of the conspirators are gone, fearing for their lives, I am able to return to my rightful place in time to have my child.

I did not return to Holyrood straight away. The idea of going back to my rooms where Davey was brutally murdered turned my stomach. To see his blood still on the floor, to hear his screams in my ears—it was too much to bear. Instead, I took up residence in one of my houses on the mall. I was secure there and away from the horror of Holyrood. However, I had to return. I had my attendants move my things to another room in the castle. I could not sleep in that room.

Yesterday, I sat in my rooms for a short while. I sat on the floor, next to the spot that still holds the crimson splash of blood, and I spoke to my friend. I told him how sorry I was that I could not save him. How much I missed him. How agonising life is without him. I just hope he hears me. While I sat, I felt that familiar breeze on my cheek, the one that told me Francis was close by. I heard his voice in my ear again, barely a whisper, but his voice still. *Be strong, my love. All is well.* It instantly soothed me. It told me that David was safe. He was being taken care of. I lay my hand across the place where he fell, and I made a silent promise to avenge his death. No matter what it took.

***

Today, I made a decision, one of the hardest I have had to make in my whole reign. I officially pardoned Darnley for David's murder. This may seem like a strange decision, one that proves me disloyal to my dear friend. However, it is quite the opposite. I keep Darnley close so that one day, when he least expects it, I will ruin him. For now, it is the safest option. I need a husband by my side to ensure my safety on the throne. While Darnley is a monster, I must suffer him so that my son and I are protected. In any case, I have no proof that he was involved in the murder. He never actually stabbed David with his own hand. I have no evidence to convict him. The truth will come out, I am sure of it.

***

This evening, I returned to my room alone. I had sent my ladies on ahead so that they could draw me a bath to ease my aching back. I was halfway up the stairs when I was unlucky enough to come across Darnley, who, again, was drunk. I had not seen him all day and had yet to tell him of my decision. In hindsight, I should have never picked an argument with him, but seeing him blind drunk and happy made my blood boil. I had dropped the pretence of a happy wife when we returned to Holyrood.

"You will be pleased to know that I have pardoned you for your role in Davey's death," I said as he passed me.

"Oh, Mary! Thank you." He grinned. It made me sick. "Thank you for believing me."

"Officially, at least. I will never forgive you in my heart."

He turned to face me, face red with rage. "There is nothing to forgive. I am innocent," he said.

There was that shiver again, that icy cold warning that signalled danger was near. Francis was warning me to keep my guard up. If only I had heeded that warning.

"I know this was your plan, Darnley," I spat, anger overtaking me. "I do not have proof yet, but the moment I do, I will ruin you."

"Ruin me!" he shouted, taking hold of me by the shoulders. "You think I am scared of you? A pathetic little woman?"

"Just as I am not scared of you. You can do nothing to me anymore."

"Perhaps I should finish the job?" he threatened. "Perhaps I should kill Rizzio's spawn too?"

"As much as I dislike the fact, the baby that grows within me is yours," I replied through gritted teeth. I could not believe that Darnley was jealous of Rizzio even after his death. "You are pathetic and weak. You have no right to walk on the same ground that David tread."

Madness took over Darnley instantly. His face morphed into the devil I was so used to. His jaw clenched together tightly, his eyes narrowed, and his brow creased. He threw me to the bottom of the stairs, where I landed on top of my now huge stomach.

"What have you done?" I cried, stunned as I cradled my stomach. Pains ran through me. How could he hurt the child that grew within me? Our child. Was he seriously so deluded that he actually believed the baby is David's? Has he seriously convinced himself that I committed adultery with David?

"Let's hope that his legacy ends here," he hissed.

At that moment, I heard footsteps as someone drew closer, and then, thankfully, Lord Bothwell turned the corner.

"My queen?" he asked, shocked. "My lady, what's happened?" He ran over to me, panicked. "What have you done?" he shouted at Darnley.

Darnley, managing to look ashamed for just a moment, turned on his heel and ran away, proving to us both that he truly was a coward.

"Your Majesty, what has happened here?" Bothwell asked.

"I fell. Nothing more," I lied. "The king was just trying to help me."

"Your Majesty, I have been in this place since you returned from France. I have seen the way the king treats you. You do not have to lie to me. We are friends." He smiled reassuringly.

"He just loses his temper sometimes," I replied. "Ouch."

"Majesty?"

"I am afraid he has hurt the baby," I said as my stomach cramped. "I need to see my doctor."

"Let me carry you to your room, my lady." Bothwell lifted me into his arms.

"Mary. You have come to my aid tonight. Call me Mary," I say.

As Bothwell carried me back to my room, I felt safer than I have in months. As he cradled me next to his chest I allowed him to comfort me. I felt protected. He took me to my rooms and sent for the doctor, who has since left after reassuring me that the baby is perfectly healthy. I allowed myself to feel a small relief knowing that Darnley's wicked plan did not succeed. However, Doctor Barlow has told me that I should start my bed rest early if I want to keep the child safe. I agreed wholeheartedly, hoping that I would be safe from Darnley in my room.

***

Bothwell, or James as I have now begun to call him, has been wonderful. Since the last incident with Darnley, he has stationed himself outside my door and sworn that he will allow no harm to come to me. Darnley is too full of shame to visit. This time, he has spared me his usual apologies.

My liking for James has grown over the past few weeks. He often comes into the room to see how I am doing and will sit with me to while away the long hours of my bed rest. When Fleming is not at her station reading to me, James takes over. He has been a great comfort at such a hard time in my life. He hates Darnley, that much is clear. He told me that if he had had the chance, he would have killed him the night he murdered Rizzio. If only it were in his hands. I wish James had been there. Things may have been different. The baby moves about in my stomach now, telling me that he is close to greeting the world. I only wish he could stay there longer, where I could keep him away from his evil father, but the time is coming close, and I must prepare to become a mother.

Chapter 29

18th June 1566

My pains started in the small hours of the morning. As I slept, I was awoken by what felt like a tearing pain in my stomach. When I cried out, Fleming was at my side in an instant.

"Mary?" she asked, still half asleep.

"I have cramps in my stomach," I answered.

"Oh," she replied, and then her face lit up when she realised what that meant. "Oh! The baby's coming!" Ladies, the baby is coming!" she shouted, waking the others.

As everyone began to rush around me and the midwife was called, I began to panic. I had never done this before, and for so many women, this was a death sentence. What if I was not prepared? As the pains got stronger, my nerves grew. I have never felt anything like it. My Marys stood around me, anxious to meet the little prince. Fleming never left my side for one moment as she gripped my hand.

As the pain ripped through me, I cried out, begging for God to have mercy on me and end the terrible labour that I was suffering. But it persisted. All day and all night, I was forced to endure the agony of childbirth. My midwives began to worry when the next day dawned and still the baby did not arrive. The pain was tight across my stomach as it throbbed. Wave after wave, the pain wrenched through me. It was so severe that it made me vomit at one point. I was desperate for it to end, as with each passing moment, it got worse.

"Is there no end to this pain?" I cried aloud when I could take no more.

"Stay strong, Mary," Fleming soothed me. "It will not be long now," she said as she dabbed my forehead with a wet cloth.

I managed to sleep a little in between the pains, and when I did, I dreamt of Francis. He had come to tell me he was proud of me and that although this baby was not of his blood, he loved him as if he was our child.

"I am tired, Francis," I whispered into the depth of my dream. "I want to give up."

"Never give up, Mary." He took my hand. "I know that this is not the end of your story."

I awoke with a shriek of pain as another contraction ripped through me. They were worse now, stronger than before. Jane, my midwife, rushed over, hot towels on hand, and examined me.

"Any moment now, Majesty," she said. "You need to start pushing. I can see the bairn's head."

I took a breath, and with every last ounce of strength I had, I began to push. The pain that tore through me was almost unbearable. I think I must have broken Fleming's hand as I gripped her with every push. I ached like I had never ached before. My back stung and my legs shook terribly. I breathed through the pain, but it was almost too much. I felt sure that this labour was going to be the end of me.

It went on for another hour before Jane finally announced that the baby's head and shoulders were out. I cried out as I forced one final push and the baby was pulled from me. For a moment, the room was silent as we all held our breath. And then, with a piercing sound, the baby began to cry. My ladies began to weep as the midwife wrapped the baby up in swaddling.

"It is a boy, my lady," Jane said as she placed him into my arms.

As my ladies wept and the midwives beamed, I looked down at my newborn son and felt nothing. I was sure that it was just exhaustion that made me feel empty. I felt a relief, at least, in knowing that he was a male. However, I did not feel that instant rush of love I had been told about. I felt empty. And then I felt ashamed of myself as this tiny babe lie in my arms, gazing up at his mother for the first time, waiting for me to love him. This little baby has been born into a world that does not deserve him. I do not deserve him. And as vile as this is to say, I do not want him.

***

For the next week, I am bed bound. The labour was a fierce one, and I have to rest. The baby is brought to me throughout the day so that I may spend time with him. My ladies dote on him. They absolutely adore him. When they pass him to me, still I feel nothing. He is a sweet little thing, and he looks up at me with such love in his eyes. Yet those eyes are not mine. His eyes are his father's, and as he looks at me, so innocent, so pure, I see the evil that he was created in. I want to love him. With every ounce of my being, I want to adore him, but I do not feel the bond of a new mother to her son. Perhaps I am every bit as evil as his father.

I have decided to call him James, for his grandfather and his uncle. Things have not been easy between my brother and me, but I know that he will protect my son with every last breath in his body. He visited yesterday, and when he held little James in his arms, his eyes lit up.

"He is bonnie, sister," he said as he smiled down at my tiny son.

"I will name him James," I replied, weakness still taking over me.

"You honour me, Mary," James exclaimed. "Our father would be proud."

"Do you really believe that, James?"

"How could he not be? Look at the stunning woman you have become." He smiled.

***

I permitted Darnley a visit after that. He does not deserve it, but to save face, I allowed him a brief audience. He picked James up and cradled him in his arms. He looked down at the child with a gleam in his eyes, a look of love which I had never seen on him before.

"He really is mine, isn't he?" he asked. All it took was one look at James to see they shared the same blood.

"Of course," I answered.

"Mary, forgive me . . ."

"I will hear none of it, Darnley. The only time we will speak from now on is where James is concerned. Apart from that, you are less than nothing to me."

"Mary, I love you," he pleaded.

"You are incapable of love."

***

As James grows, he looks more like his father every day. I spend little time with him, not wanting the hate I feel for Darnley to be projected onto him. I am so desperate to love James as I know I should, but so much has happened that I cannot let my guard down. He spends most of his time with a wet nurse while I return to my duties. I do enjoy the time I am with him. He is such a happy child, and he coos as the ladies all fuss over him. He is perfect. I just wish I could love him as he deserves.

James, Lord Bothwell, has now become a permanent member of my entourage. I find that there are not many people I can trust, and he has proven himself over the last few weeks. My council do not like him because they do not like anyone who challenges their opinions. He has become a protector to me, keeping me safe from my husband. Darnley refuses to come near me while James is by my side, and it makes me feel safer than I have in a long time.

Chapter 30

The feeling of being betrayed by someone is like no other. The feeling of being betrayed by someone who claims to love you is even worse. It is like a hole opens and swallows your whole world. This person has claimed to love you and care for you yet has done nothing to prove that. And now they have taken a dagger to your back. That is exactly what Darnley has done to me. I allowed his disgusting behaviour to continue for too long. The moment I realised the true darkness of my husband's betrayal was the moment I realised I could never trust anyone ever again. I have found out the true depth of the evil that lies within Darnley. He is sicker and more twisted than I have ever realised, and it makes me nauseous that I could have married such an inhumane creature. He is the reason my dearest friend is dead. The reason I am alone. He is the reason I cannot love my son in the way he deserves.

Just moments ago, the truth was finally revealed to me. The truth that I knew but could not prove. The truth that my husband's part in my dear Rizzio's murder runs deeper than I knew. He would have me think that he was nothing more than a pawn, that he was badgered and bullied into taking part in the gruesome deed. But none of this is true. I have seen with my own eyes his signature at the bottom of Rizzio's death warrant. It is in Darnley's own hand. His part was premeditated.

His jealousy has ruined him. I cannot bear the sight of him as he continues to act as if he is king, bashing his way around the castle, drink in hand and smug look on his face. The hate I feel in my heart at this moment is stronger than any love I may have had for him. I feel sick with grief for the friend I've lost and for the man I thought I once knew. Darnley is nothing but an illusion for the demon that lives inside of him. He is a duplicitous devil without a conscience.

My love for Darnley has been long buried under the mountain of distrust and abuse. Not one ounce of feeling for him remains. He has been erased from my heart in the most definite of ways. I wish him dead; I will not lie. I have pictured his demise a thousand time over in my mind. If only I could have him executed. It is what he deserves, and yet I refuse to murder my husband, no matter how rotten he is.

The anger that fuels me almost succeeds in stopping me from seeing the bigger picture. I must fight the rage within me and keep a level head. I will simply order him out of my home, out of my presence, and out of my mind. I will keep his son from him. The last thing I want is for my son to learn from him. He may keep his title as my husband, but he will only be such in name and nothing more. He will be less than nothing to me now. He can live out the rest of his miserable days alone and unloved, as he deserves. His stone-cold heart will be the only thing to keep him company, and when he wakes in the night, drenched in sweat and full of remorse for all of his vile acts, he will have no one there to comfort him. Our son will grow up to know that his father is nothing. Darnley will know how it feels to be truly alone in this world.

This afternoon, I took great joy in banishing him from court. He will spend the rest of his days in Kirk o' Field. I explained to him that he will never again look upon me or his child. I have not had the strength to do this before because I was so scared of the consequences, but now, no one can question my motives. He cannot hurt me anymore, for he has lost all power that he once held over me. For the first time since discovering his true nature, I do not shake from fear in his presence, nor do I back down and allow him to have the upper hand. I stand strong and firm. This is my country. I am its queen, and he is here only at my pleasure.

He begs and weeps, of course. He is pathetic, and now I have the full measure of him. Now that I have learned the extent of his madness, he can no longer hold any horror for me. He falls to his knees before me, begging my forgiveness and denying all involvement, but he does not fool me any longer. The bitter hate that has taken hold of my heart now will not allow any pity for him. I detest him in every way. His tears only make me boil over with anger.

"Rizzio lies cold in his grave while you can continue your miserable existence. Just be glad that your Stuart name saves you today."

"You cannot threaten me, Mary. I am king," he snarls at me, though I can see the fear in his eyes.

"Are you willing to stay and put that to the test, Henry?" I do not back down. "Stay and see what becomes of you, or go and live your days always watching your back. You can fear me now as I for so long have feared you."

He is speechless as I keep my eyes locked on his. For such a long time, I have avoided eye contact from fear of aggravating him, but today, I feel emboldened. I could not save Rizzio, but I can punish the man responsible for his death.

"What about my son? You cannot keep him from me."

"You're lucky that *my* son is the only thing being taken from you today. Now go before I change my mind."

As he rides away from Holyrood tonight, I feel free. Free from the grips of a madman. Free from the guilt of David's death. Free to live my life without fear of my husband. I do not care what happens to him now, as long as I never have to hear his name uttered again.

***

Now that Darnley is away from the castle, I have felt better about spending time with my son. James grows bigger every day, and as he grows, so does my affection for him. While I still do not feel the motherly attachment I believe I should, I enjoy my time with him very much. He is a sweet child who always has a smile for me. His face lights up whenever I visit him in the nursery, and it warms my cold heart a little each time. He loves me unconditionally, that much is clear. If only he knew of the battle inside my heart.

Chapter 31

In Bothwell, I have found a true and trusted friend. I had thought that after David, I would never again find such companionship, but with James, I find I can confess my soul. He has taken to being my main confidant of late, and I have found myself admitting many painful truths to him. I did not ever believe that those confessions would go further. It seems, however, that James is a very literal man. He has taken my late-night ramblings as gospel and put them into action. I am absolutely terrified of what future may lie ahead of me now. It is possible that my words have solidified my downfall.

Just a few nights ago, I allowed my emotions to get the better of me, and I broke down in front of James. I told him about everything that Darnley had inflicted on me: the bruises, the beatings, the adultery. I confessed the truth about his relationship with David and the way Darnley forced him into committing sin against me. For the first time, I allowed myself to talk about the vile details of my marriage, how Darnley had not only destroyed me but tarnished the one good thing in my life.

James grew angrier as I told my tale. With each beating I described, each fist to the face, each forced sexual encounter, his face grew red with rage as I spoke of the times Henry would pin me down and force me to submit. Usually, I would feel uncomfortable sharing such intimate details with someone, but something about James put me at ease. Somehow, after all the heartache I have endured, I found myself able to trust him.

It would be the next confession, however, that would set in motion the events of the last few days that would implicate me in a deadly plot. It may still cost me my crown, my kingdom, and possibly my life if I do not tread carefully.

"How can you suffer this man? Surely you have grounds to execute him?" Bothwell raged.

"It is not so simple. If he were any other man, I would have him banished. I would have his head. Alas, he is king, and I refuse to execute a king," I explained. Of course, I had imagined having him arrested many times, but the uproar it would cause would shake Scotland to the core. I could not do that to my already fragile country, no matter the hate I felt for Darnley.

"But Mary, he has abused you. He has beaten you. He has murdered your closest friend. How can you let that go?" James asked, shocked.

"I do not let it go. I bide my time. One day, I will have my revenge. I just have to wait," I said honestly.

"Surely you wish him dead?" he asked. "I want him dead."

"Of course I want him dead," I answered. "With every fibre of my being, I wish him dead. He has taken a broken woman and fixed her, only to break her again. The hate I feel for him burns inside of me like an inextinguishable fire. The only way that fire will ever burn out is for him to die in a fit of agony. There is a part of me that longs to watch his life slip away, as I watched the life slip out of David. You cannot begin to understand the pit of anger inside of me. I want him to rot in a hole for all of eternity," I confessed, anger taking over.

"What's stopping you?" Bothwell asked.

"I have already told you. Darnley is practically untouchable."

"I could kill him for you?" James asked. He said it so casually, as if it were nothing more than a simple favour.

"That is a dangerous thing to say," I warned. This could be deadly if anyone were to hear us.

"No one would have to know. I could snuff him out while he sleeps," James continued. The crazed look of hate in his eyes scared me.

"It's not a good idea, James. Please heed my warning."

"At least admit one thing to me."

"Fine. As long as you promise to leave it alone afterwards," I agreed.

"I will," he answered. "You would be happy if he was gone?"

"Nothing would bring me more joy."

If only I had known then that those words would be the beginning of my end.

10th February 1567

Darnley is dead.

Darnley is dead and I cannot believe it. At the age of just twenty-one, he has lost his life, leaving me husbandless for the second time. Leaving my son without a father. I am not sorry. Usually, the loss of one's husband is a traumatic experience, but living with him was more traumatising than losing him. I do not even feel sad for my son, who will grow up without his father. I feel relief that he will never know Darnley or be influenced by him. James is a blank canvas on which I will paint him the way I want him to be. He will grow up without the sickness that haunted his father.

When I was first told the news, I was in shock, but as it settled in, I allowed myself to feel relief. He is gone, and I am free from his torment.

***

Early this morning, I was awoken by a panicked Seaton as she shook me frantically to wake me.

"My Lady. My Lady, wake up." She was hysterical.

"Mary, it is early. What's the matter?" I asked in a daze.

"There was an explosion at Kirk O' Field." She explained.

I instantly sat bolt upright in bed, shock gripping me. "An explosion?" I asked, suddenly alert. "What happened?"

"We are not sure yet, Majesty. Men have gone to look now."

My mind began to spin. Was anyone hurt? Was Darnley hurt? I needed answers. I climbed out of bed as Seaton woke the rest of the ladies. I had them dress me and made my way to the council chamber, where James and other council members were gathered around, waiting for me. The severe looks on their faces told me that something terrible had happened.

"Majesty." They said collectively and bowed. They all looked exhausted, having been woken from their beds at two in the morning.

"What exactly has happened?" I asked. My mind was still reeling.

"Sister, sit down." James gestured to a chair.

"I am quite all right, James," I replied. "Now will someone tell me what is happening?"

"I am sorry to tell you, Mary, the king is dead," James said. His voice was low, his head bowed. He avoided eye contact with me as he spoke. He sounded solemn although I imagine he felt no sadness at Darnley's demise.

"What?" A nervous laugh escaped me.

The men looked at me with eyebrows raised. My reaction was not what they had expected. I think they expected me to break down and cry, but I could do nothing but stare at James in disbelief.

"Dead? Darnley?" I asked. "He can't be."

"I am afraid so, ma'am," Robert Moore answered. "His body was found a little way away from the explosion."

"Was anyone else hurt?" I asked.

"One of your husband's grooms was also found dead, Majesty," he replied. "The strange thing is, it does not seem as if the explosion killed them."

My head spun. Darnley was dead, and now I was being told that it had nothing to do with the explosion. What else could have caused it? Surely, if there was an explosion in Darnley's lodgings, then that was the culprit.

"Whatever do you mean, Moore?" I asked, confused.

"He was strangled, Mary," James cut in. "It is clear that Darnley was murdered."

"Murdered?" I asked, stunned. "Who would dare murder the king?"

James was silent for a moment, seemingly considering his answer. The men looked around, eyeing one another suspiciously. The truth was that there were many people with a motive for killing Darnley, but who would be foolish enough to murder the king?

"We will investigate. Rest assured, the guilty party will be found. It seems that the explosion was a ploy to cover the culprit's tracks."

"I want every man you have on this." I regained my composure, realising that I had a part to play.

"Of course, Majesty." James took my hand. "Is there anything you need?"

"I just need to be alone," I answered, desperate to have some space to think.

***

Once back behind the closed door of my rooms, I let out a sigh. Darnley is dead? It is terrible of me to admit that when James told me, relief washed over me, the thought that Darnley could never hurt me again prominent in my mind. It is cruel of me to find good in the death of someone so young, but with his end, I feel a weight lift off of my chest. No one deserves to die in such a terrible way, but I cannot help but think that this is God's repayment for Rizzio's stolen life. Darnley has repaid with his blood.

The knowledge that my son will never have to bear the presence of his father is a weight lifted from my chest. James will never experience the pain of being connected to a man like Darnley. We are both free of his devilish grip.

However, even in my relief, I am conflicted. I loved Darnley once. I have shared my life and my bed with him, and now he has been wiped from the world. Did he ever choose to be filled with such wickedness? Or did life teach him that? Was he born with the devil inside of him? Perhaps, it was a sickness that he had no control over? It is a sad end to a miserable life. He was so afflicted by his demons that he never stood a chance, and now he is doing penance for his deeds.

Although I will not grieve for Darnley, I will grieve for the life of a man just twenty-one years old. A life that could have been so much more. A life that was tarnished by the devil. I will have to mourn Darnley publicly. I now need to put a face on for the court, the face of a grieving widow. While I feel a relief in my heart knowing that he will never hurt me again, I will have to look to the world like a woman longing for her husband.

***

I have been back in my rooms all of an hour when there is a knock on my door, and I open it to find Bothwell. I make to call for my ladies, not wanting us to be alone together, but he hurries me inside. He seems strange tonight. He is on edge and frantic.

"What is the matter, James?" I ask, alarmed. "You know we should not be alone, especially at this time."

"I have done it, Mary. For you. I have finally done it," he says hysterically. He looks crazed, and it is unnerving.

"Done what?" I ask, lump rising in my throat.

"I have taken care of the problem."

"What problem? James, you are confusing me," I say, exhaustion hitting me.

"I have done it for you. I have taken away your pain," he says, taking hold of my hands. "I have saved you, Mary."

"James . . ." I say as realisation starts to dawn on me. "Are you responsible for what happened tonight?" I ask, not wanting to believe it.

"Darnley will not hurt you anymore."

Why did I not realise before that Bothwell is the man responsible for Darnley's death. It all makes sense now. Panic begins to rise in me as fear of what this may mean becomes clear.

"You have murdered the king?" I whisper. "James, how could you do that?"

"I want to keep you safe."

"All you have done is make me privy to the murder of my husband." I am filled with anger. "You cannot murder a king, no matter how wicked."You told me that you wished him dead," he snaps. "I have only done what I thought you wanted." Quiet, or you will get us both killed," I hush him. "I told you that in confidence. It did not mean that I wanted you to strangle him to death."

This could kill us both. If anyone gets wind that Bothwell was responsible, they will link it back to me. There is already whispers about our close friendship, and I cannot risk myself or my son.

"Does anyone else know?" I ask.

"No, just a trusted friend."

"You need to leave. This never gets found out, and you never speak a word of it. Do you understand?"

"Of course, but Mary, are you not happy?" he asks.

“How can I be happy? You have murdered my husband.”

Chapter 32

If only I knew that Bothwell would spark the beginning of my end and the series of events that have led me to where I am now.

It started out as nothing more than a rumour, a hushed word spread on the lips of my court. Yet somehow, that rumour has grown far out of my control. Everyone in Scotland is convinced that I am responsible for my husband's death. Even my own brother thinks me capable of such an act. They have no proof, only theory. However, that theory has been more than enough to spread suspicion throughout my country and tear apart the little trust I held with my court. And now, I stand on the cusp of losing my kingdom and my child.

It took only a matter of days for suspicion to spread to Bothwell, and then, eventually, to me. His groom, the man he had enlisted to help him with the job, had been found at the scene when men went to investigate. There is also a suggestion that Bothwell supplied the gunpowder. As for me, it is no secret in my court that I did not like my husband. Many had heard the vicious rows and witnessed the volatile behaviour. As gossip goes, it did not take the court long to lump Bothwell and me together. Our friendship was not a hidden one, and word spread quickly that I had recently travelled four hours to visit him at Hermitage Castle. Soon enough, the court had decided that we were having an illicit affair.

I, of course, observed forty days of mourning for my husband, knowing it was what the court would expect. However, it seems as though I have been unable to convince my court that I mourn for Darnley. I have been accused of being insincere in my grief. My brother James warns me that many believe me to be happy that my husband is dead. The truth is, the longer I am away from Darnley's shadow, the more relieved I feel that he is no longer here. Happy? Perhaps not. I would be happier if suspicion were not cast on me. Relieved? Yes. He will not be missed by me or James.

Bothwell was accused and put on trial for Darnley's murder, but with little proof, they were unable to find him guilty. The irony is that I know he is the one responsible.

My life as I know it now resembles little of the life that I lived all that time ago in France. I have spent the last few months shunned by my court for something I am not responsible for. They have no proof, but it does not stop them from talking.

Wanting to be as far from the lies as possible, I fled to Linlithgow for some time, hoping that some space from court would allow the talk to die down. It was nice to be away from the prying eyes and accusing stares, but a queen can only be away from her court for a short amount of time.

I left Linlithgow and began the journey back to Edinburgh. However, my ladies and I were met on the road by Bothwell and his men. He had supposedly come to warn me that there was trouble waiting in Edinburgh, but for some reason, I did not believe it. He seemed to still have the same crazed look in his eye that he had the night he murdered Darnley. He insisted that I travel to Dunbar Castle with him for my own safety. I refused at first; whatever trouble waited for me, I would deal with it. But he was insistent.

When I suggested that he come with me as my protection, it became clear that he was not going to take no for an answer. He took me by the arm, not caring that his men and my ladies were watching, and told me that I had no choice. His men had surrounded us, forcing us to follow.

His intentions became clear very quickly. From the moment we arrived at Dunbar, he was like a predator ready to pounce. He said he wanted to marry me, that he had been in love with me for as long as he could remember. But Bothwell is not in love with me. He is but another man desperate to take my power from me. I know this because he has tried.

Late that night, he came to visit me in my rooms and demanded that I dismiss my ladies. Mary F was reluctant. She was the one person I had confided in about the true depth of Bothwell's guilt. But there was nothing I could do. It was clear that we were being held captive in this place. I would be stupid to anger him.

He told me again that he wanted to marry me, that one way or another, I would submit. I was adamant that there was nothing he could do to change my mind, and that was when he attacked. He lunged at me, kissing me on the lips, kissing me on the neck. His hands ran through my hair roughly. I screamed for him to get off, but the more I squirmed, the more he held me down.

"Do you give in?" he breathed.

"No!" I screamed. "I will never give in."

"What you do not give to me freely, I will take from you."

It was in that moment that I realised I had been fooled again. I had fallen victim to yet another man and his quest for power. As Bothwell pinned me down and ripped at my bodice, I knew that I had to give up any hope I had left in me. I stopped fighting back. I had little care for my body; it was my soul I must protect. As Bothwell pried my legs apart, I did not push him away, nor did I scream for help. I let him have me. As he placed his lips on mine, I allowed him to kiss me. I lay there as still as if I were dead, and I let him have what he wanted.

It was not rape. I let it happen. I allowed him to make love to me. I did not fight when he put his hands around my throat and squeezed. I did not stop him from roughly turning me over and pulling at my hair. I did not weep as he finished and climbed off of me, as if I were nothing more than a paid-for whore. I did not argue when he told me that I would have to marry him now. He could use me, abuse me, tear my body to shreds. I cared no longer for what happened to me in this life.

As he held me down and had his way with me, I had one image in my mind: Francis, the one person who has never failed me. Even in death, he has stayed true. As Bothwell took advantage of me in the worst way, I had one word in my ear, one word that I know came straight from heaven. *Soon.*

***

Many judge me for my next decision, but none of them know the true details of what happened. After Bothwell's advances, I was left with little choice but to do as he wished and marry him. This is the way men play for power. They take advantage of a women knowing that she will be left with no other choice but to marry them. That is what Bothwell has done to me. He has taken my power away. He wants Scotland, and I have no fight left to keep it from him.

A few weeks after my capture, it becomes clear that Bothwell's plan has worked perfectly for him. I realised that I had missed my courses and after seeing a doctor we realised that I was carrying his child. He was overjoyed to learn that he had impregnated a queen. I only felt more miserable. I was carrying another child, by a man I did not love. This child would be another born in hate and not love.

Scotland is angry, her people need no further proof that I am in part responsible for Darnley's death. I have now married the man they believe responsible. When James wrote to me, furious at my choice, I felt less than nothing. The country is in uproar and I do not care. I do not care for the life that grows inside of me. I do not care for my crown or kingdom. I do not care if I shall live another year.

***

I could say that I am devastated, that life has again shown me all of its cruelty. I could fall to pieces and despair at the treatment that I have again been shown. However, I do not feel despair. I do not feel sadness. I feel nothing. Life dealt me the worst blows when it took Francis and then David. Anything after that is meaningless. I have not seen my son in months. I have been trapped here at Dunbar Castle against my will. I have been assaulted repeatedly and forced to marry my attacker. And now my stomach begins to grow with another child from another monster.

Death is the only answer for me now. I say that with complete certainty, knowing that death would be a blessed relief. I would kill myself and end my misery if I did not believe so fiercely in heaven and hell. I know that if I were to end my life at my own hand, God would punish me, and I will do nothing to stand in the way of the future I have in heaven.

When I was young, I thought that nothing could ever dampen the hope I felt so keenly. Now, hope is completely lost to me.

***

I have had to stay true to my husband. I cannot allow the child I am carrying to be a bastard. I do this for the life that grows inside of me and not for myself. I will happily live in this misery for the sake of my child. However, that was not good enough for my nobles, who no longer accept my rule. They wish to unseat me from my position and avenge Darnley's death. Most of them could not stand Darnley, so it is funny to me that they are so set on punishing Bothwell. I have so far refused to back down. I will not give in as easily as they wish. They sent an army to capture me, and Bothwell went out to face them.

Bothwell and I marched with our army to Carberry hill, where we waited to meet the rebel forces. Thankfully, there was still a few Scots loyal to their Queen, and we were joined by the Hamilton's and several trusted lords making our number a little over two thousand. Unfortunately, the traitors had an army just as large.

The opposing Lords approached us from Musselburgh, carrying with them a flag with the image of Darnley's death embroidered on it and the words "Judge and Revenge my cause, O Lord.". They had a message to deliver, and they were not leaving without 'justice'. I felt the nerves grow in my stomach as I saw the immense number of my supposed subjects pile up to fight against me. I longed to tell them that I was forced into this, to tell my brother that I had nothing to do with Darnley's death and that I just wanted to return to Holyrood without Bothwell, but it was hopeless. No one cared for what I had to say any longer. I had to see this through to its conclusion.

At first, we attempted to negotiate terms. After all, there was no need for men to lose their lives if we could settle this peacefully. I will always choose peace over anguish. However, the Confederate Lord's were out for blood. "We will fight the king's murderer." The Earl of Morton demanded.

They tried to draw our army out, but Bothwell quickly held them off by firing cannon at them, which made them fall back. He then offered to take on any one of the men in single combat. For the first time, I appreciated his baldness. Battle's were a gruesome thing. The day was scorching hot, and my men were thirsty. With single combat, this would be over quickly. However, when Kirkcaldy accepted his challenge, Bothwell refused to fight against someone as lowly as a Baron. Then he also refused Lord Lindsay and James Murray of Tullibardine. His arrogance always got the better of him.

The day was long and hot. No one made a move to attack. Instead, we stayed at a standstill as the hours slipped away. The rebels pushed for surrender and declared an oath that I would be protected should I agree to lay down my arms. When Edmund Blackadder and Laird Wedderburn made their apologies and left the battlefield, it became clear to me that Bothwell would not be far behind. I should have known that someone as self-centred as Bothwell would never put his own life in danger. As he turned and fled like the coward he is, I knew that I had little choice but to surrender.

He took my hand as he left. "Mary, I am so sorry. For everything. I hope you find it in you to forgive me."

"I hope you rot." I spat.

Why is it that I have surrounded myself with cowardly men? Darnley was weak and pathetic. He exerted his power over women but shrunk back when faced by men. Bothwell was happy to talk big but turned on his heel when the challenge was too great. Men are so convinced that they are the stronger sex, yet it is the women who truly carry them.

I accepted Kirkcaldy's terms and allowed him to lead me down the hill to where the Lords waited for me. I had expected to be taken in cordially, but I could not have been more wrong. The men were angry, and now that Bothwell was gone, I would face their wrath.

"Burn the murdering whore!" they exclaimed.

It all became too much for me, and I toppled from my horse. Kirkcaldy caught me and carried me the rest of the way. They led me through the streets of Edinburgh, which were lined with spectators. There was not one kind face in the crowd. I could hear them as they screamed and shouted for my death.

"Murderer," they taunted.

"Burn her!" another shouted. "The Queen of Death!"

My ladies wept as they looked upon the violent crowd baying for my blood. Never has a queen been treated so disrespectfully as I have.

"Are we going to Holyrood?" Mary B asked one of the men.

"No. You will never see Holyrood again," he answered.

I sincerely believe that he was telling the truth. I will never see Holyrood again.

Chapter 33

24th July 1567

The Lords broke their word that no harm would come to me. I was taken from Dunbar Castle to Lochleven Castle, where I have been a prisoner since. I have asked to see my son and have been refused. For all the anguish I felt at his birth, I have missed him greatly. Eleven long months I have been here without one word of comfort from anyone. I never thought that I would see the day that I missed Holyrood, but honestly I long to be within her walls now. Holyrood is a comfort compared to the cold island that Lochleven Castle sits upon.

For weeks, my traitorous advisors have tried to convince me to abdicate my throne. Of course, I refuse to give up my birth right. I am queen of Scotland until the day I die. They tell me the best thing will be for me to sign a document revoking my right to the throne and live out the rest of my days quietly. I fight and argue back refusing to ever give in. I say that I will never sign away my God-given right. However, my resolve is weakening. Their constant demands have warn me down. I have thought them back for eleven long months. I long to see an end to my imprisonment.

I have written to my cousin Elizabeth, explaining the details of my imprisonment, and asking for her aid. I had thought that she would stand by me. We both know that my situation is completely unacceptable. To imprison a queen is treason, and if she allows what is happening to me to continue, she is supporting the downfall of a fellow queen. What would that say to her enemies? It would show the world that a queen is not untouchable. She is not untouchable. I did not think her foolish enough to ignore my situation, but it seems although she empathises with my plight, she refuses to send an army. She cannot be seen to stand by a 'husband murderer'.

I tell her the truth is that I did not kill my husband. What I do not tell her is that I have envisioned his death a thousand times. That when he died, I felt joy. I do not tell her that I am glad he is gone.

It seems that now I have two choices: I can sign away my throne, or I can be put to death. While my heart leads me towards the latter, I know that neither God nor Francis would approve of such weakness. Yet to sign away the throne would be to turn my back on all that I know. I have been the queen of Scotland since I was six days old. Scotland has always been mine.

They want to make my son James king. If I agree, am I leaving him to lead the same life I have? Ruler while he is still a babe. In the control of powerful men. All of his decisions taken from him. He has no idea about the world he has come into. Unfortunately, I imagine he will learn very soon.

***

Alas, it seems my options are up, and at last, the wolves are at my door, baying for blood. I must give them a decision. I know what I will chose; I have known for a while the outcome of this situation. It seems that, finally, the people that have so hated me—Knox, Ruthven, even my own brother—have finally gotten what they wanted. A woman will no longer rule their country. They can have Scotland; I see nothing left to love in her. They can take my son and steal his childhood away from me, but they will never take away the fact that I am his mother. And I am the queen of Scotland. No piece of paper will change that. No signed document will ever change that this is my right.

As I finally agree to sign away all that I have, there is an uproar from my council.

"A wise decision, my lady," Moore comments. The council do not bother to hide their happiness.

"Have I already lost the right to be called Majesty?" I ask.

"You have just signed that right away," my half-brother, James, replies.

"And my son? What will become of your namesake, brother?"

"I have already agreed to become regent, sister." James replies coolly.

"So you have already made your claim for power? I hope that James is better than I am at rooting out the evil in Scotland."

"James will not be as foolish as you. You have lost, sister. Heed my advice: it is time to lay down your arms. Your battle has been lost."

"Your advice has always been so helpful, brother," I say pointedly as I leave the room.

***

Bothwell was to deal me one final blow before finally being done with me. The child I held within me is no more.

Late last night, as I climbed into bed, a pain began in my stomach. It started off as nothing more than a small ache, but it soon grew into absolute agony. As I climbed from the bed to call for my ladies, I doubled over in pain. When Mary F and Mary S came to help me, they realised that there was a pool of blood on my bed linens.

We looked at each other, a knowing look on all of our faces. I was losing the baby.

Fleming helped me to a chair, but the pain was too much. I fell to the floor on my hands and knees; the cramps were becoming unbearable. It made me think of when I had James, when I thought the pain would never end. How I had begged God to show me mercy, only now I begged that God show my unborn child mercy. I prayed that he would save the life within me. And yet I already knew it was too late. I knew what was happening, this baby would never take a breathe.

I know the life I carried was created in sin, but I still felt a fierce need to protect it. A mother makes a promise to her child and to God that no matter what happens, we will care for our children. I can detest their father and I can wish that the circumstances of their creation never came to be, but I would never allow any harm to come to them. However, it would seem that God had a different plan. I have failed in my duty. As I lay on the floor, agony ripping through me, and my shift covered in blood, not one but two lives slipped away from me.

Fleming sat beside me on the floor, towel in hand, ready to pick up the tiny baby that I had just lost. She gently picked up and cradled the little thing, and when she showed me, there were two tiny bodies in her hands. They were no bigger than two grapes side by side, so small. So precious.

My heart broke for the final time in that moment as I lay on the floor, shaken, exhausted, and scared. The atrocities of the men that surround me have not only ruined my life, but they had snuffed out these tiny babies before they were even given a chance. How cruel can life be to rip these beautiful creatures from my womb? These two fragile and innocent beings that have lived within me?

It is difficult to say how I feel. In one way, I believe that God has taken them to save them from the evils of this world. That like Francis, they were too pure. Too good to suffer in this world. Yet I cannot shake this feeling of utter emptiness, like something precious has been ripped from me. I feel a longing to have my womb filled once more with their tiny bodies.

It was as I lay on the ground, tears flooding from me and with an agony in my stomach, that I realised what I would have to do. If I stayed here, I would die. Just like my children had lost their lives due to the wickedness of my countrymen, so too would I. This place is volatile. It is cruel and unkind. Death hums from the walls. It is everywhere I look. I close my eyes and see my sweet Francis, lifeless and cold. I see my dearest David, as he lay on the floor in a pool of his own blood. I even see Darnley, lifeless out on a field, half naked, bruises from fingers around his neck. And finally, I see my babies, babies that never had a chance. If they had lived, they would have been born into a world with a loveless mother, a woman so bitter and twisted that she could not feel for them, a brother forced into ruling a ruined country, and men who would find the best way to use them.

Scotland is an impure place. The very island she sits on is cursed. The men that live within her are cruel and spiteful. My biggest mistake was returning to this place. I should have stayed in France. I should have never left the place that nurtured mine and Francis' love. I had expected to find a new life for myself here. I had thought that Scotland would welcome me with open arms, but all she has done is ruin me. She has taken me, chewed me up, and then spat me out again. I know now that I must turn my back on another life. I must escape this place and all of her rottenness.

There is only one place for me now, a place not so far from here, where my cousin sits on the throne. I just hope that Elizabeth stays true to her promise to support me, that she does her duty as my sister queen and helps return me to my rightful place. James can have my throne for a short time. Then I will come back, an English army behind me, and I will show this place what it truly means to be ruled by Mary Stuart.

A Love to End All

Chapter 34

19 years later…
1st February 1587

I do not write today from the comfort of my Scottish throne, nor do I write from the security of an English palace. I do not write in sadness, nor happiness. I write in truth. I write with the real and brutal details of my last nineteen years. It is safe to say that I have suffered through a great number of tragedies in my life. Losing Francis was just the beginning of a long line of loss and betrayal. However, I can tell you in all honesty that as I reflect now, I do so without a heavy heart. I am at the beginning of the end of my long journey, and as I stand on the cusp of salvation, I can do nothing but look back with utter indifference to my heartaches. At the time, they tore me to pieces. But now, as I see the end so clearly, I know that they are nothing more than temporary pain in a temporary world.

I have finally come to the conclusion of my journey. Finally, after years of misery, I can lay myself down and accept my fate. I am exhausted. All fight has gone from my weary bones. I have been imprisoned for nineteen long years. All the strength I had when I first came to England, all the will I had to have my crown returned, has completely evaporated. Even if I did have the energy to rally against my end, I would not fight it. I have no desire to live any longer. I have lived a cruel life filled with misery and little joy. When it was good, it was excellent. My marriage to Francis. My friendship with David. I have known greater love in just a few short years than many do in a lifetime.

When it was bad, it was devastating. I lost the love of my life after only a few short years of marriage, leaving me empty and hollow. That hollowness was only filled when I found a friendship so deep and pure that it mended a small piece of me. Francis was taken from me by God. It was my wicked husband, the devil himself, who ripped David and his friendship from me.

I lived with that Devil. I allowed him to abuse me, both body and soul. I let him hurt our unborn child. Now, he is dead and gone. So young and so wasted. He could have done many great things with his life. Instead, he chose the life of a drunk. I tried to change him, but some people are born wrong. Henry was one of them.

Finally, my marriage to Bothwell. My final big mistake. Another man determined to rule a powerful woman. How foolish I have been to trust the wrong people.

I have heard the phrase "casket letters" spoken about as if I should know what it means. It seems that all of these years later, Cecil and the rest of Elizabeth's advisors have found proof that I had a hand in murdering my husband. I wish I had, for I have suffered a great deal for a crime I did not commit. Whatever evidence they may have for my affection towards Bothwell has been completely fabricated. I did not love him. I had thought he was a friend, but he was just another enemy lying in wait. In any case, I leave all of this behind me now. People can choose to believe what they will. If it is easier for Elizabeth to put me to death because of a fabricated plot, then so be it. I do not judge her.

In any case, these people are gone from this world. I do not know Bothwell's fate. I do not care. I shall never see Henry again. His place is below us.

If I am to be honest, death is welcome to me now. I long to leave this world and its agony behind me. For a long time, I have seen death as a gift—the relief at the end of a harrowing journey. That is all I want now: relief from all of my woes. I want to ascend, leaving all of the tragedy behind me. I have so much more to gain in death than I do in life. I know that behind this thin veil of life, there lies the key to all of my happiness. The people who have departed this life await me in the next. I will once again see my mother, a woman who I did not know well enough in this world. David will stand with open arms to welcome me. Above all, there will be the face I have longed to see for a lifetime. A hand I have longed to hold. Lips I have dreamt of kissing. I know he waits for me. He assured me a long time ago that he would never stop waiting for me. I have always known that when my time comes, I will take my place by his side, and it shall be eternal.

I close my eyes, and I can see it. I can see him, as beautiful and angelic as the day he left me. My Francis. He has waited a long time for me. No amount of time could lessen the love between us. I know that he would wait a thousand years to be able to hold me once more. My life has been lived with a bitter hatred that could destroy the strongest heart. But in death, I shall awaken in love, a love so pure that it will mend all of my wounds. When Francis takes my hand, I will finally be home.

I sleep a little. There is nothing else to do now but wait. I dream of the days when we were young. I picture Francis and me on top of a hill. We lay beneath the stars, just like we did so many times in life. How we loved to pick out each star and give it a name of our own. Francis would say that I was the star that burned brightest in the sky. He believed me destined for greatness. If only he imagined how my rule would truly end.

I can still feel his arms wrapped around me now. It is a feeling like no other to lie peacefully in the arms of the man I love. For such a long time, I have been without that touch, without his warmth surrounding me. I will no longer have to suffer through the winter of my life. We will have thousands more moments like this one, only we shall look down instead. The stars will be close enough to touch, and everything on Earth will be far away.

When I last documented my life, I was still a young and foolish girl. I had given up my throne, my child, and everything that was rightfully mine. I had made the decision to leave Scotland and search for solace in her sister country. I had no idea that the journey I would make on that day nineteen years ago would be my last. Now, I am a withered old lady who is losing her hair and the ability to stand for too long. My Marys, who have for so long stood beside me in solidarity, now hold my hand to stop my aching legs from giving way. They place a wig on top of my head, the same fiery colour that once grew naturally, so that no one may see this famous Queen of Scots waste away before their eyes. It is a sad sight for the once great beauty. The people I have so loved in my past may no longer recognise the woman I have become.

I had thought that after my many years of exchanging letters with Elizabeth, she would prove to be a true and loyal cousin. That although we were separated by our differences, it would not stop her from coming to my aide when I needed her. I had believed not only in our family bonds, but in the bonds that made us sister queens. Sadly, like with so many other things in my life, I was mistaken.

Elizabeth would only prove loyal to me if I were not a threat to her. And although I have sworn many times to honour our friendship, she has a distrust deep within her. Her advisors do not like me. They know that I am and always have been her biggest contender to the English throne. From the moment I stepped on English land, the plots to use me to overthrow her began. Many thought to use me to their own advantage. I was made the figurehead of many plots to overthrow her. There are still many Catholics who wish to see the true religion restored. However, I can say with absolute certainty and honesty that I do not care one bit for the English crown. Deep down, I have never cared. I only wanted to be named heir. And now, even that does not seem so important.

When I first came to England, I did so with the assurance that Elizabeth would protect me. She agreed to meet me, and although I waited for hours, she never came. It seems that instead, I was fooled by her duplicity. She never had any intention of helping me; she had simply laid a trap in which she planned to ensnare a fellow queen. And I, as I have done so many times before, walked into that trap.

To begin with, I had thought that I was a guest in England, but I would quickly be proven very wrong. It was not long before the freedoms I was granted were slowly taken away, and I realised that I was actually closer to being a prisoner than a guest. Elizabeth wrote to me, full of apologies, and explained that the moment the truth of the plots was unveiled, I would be free to go. I wonder if she knew then that she was lying to me or if she honestly intended to let me go.

Of course, at first, I railed against my imprisonment. I was angry. How dare Elizabeth imprison a fellow queen? And one with the same blood as her? Yet, my protestations were useless. I have been forgotten. I was kept at Carlisle Castle, which would prove to be one of the nicest places I have been held. I spent my days ranting and raving. I wrote countless letters to Elizabeth, demanding to be set free. Demanding that she honour our family connection. I was furious; it was yet another person who had failed me. Days turned into weeks and weeks into months, and still I remained unmoved.

My initial imprisonment, in hindsight, was not so bad. I was allowed to move freely about the castle, and my ladies and I could take walks in the garden whenever it pleased us. Our host, Sir Francis Knollys, was a stern man who had made it clear to me from the outset that he did not like me much. Still, he treated me with the respect I deserved. I would ask him two, perhaps three times a day about a meeting with Elizabeth, and each time, I would receive the same evasive answer. "As soon as we get to the bottom of these plots, my lady."

I know now that Elizabeth never had any intention of meeting with me. She simply wanted to dangle me on the end of a string until she worked out what to do with me.

My time at Carlisle Castle was to be brief, although it did not seem so at the time. Two months after being taken prisoner, I was moved to Bolton Castle. At Bolton Castle, I was again awarded the respect of my station. I was allowed to keep a modest household and the freedom of roaming freely. I continued to ask after Elizabeth, and my letters to her became more frequent. Only she would no longer reply to me.

We stayed at Bolton for around eight months, and while there, we were lulled into a sense of false security. All was well. We were not treated like prisoners, but more like important house guests. The only difference was that we could not leave. My hosts were kind. We were allowed to use the castle as if it were our own, only it was not. It was another unfamiliar place far from home.

In the beginning, I was still foolish enough to believe that everything would be well. For some strange reason, I clung on to hope. I believed that one day Elizabeth would free me, and then she would help me retake my throne. I still had the foolishness of a child. I still could not see through the surface and to the heart, where the true evil lies. And then I was moved to Tutbury . . .

We moved to Tutbury on a particularly cold and wet day in January, almost a year after Elizabeth had first imprisoned me. If I never see another place like Tutbury again, it will be too soon. I wrote about it then. It was the last thing I wrote for a long time. It was here that depression truly closed around me.

This place is the perfect symbolism for my inner demons. Its dark and dingy walls represent the darkness of my own soul. I feel trapped within my bad mood as I am trapped inside this prison. It is not hell, but it is not far off. It serves as a personal hell, so far away from all that I love. It makes me aware of all that I no longer possess. It is bleak and only serves to remind me of the terrible blackness that takes over my whole world. It is unloving and unkind, much like a mirror of my own life. By moving me here, Elizabeth has finally succeeded in breaking any fight that I might have had left within me. I long for my days to end. I pray that this is the last dreadful place that I will be kept in in England. I know that by sending me here, Elizabeth is praying for me to disappear, to shrivel up and die here without one trace of me left. She hopes that while I am here, I will be forgotten about. That the people who rally for my cause forget about the queen they hold so dear. In this place, I feel forgotten. I have slipped away to a dark corner of England, never to resurface.

Oh Francis, if only you could hold me now. You would never forget me, would you? I hear his words as keenly as he were still here. "Never, my love." His warmth is all around me at once, his presence felt once again in my moment of need. Today, however, it does not bring me comfort. Today, it is a cruel reminder of all that I no longer have. It is a sharp pain, as I long to have his arms around me but am not granted the one thing I need. He is here, but I cannot feel his touch, the touch that would make all of my woes fade into dust. "Soon." That familiar voice echoes in my ear. But I am left with one thought in my mind as his image fades. "Not soon enough." Although his presence causes me pain, I still feel the dull ache as he leaves me.

It is obvious as grief takes hold of my heavy heart once again.

No one in this place brings me any comfort at all. Even my ladies, with their familiar smiles and warm embraces, hold not one bit of solace for me. I long to feel safe and secure again, to have the loving arms of a mother around me. I wish I could go back to the days when I was young and carefree. When the care of a loved one easily nursed the sickness away. When Catherine would soothe all my ills away or my dear grandmother would sing me to sleep. How unaware we are at such a young age. How at the time we feel as if the whole world rests on our small shoulders when in actuality, life has not yet begun to display its cruel ways.

It was at Tutbury that the ache in my bones began to set in. My body was reflecting the way I felt inside. My ladies tried to comfort me, but we were all weary. For all of my downfalls, they had been right beside me. Mary F with her guidance and support. Mary S with her undeniable way of making me laugh. Mary B, who has suffered the most from the cold, and Mary L, whose optimism and hope have kept us all going at times. But Tutbury broke us all. It was Tutbury where hope came to die. It was Tutbury where I realised that I would never leave England again., whether that be because of the dismal setting or the mood that had befallen all of us. I knew that England was the last stop on my journey in this world.

And now I begin my journey into the next.

***

7th February 1587

I have finally come to the end of my tragic journey. Finally, I can lay myself down and give in to the fate which has been decided for me. I have no fight left in any case. I have been imprisoned for nineteen long years, and I am exhausted. I am both mentally and physically drained in every single way. I do not have the strength to rally against my chosen end. My bones have grown weary, and I find that my legs can scarcely bear to carry my weight. My willpower has left me completely. I neither have the physical strength nor the mental capacity to carry on. I have finally come to the end of my life, the end I have been seeking for as long as I can remember.

I have worn out any use that this world may have for me. I long to die. Death is a gift to me now. Life has battered and bruised me in the cruelest of ways, and I no longer feel the need to prolong it. It has given me little hope or reason to wish to drag out my days any longer. I have so much more to gain in death than I do in life, for on the other side their waits a welcoming party like no other. I will be taken in with open arms and love. I leave only hate behind in this life. A bitter hate that I shall be glad to be rid of.

I will be put to death in hate, but I will awaken into a love like no other. I see Francis' face so clearly now as he smiles. His smile is the warmest I have ever witnessed. It is true and loving. It is just for me. His arms are wide and ready to take me home. I so desperately want to run to him. I feel the pull to him now as strongly as I did when we were together. My life has never been complete without him.

I long to close my eyes and awaken in a world of peace. I have been sad for as long as I can remember. My weary soul can scarcely stand another day. If I could lay down and die here in this moment, I would. If I could cease to breathe and be carried away now, I would want nothing more. I have pulled myself through this life. I have stood strong and tall with each and every heartbreak, but I can do it no longer. I hurt. I hurt from the inside out. I long to be far away from this place. I long to be in France.

I picture Francis and me, happy in his home. We sit at the top of a hill, and we lie beneath the stars. How we loved to gaze up at the stars. He would hold me to protect me from the cold, and we would forget about the world around us. When I pass over, we can have endless moments like that, as many as we want. I know now that I do not have long to wait, at least. I have been told today that my fate has been decided.

Elizabeth, after years of deliberation, has finally decided that the only way to truly feel secure in her reign is to remove me. I hold no anger towards her or the decision. I receive it with gladness in my heart. I smile upon the woman who condemns me. She is doing me a kindness. I will finally leave this Earthly plane and all of the pain behind me. I know that I am ascending to a kinder place where I can finally lay down my losses and begin anew.

The ache in my bones is nothing compared to the ache in my heart, and that heart now has nothing to hold on to. My son is a grown man ruling our kingdom. He is in no more need of me than I am of him. I have learned to live without him as he has learned to live without me. We will reunite one day, I am sure of it. But until then, I have come to terms with leaving him behind. The son I know is the small boy I left all those years ago.

It is time to let go. I leave with no worries for his safety. I leave knowing that he is secure in his throne and will one day unite the two nations of England and Scotland. If I will be remembered for little else than my mistakes, at least I know that I brought the two places together. I will know that because of my son, there will be a peace like none before.

I look around me and see nothing but shadows, memories of a tragic life. I see my brief moments of happiness while Francis was alive, but the rest is complete darkness. It cripples me with despair. I see the faces of the men who betrayed me. I see the face of my son, left behind so young. I see the babes that never were. I see my mother, long gone and unappreciated. I can still see Rizzio. I see as he pleads with me to save him, as he begs with his eyes for mercy, and I see as he is wiped from this world. I see Darnley, young and foolish, an evil man with an evil agenda. I see the pain he caused me in our short marriage. I picture him lying cold on the ground shortly after his murder.

As I look around, the disappointed expressions on the faces of my people fill my mind and the anger from my brother as he lost all belief in me. It is hard to see the light when your life is always so overcast. Nothing since Francis has ever been well. I shut happiness out. I locked my heart away. I never allowed myself to swim. Instead, I drowned.

I am drowning now. The waves consume me. They batter me, and I am never allowed up for air. I no longer wish to keep my head above the water. I want the grief to carry me away now. I care little for survival. It is over. I smile to myself as they tell me of my fate. They must think me mad. As they read the final document, I allow my heart to feel light again. I allow myself to see him again. I close my eyes and revel in the moment. They think me so strange. Others would beg and argue, but I receive the order with a song in my heart and Francis' words in my head. *We will be reunited once more.*

He made me an eternal promise all of those years ago. He promised that he would never leave me. And he never has. I have carried him in my heart every single day. I can hear his voice as clearly now as if he stood beside me. In my moments of grief, I am sure that I can feel his hand on mine. It is a comfort like no other. It has carried me through the years, but to feel his presence is not enough anymore. I need to be able to hold him. I need to be able to kiss him. The only answer for me now is death. I must give in to the blackness and allow this mortal body to fade from existence.

I had a dream last night. For the first time in a long time, I dreamt about Rizzio. It used to be that his murder would be on constant image in my mind, but eventually, it had become less and less apparent. Last night was different. I saw him as he used to be. We did not talk. He simply sat in the corner of my room in a large chair and smiled at me. For so long, I have blamed myself for what happened to him. I have let the guilt of his death weigh on my shoulders. I just know that this was his way of making me see that I should let go of that guilt. He still loved me. He had never borne any ill will towards me. With this, another loose end was tied, and I feel like nothing is holding me back from finding peace.

I feel a slight fear of the axe. I have heard that it is a painful way to die. I do not like the idea of pain in my final moments. If I could change my fate, then I would pass peacefully in my sleep, dreaming of my love. But I have no control over the way I shall depart this world. I tell myself that the amount of pain I will feel will be brief compared to the eternity I am about to embark on.

I do wonder how Elizabeth feels. I do know that this cannot have been easy for her. I do not believe her a cruel woman. I do not think for one moment that she does this easily. She would have thought long and hard and found no other conclusion. Now that there is evidence against me, however fabricated it may be, she has little choice. Her spies have found me to be involved in a plot. I am, of course, innocent, but I feel no need to plead my cause against any of it.

This is the last push for Elizabeth. She must show her strength now. Once I am gone, she will no longer have to worry that I am a threat to her life or her throne. I understand.

And if the roles were reversed, I cannot say that I would do any different. She has refused the advice of her closest confidants for nineteen long years. She can ignore them no longer, especially as they have offered her hard proof in the form of my letters.

It is enough to make me chuckle to myself. As if I have it in me to plot and scheme any longer. I care so little for who sits on the throne.

I do not hold any ill will for Elizabeth. I hold no hate for her. She has done what she had to, and I cannot blame her for matters out of her control. I do not wish to die with hate in my heart, so I choose to let go of the hate I feel. The hate I have for Bothwell, for Darnley, for John Knox, even the hate that I have felt towards my brother James. What is it worth to me? I do not wish to spend my last few days heavy with the burden of hate. I will never again have to see any of those men. Darnley does not wait for me behind heaven's doors. He has gone to another place. I know this without seeing. A man so evil does not belong in heaven. My hate has no effect on him now.

For so long, I have been so sad, so tormented by the past. With news of my death, I feel that I can let that go. Why should I let the chains of this world hold me down any longer? A peacefulness I have not felt for as long as I can remember has washed over me. I have not felt for as long as I can remember.

I lie on my bed now. The men who delivered my verdict have left, and they make preparations now for my execution early tomorrow morning. My ladies weep around me, but I do not shed a tear. I feel as if I have to comfort them. They are sadder to lose me than I am to go. They have been so loyal to me all of these years. I shall miss them. I am so used to seeing them every day. But this way, they can all go on and live their own lives. No longer will they have to suffer through my imprisonment with me. No longer will they have to stand by a queen who makes questionable decisions. They are free, and I only hope they live the rest of their days in happiness.

They all kneel at my feet. Their faces are wet with tears. I tell them not to weep for me. They should weep for the living and not the dead. I do not wish them to hold sadness in their hearts. I know I will see them all again. They are good women who lead good lives. They will be accepted as readily by God as I hope he will accept me.

I have a few things to set in order, but these are all trifles. I wish only to write a will. I want to ensure that each and every person who has been loyal to me receives something to remember me by. I also wish to write to my son a farewell. I need him to know that I am at peace with this decision. I would not feel right leaving this world without one last word to James. I have accepted and welcomed death gladly, and I need him to know that I will be at peace.

There are people who have been loyal to me for longer than I can remember, and I must write to them. I will write to my brother-in-law, Henry, and thank him for his continued support. The Valois loyalty has never failed me. I could weep with joy at the love I have felt from France. My only real regret is that I ever left. France was my home, and nothing since has been able to fill the void it left within me. I only wish that I could see her once more, to stand in the Cathedral of Notre Dame one more time, the place where Francis and I took our vows. I felt closer to God there than I have anywhere else. I would love to once more feel like part of a family, to feel as if I had a mother. Siblings who cared for me. A husband who loved me unconditionally. To see Catherine once more. She meant so much to me.

I wish I was young again. Young, free, and happy. How it would feel to ride again, to sit atop a horse and feel the wind in my hair. Or to dance. I have not danced in such a long time. I hope there is dancing in heaven. I could not dance now even if I wanted to. My legs would buckle underneath me before long. How it felt to dance with a handsome man, to feel as light as a feather as I was whisked around the room.

I was a young, beautiful queen once. Francis and I were a magnificent couple. We were the envy of the French court. I would love to be that beautiful again, for my red hair to fall in waves down my back. My face is now filled with wrinkles in place of smooth skin. My sculptured face is now overly thin and worn. The years of sadness show themselves in my cheeks.

How happy I used to look as I stood across from Francis, the blush of love in my cheeks. Our eyes danced with the passion that we held for each other. I remember how when I used to see him, it would feel as if my soul had floated out of my body altogether. We were in another world entirely. I used to dress in the richest of clothes. The brightest of colours. How I would love to feel like that again. Happy. Unconditionally happy.

I will wear red tomorrow under my dress. My petticoats will be of the deepest crimson, and I will know that I wear them for Francis and for my faith, faith that has never wavered. Even through all of my trials, I have known that God has a plan for me. That plan has led me to today, and I stand on the cusp of my beginning.

How I can still see us so clearly. I have the same flutter of love for him in my stomach as I did then. For a long time, every time I thought of Francis, my stomach filled with dread. I could not escape the pain of his death, and I could not cease thinking about him. When I think of him now, I feel an excitement in my stomach. It is like before we married, when I would be filled with excitement for the next time I would see him. That is how I feel now, consumed by the joy that he is only a day away. My love has never faltered, and it never will.

Oh, how it will feel to be touched by him again. For his hand to stroke my cheek. To feel his breath on my face. His words in my ear. A whisper of *I love you.* It is a moment I have dreamed of since he left. I just wish to be enclosed in his arms again. There is no safer place than in the arms of my love. To see him laugh again and once more feel my soul lighten with complete joy. For his smile to lighten up my entire world. He could wipe away all of the world's woes with that smile.

My heart is light when I think of him. For a time, I lose myself in his presence. I can smell him still. He always smelled so sweet to me, like a rose freshly plucked. I know that when I smell this, he is not very far away. His spirit surrounds me. I close my eyes and let him in. It is the warmest feeling in the world.

My achy bones cease to bother me for a moment. My head stops pounding, and I find that I am calm. The brush on my cheek tells me that he has cupped my face in his hands. The love I feel is undeniable and exciting. My heart races with the need to hold him.

But then the ache begins, the ache of not being able to kiss him, to hold his face in my hands, to stroke his hair. It sets in and he is gone again. I must will myself to carry on just for one more day. One more day, and I will be finished with my agonising journey. Oh Lord, please give me the strength to get there. You have kept me going for so long, and without the faith in you, I may have never gotten this far. Help me through just one more day. A few more hours. Give me the strength to say goodbye to the living and move on in peace.

Everything seems so still this afternoon. There is an indescribable silence that fills both my mind and the air, a sort of calmness that steadies me. My ladies weep around me. Mary Seton, who has been a dear friend to me since we were babies in the cradle, for once cannot contain the pain in her heart. She has always been so strong, always been the strength I need when life has beaten me down, but this is too much for her to handle. She is not prepared to lose me, and I feel my heart break for my loyal friend. She is more a sister to me than a lady, and I hate to see her filled with such sorrow.

She is growing old now, like me. The lines fill her face, as they do mine, and she complains of a bad back. I wish her to be free. I want her to spend the years she has left in service to herself. She has served me so well and almost forgotten to live. She refuses to face me, but I can see the tears gleaming on her cheeks as she stares out the window. I go and sit with her, away from the others, who all console one another. I place my arm around her and feel as she heaves in a great, shuddering cry of pain. I love my Marys so dearly. How can I bear the pain she feels?

"Mary, please do not weep for me." I wipe the tears from her face. "I am not sad at this news. You know how I despair at this life."

She does not move to reply. She sits with her head in her hands. I know that she is trying to
compose herself. I stroke her hair gently. It reminds me of when we were girls and we would play at doing each other's hair. She would put mine up and spread rouge on my cheeks. We would cover ourselves in all of the jewels that we could find and prance around the castle.

"Mary, darling, it is all right. Please believe me. I could not be happier," I explain.

She turns at this, her face confused and hurt. She has never understood my longing to leave this place. She sees it as a betrayal, as if I am doing it because I wish to leave her.

"How can you be happy, Mary?" she asks, a hint of anger in her words. "I cannot rejoice at losing you." She turns her back on me again.

"I do not take joy in leaving you." I take her hand. "Please understand, I am tired. I cannot stand to miss him one moment longer. It has broken me, Mary. You have seen how it defeats me. I just want to rest. I want to rest with him." The tears roll down my face now as the hurt overcomes me. I need her to understand. She is my oldest friend. I need her to accept this, even if no one else will.

"Francis?" she asks, his name a whisper on her lips.

"I cannot do it anymore. I cannot get up each day and feel the weight of his loss on my chest. I cannot plaster a fake smile on my face and continue on with a life that has brought me such
devastation."

The tears begin to dry on Mary's face as understanding dawns on her. "There has never truly been anyone else, has there?"

"There hasn't." I smile weakly at her. "That is not to say that I do not love you or the others. But I
cannot stay for your love when I know that his waits for me." I hold her hand tightly in mine.

I begin to notice that the other ladies have joined us. They sit now on the floor with their legs crossed, like children eager to learn.

"You are certain he will be there, Mary?" Mary B asks. "How can you be so sure of it?"

I think for a moment, but I know the answer almost instantly. "Because a love like ours does not simply go away. Francis told me a long time ago that even death could not separate us. I did not believe him then. Death was so final. But the years have taught me differently. I feel him on every breeze. I sense him in every rain drop, see his face reflected in every star. He is no more gone than you or me. I believe that he is with God, waiting patiently for me to join."

At this, Mary Beaton begins to sob. She sits with her knees pulled up to her chest. Her long hair falls in waves, covering her beautiful face. She is so delicate. So sensitive. I hate to cause her any pain. It hurts me to see her so affected. Each and every one of these ladies has been such a monumental part of my life. I look at each of them. Most try to hide their pain from me, but Mary B cannot contain it. I stand and pull her to sit beside me, holding her gently in my arms.

"Mary, I am so sorry that I have to leave you. Believe me, you ladies mean more to me than you will ever know. But please understand that I have to go." I stroke her hair as she weeps on my shoulder. I doubt that they will ever completely understand.

"I just don't know how you can be so sure," she explains, "why you cannot fight this."

"Because I do not want to fight it. I long to be far away from here, with the man I love. With God. Ladies, please understand. This is not about you. This is not about Elizabeth. This is about me and
my need. I need to rest. I am exhausted from life. You have seen how each day I get wearier. I do not have long left in any case. Let it end here."

"I hope you are right, Mary," Mary F finally speaks.

"I have faith in my God. I have always had faith in my God. I go to the scaffold a Catholic woman, in the true faith. My belief in him has never wavered." I smile at each of them. "Be sure that we will meet again."

"We will miss you so much, Mary. How will we stand it?" Jane asks.

"I will miss you too. But you should be confident in the knowledge that we go to the same place." I wipe my eyes and stand before them. "Now let us spend the night thinking about the good times and not the bad. I will hear no more sadness."

We sit like this for a little while. We talk of everything and nothing all at the same time. We recall our younger days. How much life has changed us over the years. When I was a girl, all I could see
was the future for Francis and me. I could have never in my wildest dreams imagined

that I would be in this place awaiting my execution.

It is strange that we have no control over the path life has set out for us. Was I really born for nothing more than a tragic life full of loss and heartache, or was I here to play a greater part? If so, what was that part? It was not simply to be queen of Scotland or queen of France. I must have had some meaning. I do not believe that God puts us in this world just to torment us. He would have had some greater plan. Perhaps it is my son. Perhaps I was put here so that I may give life to the monarch of two nations. I am sure that one day, years from now, my purpose will become clear. But in this moment, I see nothing more than sadness.

At the end of the night, each of my ladies kisses me goodnight for one final time. All of them bless me as their lips graze my cheeks. They hold back their tears and promise to see me in the morning. This is the moment where I can stand no more. In the cold darkness, I feel the tears escape me. It is an odd mixture of happiness and sadness, of apprehension and longing. I am overjoyed yet so taken aback by the finality of everything.

The idea that tomorrow my misery will end is a foreign thought to me. I have grown so used to the idea of being married to my pain. I stopped feeling for such a long time, and now I can feel again. It is as if my heart has been opened again after these long years, and I am able to allow all of the feelings back in that have for so long been nothing more than a numbness. I have written my final farewells. I have written my will. I have set everything in order, and now all I have to do is sleep and take the short walk to my final stage, to address the crowd as a queen one last time. I only need my strength for a while longer, and then I can give in.

I must remember that in my end is my beginning.

Chapter 35

8th February 1587

I have awoken to a buzz all around me. Fotheringhay is busy today. People prepare for the event about to take place. I feel a solemn mood come over me. It is not necessarily sadness. More a quiet peace. My time on Earth ticks away now. The light spills into the room, illuminating all of the dark corners, and I see each of my ladies as beautiful as the day we met. I see them differently now, as if the years have not aged them at all. I wonder if I look like that: blush returned to my cheek and lines erased. Or is it my imagination picturing us when we were young and longing to return to those days?

I look out of my window and towards the clouds as I silently thank God for bringing this day to me. My lips utter an almost silent "See you soon, my love" to Francis, and I begin to ready myself. We are told that the hour draws near now. I make my final prayers. They offer me a Protestant minister, but I will not turn my back on my true faith in my last moments. I die a Catholic, and my red undergarments tell the world just that. I made peace with my maker a long time ago. I have been ready for this for twenty-seven years.

The refusal of a Catholic priest is the final way for Elizabeth to hold her power over me, but I brush it off. She can do me no harm now. Nothing in this life will trouble me today. I know where I am going, and I also know that the lack of a priest will not stop me.

My darling Mary's dress me one last time. Like they have so many times before. They pin my hair up and place a wig atop my head. My hair is no longer the fiery red it once was. It is now replaced with grey. I do not wish the world to see me like this. I long for them to see the Mary I am on the inside and not the wretch that has been made in these years. When I gaze into the looking glass, I see myself as I was all those years ago: the blush of love fresh in my cheeks and the sparkle of happiness in my eyes, the sparkle that comes whenever I think of him. I allow his name to lift my spirits. I see him as he waits. His arms are open wide, and he is ready for me. Once I leave this frail body, I shall be able to run to him. He takes all of the fear away and shows me that only love lies ahead. I bask in the light that is so near now.

Although I am smiling, my ladies no longer try to conceal their pain, and I do not wish to stop them. They weep as they dress me, and I choose to allow them this. I know the hurt they are feeling. I have felt it many times myself over the years. To lose someone you love is to have your heart ripped from your chest. This is what they feel now. They feel the pain of losing a loved one.

They kneel with me so that they may pray. I pray for everyone I leave behind. I pray for my son. I pray for James, my half-brother. I pray for Elizabeth and wish with all of my heart that she has a long and fruitful reign. I pray that my son, James, knows only the joys in this world and never the misery. I pray that one day, he reigns long over Scotland and England as one. I pray that my ladies take some peace in the idea that I am going in love and not hate.

My silent prayer is over to soon, because finally, the time comes, and we are instructed to leave these rooms that for a long while have been home to us all. I take each of them into my arms one last time and place a kiss on their cheeks. Then, for the final time, I lead them, walking before them as their queen. I smile at Paulet, my cruel jailor, as him as he comes to lead us out. He has been wicked in the years that I have been held here, and I know that in part he is responsible for the lack of courtesy I am shown today. He is taken aback but does not return the gesture, refusing to be kind even in my last hour. I think he expected me to stall, but I follow him gladly. Today, he brings me a gift and I cannot hate him for his task.

We take the short walk from my room into the great hall. My ladies weep behind Me, and I can hear as Mary S once again tries to hold back her sobs. I am not sure she has the stomach for this. As much as it is her who I would like up there with me, I make the decision now to leave her in the crowd, for her sake and not mine. I am not scared. I remind myself repeatedly that it is one more moment of pain in order for me to have a forever of happiness. And I truly deserve a forever of happiness.

As we enter the room, I am shocked by the amount of people gathered to watch. The room is full to the brim. I can barely see ahead of me, but as the crowd parts to allow me through, I see the scaffold in the centre. The executioner stands ahead in his black mask. It is a sight to put the fear of God into anyone, yet I barely flinch. I need to keep my composure just a little longer. "Just a few more steps." Francis' voice is at my ear again.

I take the hands of two of my ladies, and we walk the small way to the scaffold. My stomach turns with nerves as I look about me for a kind face and find that they are few and far between. Mary F smiles at me as she fights to hold off the tears. I remind myself that this is not goodbye.

The executioner seems eager to begin. He can barely stand still with anticipation. The scaffold I stand on has been draped in black. The room looks solemn for this solemn deed.

This is the last thing I shall see before heaven's doors, and I could giggle to myself with the severity of it all. Why should I care that these people look at me in distaste? For they have to stay here in misery while I move on. I put them from my mind and bend my head in prayer.

Again, I am only offered a Protestant for my final prayers, and still I refuse. God knows I am coming. He does not need a minister to accept me. I feel warmth all around me now. It is as if I am standing on the very edge of this life before stepping into the next. I only need to take one more step. I pray aloud so that the room may know that my last words were in service to God. The executioner does not like my praying in Latin and tries his hardest to conceal my words by interrupting. I continue anyway. He will not stop me from speaking to my God.

I only have to endure a little more. My ladies remove my dress, and the crowd let out a collective gasp as my crimson underclothes are shown. "How dare she present herself as a martyr?" they whisper. "This is an insult to the queen." I hear. But they mean nothing to me, and their opinions mean even less.

It is time to kneel now. A solitary tear escapes me. It runs down my cheek as the last that I will ever shed. This is the final time I will ever have to cry from pain or anguish.

This is the last time my heart will ever ache. I take slow and deep breaths as I allow my last words of prayer to escape my lips. Mary ties a handkerchief over my eyes and gently touches my cheek in one last gesture of love. Now the tears fall freely. I do not cry for this life. I cry for the loss of the people within it.

They want me to kneel at the block now. My trembling legs struggle to bend, but I do so gracefully. I do not visibly shake, for I will not appear weak in my last moments. I am the Queen of Scotland and dowager Queen of France. They will never see me break. I kneel before the block and hold my head high. All I see at first is darkness, a never-ending darkness, and I feel the fear of the unknown hit me. But as I am made to lay my head down, I see everything so clearly.

There he is. There is my Francis. He is standing before me, and everything else fades away. The room goes quiet, and all I see is him. He is before me now, his arm outstretched and that beautiful smile etched onto his perfect face. I remember in this instant exactly what it feels like to be loved. feeling long ago lost on me. He is as perfect as the day he left me.

I am coming, I silently promise.

He laughs and gestures me to hurry up. "Come, Mary," he says. He has been waiting nearly thirty years for me. In this moment, I am truly happy, a feeling which for so long I have forgotten. This is the start of my eternal promise. Of my forever.

I am interrupted as I hear the axe swing through the air. My arms stretch out and a smile appears on my lips. I have one final thought in my mind and one final word on my lips.

"Francis!"

ACKNOWLEDGMENTS

There are so many people that I need to thank, not only with Eternal Promise but for being a constant support throughout my life.

First and foremost, I would like to thank Kathi, my friend and publisher, who has believed in me from the moment she decided to publish The Most Happy. Thanks to Kathi and Churchill Publishing, I have not only published my second book, but also now work with her to help others publish theirs.

Next, I would like to thank my boyfriend Tom, who believes in me when I do not believe in myself. He has pushed me to get this book finished every day, and it is thanks to his love and support that I am where I am today. I love you.

I also want to thank my best friend, Ashley, who is not just a best friend but also a brother. He is there for me every single day of my life. I am so blessed to have a best friend who never lets me down. I would also like to dedicate this to his twins, who will be born later this year!

Also, huge thanks to my ever-growing family! To my mum, who has read three drafts of this book, to help me make it as good as it can be. Thanks to My Grandad, who has been a father to me and helped guide me into the person I am today. To my siblings, Courtney,

Chelsea, Jacob, Lucie-May, Sophia and David, who make me a proud big sister every day. And to my nieces and nephews, Jayden and Alaya, and the newest addition when Courtney has hers later this year!

Thank you to everyone that has supported the creation of this book, Jenna, who works tirelessly over my cover. Amanda, who has edited it beautifully. Linda, who reads every last word. And thank you to everyone who reads my books and for all of your continued support.

Finally, I want to thank the people who are not here, but this book would not be possible without them. Of course, first to my Nan. What a hole you have left in my life. A hole that is only filled by all the things you taught me. By all the love you left behind. I will never stop missing you. Much like Mary met Francis again, I truly believe I will see you again.

To my Auntie Pam. You helped me through the worst time in my life, and I will never forget that. I know that you and Nan are up there looking down on all of us.

And lastly, Mary. What a journey we have been on. A journey of twists and turns and ups and downs. I have laughed writing this book, and I've cried. What a life you led. A life that was determined to beat you down, and you handled it like the badass you were. You made your mistakes, sure, who doesn't? Getting to know you has been an honour. I can only hope I have done you justice in this book.

Eternal Promise: The Soul of Mary Stuart is the second novel for author Holly-Eloise Walters. Her first, the brilliant *The Most Happy*, a novel of Anne Boleyn, was an Amazon bestseller.

Ms. Walters resides in Bristol, UK and loves all things Tudor.